Escape to Alaska

Mary Wasche

Cover design by Mary Katzke, Affinity Films.

Book design by Lizzie Newell

This book is dedicated to Jesica Sartell, sister and editor extraordinaire.

Special thanks to my husband, Marty Wasche, for his unwavering support, and to my son, Ken Wasche, for his advice and encouragement. Heartfelt appreciation to my readers, Sue Kerans, Teresa Lueck, Ethann Oldham, Loren Clifford, and McKinley Kerans, who helped craft a story that works. For their invaluable technical assistance, critique skills and inspiration, acknowledgement must go to fellow members of the Chugach Writers Group; Chris Boone, Patricia Watts, Keenen Powell, Vivian Mendenhall, Gigi Lynch, Stan Jones, and Mary Katzke.

Chapter 1

September 1963

LILA PULLED INTO the rutted parking lot, switched off the ignition, and stared at the distant, dark opening of the tunnel that would lead her to safety. Tired of running, tired of being afraid and alone, worn out by too many days of perilous driving through unfamiliar wilderness, she wrenched the driver's door open and kneaded at the tingling in her hip. As she swung her feet out, hot tears of weariness and relief began to trickle down her cheeks.

A flash of movement beyond the back fender caught her eye. She turned to see a man in a blue jacket with a gold Alaska Railroad patch above the pocket approaching. He reached her open door, studied her face for a moment, then stepped over and folded his long legs into a crouch in front of her. Loose dark curls sprouted from his uniform cap and warm eyes, copper brown as pennies, searched hers.

His voice carried a hint of hesitation. "Are you all right?"

Lila swiped a sleeve across her eyes, managing only a shrug in response.

With a fleeting, uncertain look, he rose, dug into his back pocket and thrust a folded red handkerchief toward her. "Here."

Lila reached for the handkerchief, clutching it as he pushed it into her palm. She crammed it tight against her eyes in an effort to stop the sobs that now rippled through her.

After a few minutes, she felt a tentative touch on her wrist. She gave a heaving breath, lowered the handkerchief, and blindly grasped the man's outstretched hand, allowing herself to be drawn up from the driver's seat. As soon as she was on her feet, she twisted her hand from his and wiped her face, then stumbled back against the car, legs trembling with exhaustion. Sudden unease about this strange man being so close to her caused her throat to tighten. She looked around to see if anyone else was near.

He must have noticed the flash of anxiety that crossed her face. With a self-conscious look, he backed a few steps away. "I'm Paul. I'm with the railroad. You going through to Whittier? Train's due to load in half an hour." When Lila didn't answer, his brow tightened. "Are you all right?"

Lila wiped away the last of her tears with the sodden handkerchief and looked up, noticing the high cheekbones and arched black eyebrows dominating his features. A hesitant half-smile played across his face when their gazes met. At this, she fought a bewildering desire to clutch his warm hand again and hold it tight against her, surprised by this wantonness. It wasn't like her to act so needy or forward, especially with a stranger.

"I'm… Yeah…" She took another faltering step backward and leaned into the car door. "But your handkerchief…it's a mess."

"That's okay. Keep it." A lilt she couldn't identify wove through his words.

"I'll bring it back to you," Lila promised.

He shrugged while Lila stuffed the damp handkerchief into the pocket of her jeans. She paused, suddenly embarrassed and shy, and used both hands to shove the honey-colored tangle of curls back from her face. After a deep, steadying breath, she met his gaze again. "I'm Lila. And thank you. I…I don't know what got into me."

"You're welcome," he replied. His eyes darkened, curiosity flickering through them. "Are you in some kind of trouble?"

"Well…yeah… I just got here. I…drove from Minnesota. I need to get through the tunnel to Whittier. Right away."

Paul's gulp was obvious. "You drove the all the way from Minnesota? By yourself?"

Lila nodded.

"Are you in trouble?" he repeated, the odd accent now more pronounced.

Lila looked away, struggling against growing anxiety. Her hands fluttered to her throat, pressing for the trace of pain that lingered even though it had been a little over a week now. "Yeah. I heard that once you get through the tunnel, you're protected. That there's no other way for someone to get into Whittier?" Despite Paul's stunned expression, she went on, words tumbling. "I just need to get into Whittier. I heard about it… and, well…I have to get there…right away."

Paul muttered a word Lila couldn't understand and took a step away. He studied her for a long minute. Lila looked away from his scrutiny, feeling tendrils of anxiety begin to nip at her consciousness, then raised her head, determined to regain her composure. Was he the person she should tell about this? Was Whittier really a protected place?

Paul looked up, then pulled a pen and tablet from his pocket. "So you're looking for a place to hide?" When Lila dipped her head, he went on. "Yeah, people do hide out in Whittier."

"Well…good…" Lila stammered. She must sound flighty, and look a mess, besides. She swiped again at her reddened eyes and wet cheeks, smoothed her jacket front, and stood straighter.

Worry and curiosity played across Paul's face. When Lila didn't say anything else, he finally spoke. "You're running from someone, aren't you?"

Lila hesitated, gulped hard, and managed to whisper, "Yes."

4

"We can keep out strangers trying to get through the tunnel. Just trust me enough to give me a picture and I'll take care of it."

Lila dug into her purse and handed him a picture of a dark-haired, sullen-looking man. Paul studied the picture and shifted his gaze to Lila before tucking it into his pocket. His eyebrows knit. "Do you know someone in Whittier? Got a place to stay?"

She shook her head.

"Does anybody know you're here?" he asked, his voice deepening with concern.

"Nobody. Oh, wait. There's a couple I met in Montana where I stayed one night on the drive. They're the ones who told me about Whittier and how to get here." She spread her hands and added, "But I didn't tell anybody where I was going when I left home. I just took off." Reassured by the kindness in Paul's eyes, she added, "I just need to get through that tunnel. Then I'll figure things out."

Paul stuck the pen and tablet back into his pocket and shook his head. "You know there aren't any motels or hotels in Whittier. There isn't even one single house." At her look of dismay, Paul's voice rose. "Hey, don't worry. I live there, and I have a friend who'll probably let you stay with her 'til you get things figured out. But Whittier's a real strange place. Not like any other town in America."

Lila stared at him wordlessly while he added, "I'll be there when you get to the other side of the tunnel. Then I'll take you to meet my friend, Nan. Okay?"

Lila managed to nod, and he glanced over his shoulder. "Well, I need to get back to work now. It's almost time to start loading the flatcars, and a few more vehicles just got here, so I have to check 'em in."

Paul turned and walked away. Lila's head grew light. She leaned back against the car again, fighting dizziness. What had she done, coming to this strange place all alone? And now ready to rely on a man she didn't even know?

She drew in deep calming breaths. It seemed so long ago that she'd headed west out of St. Paul on impulse, dazed with terror, driving on and on through solitary, dream-like days, following the map west and north. She hardly remembered eating or drinking, and the gas stations and decrepit motels along the Alcan Highway were only a blur.

The all-consuming trance had begun to lessen only minutes ago at the sight of the wooden building with the red and white billboard across the roof proclaiming; WELCOME TO THE ALASKA RAILROAD. PORTAGE DEPOT. WHITTIER TUNNEL. The brittle sense of unreality that had consumed her for these past two weeks began to fade now that she was finally here and about to get through the tunnel to refuge.

She turned and sank back into the driver's seat, filled with relief. But that relief was quickly replaced by growing doubt. Why would she trust what a stranger was telling her? A nearly overwhelming sense of impending doom followed.

What if this doesn't work? Where will I go?

The weight of the miles she'd traveled to get here hit suddenly. So did the fact that she knew nobody and was utterly alone.

Then, a spark of excitement chased her trepidation and weariness. A tight smile of pride and a burst of strength overcame her. She'd taken action to protect herself. She steadied herself against the memories, but couldn't stop the shards of familiar fear that twisted through her. She fought the feeling off and within moments a surge of hot, brooding anger replaced it. She drew herself upright, gripped the steering wheel, and vowed that whatever lay ahead, she would handle it. "Damn you, Lou. Damn you for making me run for my life," she muttered.

Strengthened by the passion of her anger, she looked ahead to where a half-dozen other vehicles waited in single file in front of the depot. A decrepit yellow school bus led the line, sagging curtains at the windows and carelessly painted-over lettering on the sides. Behind it were two pickup trucks with camper units perched in their beds, a deep-sided aluminum boat on a trailer hitched behind a dusty red truck, a few passenger cars, and a high, square white bakery truck with a faded bread loaf logo on its doors.

Train tracks ran alongside the line of vehicles and disappeared into the shriveled grass and dry brush of a meadow ahead. The meadow lay half-shadowed by stately mountains tipped with snow as pure and white as powdered sugar. A high, pitch-roofed, green metal doorway framed the dark mouth of the tunnel in the distance.

Lila settled back and gripped the steering wheel tighter. She was so tired of sitting in this car. So tired of running and worrying and being afraid. She'd made it this far on her own. She pounded the steering wheel again and sat up straight.

Her thoughts returned to the railroad worker when she noticed him begin a brisk walk toward her. She couldn't help admiring the confident way he moved and the little bounce in his step. He must be coming to check her in.

Paul reached the car window and motioned for her to roll it down, then checked his clipboard before giving her his full attention. He looked at her for a long moment before asking, "Lila, would you let me go over a few things with you so you know what to expect?"

Lila returned Paul's gaze, biting her lower lip before answering. "Sure. Thanks. What do I have to do?"

"The vehicles drive onto railroad flatcars and then the train takes them through the tunnel. If you want to read about it, you can walk over to the depot. There's a brochure that explains everything, and some maps, too. It's still twenty minutes or so 'til we load the vehicles, so you've got time to find out all about it. But be sure to be back in your car by the time the train pulls in for loading. You'll hear it coming."

His lilt, the slow cadence and clipped word endings, caught her attention again when he continued. "If you have any questions, I'll be here around the line of vehicles 'til the train loads. Just give me a wave." He gave a barely visible dip of his head. "Well, I need to take your payment now. It'll be five dollars cash, no checks. You pay only to go through into Whittier, not to come back out. And I need to see your identification."

Lila rustled into her purse and handed over her driver's license and a five-dollar bill. Paul recorded it, then laid his hand on the hood of her car. "Hey, is this one of the new Fords?"

"Yeah. A '63 Galaxie."

"Oh," he murmured. After a long look filled with curiosity, Paul turned away and began to walk toward the bakery truck in front of her.

Lila sat for a moment. Men always noticed her, locking gazes with her a little longer than was necessary or polite. She was the one who ended up looking away first, flustered and self-conscious. Once, a dignified man in a suit and tie had walked up to her in the produce area of the grocery store and complimented her on her "delightful and unusual hair style." At the memory, she ran her fingers through the mass of curls over her shoulders.

She shook off the thoughts, climbed out of the car and walked to the depot. She sat on the lone wooden bench and read through the informational brochure. Three miles from this station to the actual community of Whittier. The tunnel, running for two and a half miles through the solid rock base of a mountain, had been built by the military in the early 1940s in an effort to change a vulnerable Alaska into a defensive outpost as World War II loomed. Whittier's long-standing isolation due to lack of road or air access meant only experienced commercial fishing crews and huge cargo or military ships were able to navigate Prince William Sound's unpredictable waters, weather, and dangerous shoreline to reach its harbor. The picture of the mouth of the big tunnel fascinated her—such a small opening in such a huge mountain.

She sighed and let the brochure fall to her lap. What would it be like on the other side?

Chapter 2

WHEN SHE WAS back in her car a few minutes later, three loud whistles pierced the air behind the line of vehicles, startling her. Lila looked back over her shoulder to watch a monstrous blue and gold engine chug into view beneath a rolling column of smoke. Soon it was her turn to drive up a gouged wooden ramp onto one of the rust-covered, metal flatcars the engine pulled. Paul appeared at her window just before she drove ahead.

"You ready?" he mouthed.

Lila smiled and returned a silent thank you through the glass. She shifted away from the damp wadded handkerchief pressing into her hip and rolled her shoulders to loosen them before pushing the accelerator. Paul waved her onto the ramp, then directed her forward along the connected flatbed cars until she was within inches of the bakery truck parked ahead. She turned off the engine and twisted around in her seat to watch the rest of the vehicles being guided onto the train. When they were all loaded, three more shrill blasts sounded, and the train bumped clumsily forward before steadying into a slow roll.

It picked up speed, rumbling along beside a shallow river of turquoise-tinted water tumbling over a rocky bottom. Meadows filled with brown grass, skeletal brush, and withered plant stalks stretched from the river toward steep mountains. An immense bluish-white river of ice drooped between two mountain peaks to the right of the train, dominating the view, and a wooden sign flashed beside the tracks, identifying it as Portage Glacier. In front of the face of ice lay a large bowl of aqua water with chunks of blue-white ice floating on its surface. The sharp, irregular chunks, some the size of cars, some much larger, bobbed lightly on the tranquil surface. Lila wished Mom could see the exquisite sight. The train rolled along over a wooden bridge, past another small meadow, and across the second bridge.

Immediately, an imposing mountain ahead darkened the sky. Workmen ran to a log hut ahead when the train began to slow, and she recognized Paul as he strode down the line, checking vehicles against the clipboard he held. He raised his head and gave her a brief grin as he passed her window.

When the train growled back into motion, Lila sucked in a deep breath of anticipation. She gasped as all natural light vanished the instant her car passed under the entrance door. Dim, oversized light bulbs hanging on the rock walls at far-flung intervals cast an eerie yellow glow and there was a noticeable change in the air even though the car windows were closed. Lila breathed in the musty, cold, dead air, fighting panic. The tunnel was so narrow. It looked like she could almost reach out and touch the scarred, glistening rock walls on either side of her car. The dark, arched ceiling, rising only feet above the roofs of the vehicles, revealed symmetrical gashes in the rock, their jagged contours undoubtedly made by dynamite blasts. Drips of water splashed onto Lila's windshield at random intervals, startling her each time one hit. Those drops, and the muted, rhythmic clattering of the train wheels made up the only sound.

A burst of terror seized Lila when a large white sign flashed by, alerting her to the location of "Safe House Number One." She whipped around to check the cars behind her. A man's calm, pale face returned her stare through the windshield behind. His passive look became one of surprise to see her turn around so abruptly and face him. He gave a faint smile. Lila gave him a fleeting, sheepish half-grin in return, and faced forward, a bit comforted by his calm demeanor. She settled back into her seat, straining for a first glimpse of light at the end of the spooky, seemingly endless tunnel. The minutes dragged.

At last, there it was, a hint, a glimmer, a growing pinpoint of light ahead. Then the train burst into a blinding flash of daylight, making Lila squint. It slowed while pulling out from the tunnel and she heaved a sigh of relief. She looked around, eager for her first glimpse of Whittier.

A clump of white metal fuel storage tanks the size of small houses sat in a clearing to her left, protected by a rock barrier along the ocean shore. On their tops, metal boardwalks with complex railings dripped streams of rust down the sides of the tanks. Frisky waves lapped at the rocky shoreline in front of the tanks, skipping away to meet forested cliffs rising from the other side of an immense blue bay. Wispy patches of snow lay scattered against rocks in protected shady areas along the tracks even though it was only the end of September. Mucky gray ground bordered the right side of the tracks before angling up to meet mountain slopes where dense patches of dark evergreens climbed toward the mountain tops.

The crew materialized while the train rolled to a sluggish stop, directed the unloading of the flatcars, and soon it was Lila's turn to back down. Before she knew it, she was driving forward on a narrow dirt lane beside the tracks. She strained for a glimpse of the town while still in line with the other vehicles.

Ahead on the left, in a harbor nestled against a rocky seawall, an assortment of boats bobbed on their tethers alongside a weathered wooden wharf. Indigo waters stretched far across the bay to meet the surrounding mountains.

A cream-colored brick building, its top four rows of bricks accented in alternating pale blue and orange, rose to the right. A lone sentinel, it reached for a dozen stories above a cluster of small sheds and huts. The building, the tallest Lila had seen since leaving home, looked like it belonged in Minnesota instead of here in this secluded seaside community.

A hulking gray building with hundreds of vacant, broken-out windows directly ahead on the far side of the settlement caught her attention. Set at the base of an enormous mountain, it looked like an out-of-place, abandoned prison plucked from Siberia. The mysterious vacant building comprised the far border of Whittier, as best she could tell.

The tiny community was nothing but the two apartment-like structures, a dozen sheds, several shabby warehouses, and multiple sets of railroad tracks, all surrounding a large gravel and dirt parking lot. The lot held a wasteland of boat trailers, abandoned cars, rusted heavy equipment, and huge, water-stained wooden spools. Several windowless, ancient dump trucks squatted in the dirt. A few small, two-story wooden buildings that appeared to be stores or restaurants formed the far edge of the parking lot in front of the abandoned building. Scattered rows of rusty boxcars filled a small railroad yard next to them.

A steady wind kicked up swirls of dust and shook the limbs of the scrawny, bare-branched trees bordering the town. A bite of cool air whistled in along the top of Lila's window and she cranked the handle to roll it up tighter.

She looked around in dismay. The tunnel and its mountain lay behind her. More mountains, rising beyond the huge gray building and the railroad yard, defined the far border. The tall apartment building to the right, hemmed in by the wall of mountains behind it, comprised one side of the community, and the ocean and wharf made the opposite border. This was all there was, just a narrow scrap of land, only as big as a neighborhood back home. And Paul was right. There wasn't a single house in sight. This little place, so barren, so small, so grim, wasn't anything like she'd expected. What if Lou found her here? Would she be trapped? A shudder of fear twisted through her, followed by a vision of Lou's scowling face.

Her anxiety was interrupted by a honk as a dark blue pickup with gold lettering on its door nudged its way along the line of traffic and pulled up beside her. Paul grinned from behind the wheel and waved her forward to follow him. She steered the car out of line and followed Paul's pick-up until it pulled up in front of the tall brick building.

Paul got out and strode up to Lila's car. "Well, here we are. This is where we all live. It's an apartment building called the Hodge."

Lila stared. The twelve-story building could have been a school or office building back in Minnesota. Metal railings bordered matching sets of concrete steps at either end. Hundreds of identical aluminum windows and the pale color of the bricks matched those of her elementary school. Incredible! All the residents of Whittier lived in this same building.

Two boys burst from the far set of doors. "Hi, Paul," they shouted as they bounced down the steps.

"Hey, Jeff, Bobby. What's up, you two?" The boys stole a curious look at Lila as they tore past, headed toward the harbor, jackets flying open. One called back over his shoulder, "A big boat's comin' in to the dock! We're gonna watch!"

"Come on," Paul said, turning back to Lila. "I'll take you up to Nan's. She's the unofficial building manager. Usually, she puts up visitors and new residents until they get settled. She has to like you, though, or you're out of luck. Over the years, a couple guys Nan didn't take to ended up sleeping in their trucks for a few days until the tunnel opened to let 'em back out. Nan's honest and knows everybody and everything. She's been here forever. Sound good?"

Lila turned toward him, feeling slightly numb. "Sure. Thanks."

Paul led Lila through the nearest set of entry doors into a deserted lobby with a scuffed floor of faded green linoleum. A large, plastic plant, leaves laden with dust, dominated one corner where it leaned against a worn and crackled black leather bench. Lila, filled with growing curiosity and still uneasy, followed Paul through the lobby and along a narrow corridor, its pale yellow concrete block walls nicked and cracked. The air smelled vaguely of other people, with a hint of stale cooking odors. Paul turned into another small lobby and the ping of the elevator brought her to his side. She moved into the elevator car beside him, the heavy metal doors clanged shut, and they were lifted upward to floor nine, gears growling and grinding. Lila, although grateful for Paul's presence, tried to ignore a gnawing sense of misgiving at being in this strange place, following a man she didn't know.

Chapter 3

PAUL STEPPED OUT of the elevator, held the door for Lila, and walked toward the end of another dim corridor with the same deteriorated linoleum floors and sickly yellow walls as the lobby. Lila scurried at his heels. He stopped before one of the mud-brown metal doors lining the corridor, all spaced about fifty feet apart. The door swung open promptly at his knock and a stout, fiftyish-looking woman peered out. Her face, crisscrossed by wrinkles, dark eyes half-hidden beneath pouched eyelids, lit up with a broad smile.

"Hey, Paul. Long time no see." They chuckled together, as if sharing a private joke.

Paul pulled Lila forward. "Got another one for you, Nan. This is Lila. She'll be needing a place until she gets settled."

The chunky woman's bare feet ended in pudgy, crumpled toes. A baggy once-white sweatshirt, adorned with a pair of faded red cardinals, hung over denim pedal pushers. The half-smoked cigarette dangling from the corner of her mouth gave off a wisp of smoke. Blunt, chopped hair, a strange shade of reddish brown, contrasted oddly with her penciled black eyebrows. Lila stared back at her.

Nan looked Lila up and down "Ya mean another one needin' to hide out?" the woman asked, turning to Paul, her eyebrows lifted.

"Yup."

Nan stepped back and motioned them in. Lila paused inside the door, her attention drawn to the rectangular window taking up half the living room wall across the apartment. Nan and Paul stepped aside, motioning Lila to move past them to the window.

She looked down to see the harbor below bristling with boat masts reaching for the sky and jostling for space. The glassy blue water of the bay touched the far shore before widening and disappearing into the distance to the right. Seagulls tumbled in every direction over the harbor like white confetti, their squawks a distant chorus. The rugged points of snow-topped mountains on the far shoreline lay against a cloudless sky as true blue as in a child's painting. Sheltered, bluish-white glaciers spilled down the crevices that folded the mountains into each other. Above the cliffs and rocky shores, forests of dark spruce draped the steep mountainsides. This view hadn't been visible from the ground. It was an entirely different look at Whittier, and it took Lila's breath away.

After a moment, she felt a change in the air and sensed Paul beside her. "Pretty incredible, huh?" he asked.

Lila turned to him, wide-eyed. "Yes, it's amazing!"

Nan laughed behind them and reached to turn off the country music softly playing from the radio on her kitchen counter. "Yeah, the view kinda makes it all worthwhile," she said. "Winters get real long and nasty here. But then, every spring, the gray skies disappear. The view's different every day and I always end up feeling I just have to stay. I started to leave maybe a dozen times or so, but never did. Lotsa folks only make it through the third winter, if that, before they go kinda crazy and hafta get out. But some of us, well, we just never manage to leave."

Nan puffed her cigarette, drawing smoke deep into her lungs, and tipped her head back to blow it out toward the ceiling before continuing. "It's a cheap place to live. There's not much to spend money on, especially in the winter. There's seventy of us in the building now. Before the military finished pullin' out years back, we had lots more people."

Taking another deep drag on her cigarette, Nan puffed a series of perfect smoke rings across the living room. She admired them for a moment, then looked at Lila. "So what about you? Got a plan?"

"Not exactly," Lila replied. "I need a job and a place to live. Is there any work? How much are apartments? Rent, I mean?"

"Well, Dearie, that depends. Depends on lotsa things. What kinda job you'll do, for one. Ever worked in a grocery store or a bar or handled a cash register? The general store's lookin' for somebody to run the counter and clean the place. It's the town waterin' hole, too, so you might have to bartend a bit. You old enough? Oh well, it don't matter. Nobody ever checks. Ruth, she did it for the last year or so. But she up and left last week. Probly 'cuz winter's comin' on so soon now."

She paused with a disgusted shake of her head. "Ruth drove onto the train last Saturday morning with her car loaded. Never said a word to anyone about leavin'. Her apartment might have some stuff left in it, now that I think about it. Building's got a hundred apartments, lotta 'em empty, so findin' a place to live won't be no problem. Lotta folks just take off like Ruth, so there's stuff left behind all the time, and everybody sorta helps themselves to whatever they need. I can show you around."

"Well, I'll be twenty my next birthday. I haven't run a cash register before, but I can learn. And I know how to clean. My mother taught me when I helped her clean houses for her clients in St. Paul," Lila assured her.

At Nan's encouraging look, Lila went on, "How much is rent?"

"Starts at seventy-five a month for a back apartment, one bedroom. Front ones highest up, two bedroom, go for a hundred and fifty. Plus, you gotta pay utilities…" Nan paused, her face expectant. "You bring any stuff with ya? Furniture? Anything like that? You got any money?"

Lila nodded her head and did a quick mental calculation. She could get along for a while with the money she had left. And if she could find some furniture someone had left behind, or at least drive back into Anchorage to pick up some cheap essentials, she'd be able to make it just fine, especially if she got a job.

"How do you get groceries?" she asked.

Paul answered this time. "We go into Anchorage, or have somebody else pick stuff up for us when they go. The general store here's pretty small, and it's usually out of what you need, anyway. Right, Nan?"

He looked to Nan, who nodded in agreement. "Yup, we stock up at the Red Owl when we go into town. An' we help each other out. Lotta borrowin' and payin' back. There's potlucks, too. Nobody goes hungry."

Paul continued, "You know what people are cooking because the smells waft through the shafts. Especially fish and cabbage. Or if somebody bakes brownies." He gave a laugh and went on. "This building was built in separate pieces with shafts between the sections so it could withstand earthquakes, but wind and odors drift their way

23

through it. In the winter, the halls get really cold if the wind's blowing from the north. Sometimes, it blows through the hallways so hard people have trouble getting out their own front doors."

With a smile at Lila's unbelieving face, Paul went on, "This building is one of the few in the entire state that was built like this. It just stands here and rocks."

Lila's eyes grew wide and her mouth fell open. Paul and Nan chuckled at her expression.

Nan's eyes crinkled. "Don't worry. It's about the safest building in Alaska. Built by the military, you know. And the chance of one a' them big quakes happenin' ain't likely. We don't worry about it. It's the winds that'll get you."

She tapped her ashes into a bulky glass ash tray. "In winter, windows rattle all day and night in the whole blamed building. Wind blows fifty, sixty miles an hour. Sometimes for a week straight. Folks hafta wear ear plugs to get a break from the noise. And the snow blows so hard sometimes you can't even see across the parking lot. Kids go underground through a tunnel to school. An' old people have to wait for a still day to go outside so they don't get blown away. Dogs been blown half-way cross town quite a few times."

Nan grinned at Lila's stunned expression, stubbed out her cigarette, and rummaged for a fresh one. She lit it, sucked in a first drag, then continued, words quick, eyes bright, eager to tell Lila more. "Honest to God. Couple years back, a black Lab went out the front door in a near eighty-mile wind. Ended up plastered against the side of the harbormaster's shack along the shore, clear across the parking lot. Took two men to get him off that wall. Dog still won't go outside if he can hear the wind."

Paul added. "Yup. All true. And twenty feet of snow is nothing. Some winters it's near forty. The drifts cover second story windows and bury cars." He glanced toward the door. "But enough of that. Let's get you settled. Can you take over, Nan? I better get back to work."

Nan tapped the ashes off her cigarette again and looked hard at Lila. "You got anything to tell me before I put you up? Sick? In trouble with the law?" Her eyes glinted in a friendly manner, but her words were tough. "I ain't about to get involved if you're just gonna take off right away. And I don't want any part of it if you're bringing big trouble with you. Understand what I'm sayin'?"

Lila replied, "Yeah, well, I am in trouble. Not with the law. I didn't do anything wrong, but I saw something I shouldn't have and I need to hide. I'm sure he's already trying to find me. I'll have to get a job, too, as soon as possible." Her breath came fast and her stomach clenched. Would Nan send her away?

"Good Lord!" Nan shuddered, stubbing her cigarette among a heap of others. "You're in deep shit, huh?" She waved an arm around the apartment. "All right, then, Dearie. You sound like you're bein' straight with me. So, fine, you can stay. We'll get you settled in and I'll take you over to the general store and bar first thing tomorrow to see about a job. I know Ol' Tom's desperate for some help."

"I won't know what I'm doing behind a bar, but I can learn," Lila replied. "I need a job. I know I'll be able to do it."

"Good," Nan replied. "And we'll take a look at empty apartments in the building, tomorrow, too. Sound good?

When Lila nodded, Nan turned back to Paul. "You guys'll be checking any strangers tryin' to come through, right Got a picture?" She finished grinding out her cigarette, tapped another from the pack on the kitchen counter, struck a match, and huffed out a cloud of smoke while she waited for him to answer.

Paul turned to Lila, his voice low and firm, authoritative. "Everyone has to provide identification and get a ticket from us to get through the tunnel. We're very diligent about checking everybody, especially strangers. We'll start that right now, but you'll have to tell us more."

Lila looked away. She couldn't tell these people everything right now. She didn't really know them. What would they think of her? She needed time to think about how to tell them. She shrugged and turned her gaze away from Paul.

Paul hesitated, waiting, and when Lila didn't say anymore, turned abruptly, gave Nan a small wave, and left.

Lila took a deep, settling breath and turned to Nan who had busied herself at the kitchen counter. "Should I bring my stuff up? My car's parked in front."

A half hour later, her sleeping bag and pillow, duffel bag of laundry, purse and suitcase were piled in Nan's spare bedroom. The bedroom's block walls were painted a soothing pale pink, the window overlooking the harbor was bordered by ruffled white curtains, and a quilt of rose and white squares covered the single bed. Nan showed Lila the common laundry room down the hall and gave her some powdered detergent and a roll of dimes. How good it felt to be doing routine chores and having clean clothes again.

After a supper of rice and baked salmon with creamy dill sauce, Lila sat down with Nan to watch *Bonanza* on the tiny, black and white TV with its slightly tilted, snowy picture. But her eyes quickly became too heavy to keep open. She shuffled off to bed with a murmured "Good night" and crawled beneath the heavy quilt, sinking under its weight and warmth, finally feeling safe.

Chapter 4

LILA WOKE THE next morning, swung her legs off the edge of the bed and bent over to ease the bite of nausea that had begun her mornings lately. Surely now she'd reached safety, it would start easing up. Her stomach settled enough to stand after a few moments, and she dressed to the sound of the Righteous Brothers crooning "You've Lost That Lovin' Feelin" from Nan's kitchen radio. The song brought thoughts of what she'd left behind, and her heart quickened. She trembled, remembering, and massaged the lingering soreness in her neck. With a determined shake of her head, she walked out of the bedroom.

Nan twisted away from the kitchen sink and without taking her hands out of the dishwater, asked over her shoulder, "Get enough sleep?"

"Yes, thanks," Lila answered. "It's so quiet here. And that quilt was nice and warm. I was really tired, I guess." She hesitated, "Thank you so much, Nan.

Thank you for letting me stay here. And for helping me." She smiled her thanks at Nan, feeling the stiffness in her face begin to loosen. It had been a long time since her last real smile.

Nan's eyes, glimmering with curiosity, lingered on Lila for a long moment before she turned back to the dishes. "You're welcome, Dearie. Now, let's get down to brass tacks. How much money you got?"

When Lila didn't answer right away, Nan turned around, wiping her dripping hands along her pants. "C'mon. If I'm gonna help, you gotta let me know everything. Starting with money. How much? And what other work have you done?" The authority in her tone, accompanied by a coldness that hadn't been apparent yesterday, left no room for argument.

Lila gulped. "Just over four hundred dollars. And I have the Galaxie I drove up here. I don't know if it's paid for. I just took it," Lila offered.

Nan's eyes widened, but she remained silent, moved her hands to her hips, and waited for Lila to continue.

Lila went on, her voice now tinged with apprehension.

What must Nan be thinking of me?

"I babysat the neighbors' kids during summers while I was in high school. And I helped my Mom clean houses while I was growing up. She has her own cleaning business. But my husband wouldn't let me work after we got married. I'll need to make money…" Her voice trailed off.

29

Nan grimaced, then nodded. "No real job experience then. Well, I'll take you over to see 'Ol Tom at the store this morning. I bet I can talk him into giving you a chance. We'll get you that job."

When Lila didn't answer, Nan continued. "This trouble you're in. How bad is it?"

"Bad," Lila replied. "Really bad."

Nan shook her head, her face scrunched with worry, and turned back to the sink. Lila walked to her bedroom, closed the door and leaned back against it, overcome by memories. She shuddered, feeling again the panic of not being able to breathe and of powerful hands closing like steel around her throat. Weak-kneed at the memory, Lila stumbled over to her bed, sank onto it, and tried to stifle rising sobs.

The bedroom door squeaked open. "Dearie, are you alright?" Nan's concerned face peeked around the door frame. "I thought I heard you cry out."

Lila turned to Nan, her eyes overflowing with tears, her breath catching in her throat. "I thought I was going to die. Everything went black...he...he..."

Nan's eyes stood out like glowing beacons in her ashen face. "My God! Someone tried to kill you?" She rushed into the room and drew Lila up, enveloping her in her arms. The smell of Nan's cigarettes and the toast she'd been buttering formed an oddly comforting cloud around Lila. "You're safe here, Dearie. It's okay. It's okay," she murmured, patting Lila's back.

Lila folded herself deeper into Nan's embrace and hiccupped with relief. Soon, she pulled back a little from Nan's arms and swiped again at her tears. "I'm sure he's trying to find me by now. I didn't tell anybody where I was going when I left home. I hope he doesn't bring trouble here to you. He won't be able to get past the tunnel guards will he?"

Nan shrugged away. "No, he won't get through. Those guys are real careful about who they let through." She tossed her head. "You poor thing. Some breakfast and a cup of cocoa. That's what you need."

Nan soon called Lila for toast, scrambled eggs and hot chocolate, explaining that good old-fashioned home cooking would make Lila feel better. Neither mentioned what Lila had just told Nan.

After the dishes were done, they walked across the parking lot to the log-fronted general store, and Lila soon found herself listening to instructions on how to run a cash register. Nan leaned against the bar and lit a cigarette while the scrawny old man began.

"Can ya start tonight?" Old Tom asked. His opaque blue eyes searched Lila's from within their nest of wrinkles. Lila couldn't keep her eyes off the smoky-gray beard and moustache covering his cheeks and mouth and hanging over his chest like a large, shaggy bib. How many years had it been since he'd shaved and how did he manage to eat with all that bristly hair in the way?

He ran a grimy rag over the scarred wooden countertop beside the cash register, seeming unaware of Lila's fascination, and continued, "I been doin' everything since Ruth up and left and I'm beat. Too old for this. Can ya be back here by four today and stay 'til closing at ten? Shouldn't be busy. Be a good day to learn."

At Lila's eager head bob, he went on, "When ya get here, I'll stick around for a while to kinda break ya in before I head back to the Hodge. We all know each other around here, and almost every damn thing about each other, too. So ya should do fine. It'll just be the regulars and I know what they drink, and how much."

He wiped a gnarled hand across his brow, and leaned away from the counter, "Ya gotta write down everything ya sell, and I'll give it a looksee in the mornings. If somebody wants a drink, they kin tell ya how to make it. Mostly, it'll be opening beer bottles, though. Turn off the lights with this here switch and bang the cash register drawer shut hard. And flip this little lock over it when ya leave." He stopped for a raspy breath. "And whoever's still here'll head out the door when ya start shuttin' off the lights. I can see the place from my window and nobody 'round here is hardly ever out and about after ten or so."

He scratched bent fingers around in his beard while he waited for Lila to answer. When her head bobbed again, Nan gave an approving smile and tapped her ashes into a battered tin ash tray with

"Budweiser" spelled out around its rim in peeling red letters.

The old man added, "And can ya do the cleanin'? Doesn't have to be much, but I don't like doin' it. Ya gotta sweep out this big room and the aisles every day and clean the toilet room and kinda keep the place to rights. I need ya as many hours as ya wanna work. Mostly afternoons and after supper. I git up early so I'm here in the mornin' by ten or so. Most folks 'round here ain't really up and around 'til noon, anyway. Not much happens 'fore then."

He paused, shuffled in his stained leather boots, and looked at Lila for a reaction.

When she tipped her head in acknowledgement, he continued, "I'll pay ya cash, three bucks an hour, once a week. You kin write down yer hours and turn in the slip Fridays. I'll be around every day, and I'm in apartment 620 if ya need me. Got no phone. Never did, never will. Durn things don't work half the time anyways, so why waste the money? Sure as hell don't need one around here—ya can jest holler and everybody'll hear ya and pass it on." He chuckled at his joke, his face crinkling into a maze of wrinkles. "So, sound like somethin' ya can handle?"

"I can do it, I'm sure," Lila answered, trying to absorb all the information the old man had rattled off.

She looked around the dim bar and dusty, haphazardly-stocked shelves of groceries. Wash off all those wooden shelves and set the goods out in order, clean the gritty wood floors, wipe dust off the liquor bottles, clean the glass fronts of the coolers, give the whole place a good going over, that's what it needed. Some worthwhile activity, and earning money of her own was just what she needed. Twenty or thirty hours a week would be more than enough money for rent and food. And cash, no records sent off to the government that someone might be able to use to track her down. Perfect.

"I'll start this afternoon then." Lila confirmed, trying not to sound too eager.

Nan moved to Lila's side while Tom rasped, "Sure. Good. Be back here 'bout three or so." He scratched beneath the chest pocket of his blue coveralls and gave Lila a shrewd look. "Anythin' else?"

"Nope. I'll work hard, I promise. And I'm honest," Lila replied. "Thank you for the job. See you at four. Bye."

Old Tom gestured them toward the door. "Yup. Later."

Now she couldn't wait to get back and find an apartment. When she and Nan stepped outside for the walk back to the Hodge, a damp, stinging wind bit at their faces. Lila hugged her arms across her chest.

"Winter wind," Nan observed, sniffing the air. "I can smell a big snow on the way. Winter comes early here. There's already been a few flakes. Couple of weeks from now, middle of October, there's gonna be snow that stays. And it'll prob'ly rain, or even snow a bit, almost every day 'til then, to boot. Sure you're gonna be able to handle this? Winters are long. Really long. And dark. No sun for almost six months. Got a good jacket?"

Lila shook her head. "No. I didn't think to bring my heavy one from Minnesota. I left in such a hurry. My jacket was old, anyway, and the zipper always got stuck halfway. I'll get a warmer coat as soon as I can." She paused and turned to Nan, the wind making her eyes water. "And I can't thank you enough for helping me, Nan. I can handle this, I'm sure."

Nan shrugged and turned away, head bowed into the wind. "No big deal, Dearie."

The rest of Lila's day was spent tramping through the Hodge with Nan. They settled on a one-bedroom apartment on the floor below Nan's for one hundred a month. Although the back apartments were cheaper, Lila was sure the view of the harbor would be worth the extra money.

She signed the simple one-page lease at the building's office in the lobby, transferred the heat and electricity into her name, and paid cash for the few remaining days of September's rent. The key felt good in her hand and Lila took immense pride in having a place of her own for the first time in her life. Although the apartment's rooms were completely empty, the worn linoleum smooth and cold underfoot, and the windows bare, she visualized it furnished and couldn't wait to start accumulating household goods and other things. Nan agreed to walk through the Hodge with her the next day and see what they could find.

Lila bought stamps and an envelope from the closet-sized post office in the corridor next to the lobby. It was time to let Mom and Judy know she was safe since the worry they must be feeling gnawed at her. Being able to send the mail through the couple she'd stayed overnight with in Montana eased her mind some, but the danger of it being traced still worried her.

Her heart fluttered. Had Lou alerted law enforcement about his missing car and money? Was he harassing Mom and Judy? Were the police looking for her? Was anyone on her trail? She visualized him gripping the wheel of a pickup with those wide knuckles. She shook her head to clear the image of the scowling face that would be twisted with rage as he followed the Alcan Highway if he'd somehow already figured out where she went.

That night at Nan's kitchen table she wrote a letter.

Dear Mom and Judy,

I'm sorry for taking off like I did without telling you. There's a good reason I had to leave. I'll tell you about it when I can.

I have a job here already, so I'm getting by just fine. I've met some nice people who are helping me get settled and I already have my own apartment. I don't know when I'll be able to come back home, or even when I'll be able to call.

I worry about you and hope you'll write back as soon as you can. Use the return address on this envelope to mail a letter back to me. These people helped me out when I drove through their little town in Montana, and they said they'd forward mail so I don't have to put my real return address on the envelopes — that would be too dangerous right now. I miss you both very much. But don't worry about me. I'm safe here. I'll write again as soon as I hear from you and I'll try to figure out a way to call you soon, too.

I love you, Mom. And Judy, you know you're the best friend anybody could ever have.

Love, Lila

Lila tucked a note into the envelope assuring Dee and Chuck in Montana that she'd made it to Whittier and thanked them for being so kind and helpful during her overnight stop, as well as for being willing to forward her letters back and forth between Alaska and Minnesota. Dropping the envelope in the slot of the little post office door lightened her heart. Soon the people back home she loved most would get word that she was fine.

Chapter 5

LILA'S MOTHER STOPPED short at an envelope addressed in her daughter's familiar hand, dropped the rest of the mail on the kitchen counter and tore the envelope open with trembling fingers. A sob escaped and tears coursed down her cheeks as she read. Crying and smiling at the same time, weak with relief, Margaret hurried to the kitchen wall phone and spun Judy's number into the dial.

"Oh, Judy! I heard from Lila! I got a letter!" she blurted over Judy's hello.

"Margaret, thank God!" Judy cried. "What... Where?"

A loud knocking in the background caused Margaret to interrupt. "Wait a minute...there's someone at the back door. Just a second..."

Judy could hear insistent pounding in the background. A few seconds later it stopped, and a muffled squeak came through, followed by a low, muttered cuss word. Then the receiver was slammed down with a bang and the line began to buzz. Judy flung her phone into the cradle and dashed for her husband.

"Jerry! Something's happening at Margaret's," she gasped the second she reached the garage. "We were on the phone... She got a letter from Lila... There was knocking at her door and then the phone got hung up, hard! I've got a really a bad feeling. Oh, God! We gotta get over there."

"Oh, crap!" Jerry answered, stuffing his wrench into his back pocket. "I've been afraid something like this might happen." He jumped to his feet. "Come on!"

He brushed his hands off along his pant legs, shoved his glasses onto the bridge of his nose and sprinted for the driveway. His truck was already in reverse by the time Judy scrambled in and swung her door shut. They backed out of the driveway with a screech and sped toward Margaret's house two blocks away.

"What did you hear?" Jerry yelled, as he blasted through a yellow light and careened around the corner. "What?"

"She got a letter from Lila," Judy cried. She rocked back and forth in the vinyl seat, hands clutching the dashboard. Her breath came in gasps. "But before she could tell me anything else, she had to answer the door. Then I heard loud pounding, strange sounds, the phone slammed! Oh, God! I'm so scared it was Lou! Hurry!"

Jerry peeled the truck into Margaret's driveway. They jumped from the cab and rushed up the back porch steps. The screen door hung open. When Judy reached the kitchen doorway, she screamed and clutched her fists to her mouth. Margaret lay unmoving on her back on the white speckled linoleum, eyes closed, one arm askew over her head, blood pooling beneath her neck.

"Oh, my God! She's hurt! Call for help!" Judy snatched a dishtowel from the counter, fell to her knees beside Margaret, and pressed the towel to Margaret's bloody neck. She murmured words of comfort, oblivious to the blood soaking the legs of her new white jeans.

Jerry grabbed the phone and dialed the St. Paul police emergency number taped to the wall. A few minutes later, an ambulance screamed to a stop at the curb in front of the house, red lights flashing. A small crowd of neighbors and passersby gathered in the shade of the tall elms along the sidewalk as the medics carried Margaret out on a stretcher. She hadn't regained consciousness despite Judy's frantic pleas and gentle touches.

Judy and Jerry ran to their truck and followed the ambulance to Midway Hospital, parked recklessly in an "Emergency Vehicle Only" space and dashed in just in time to see Margaret being wheeled away on a gurney. Her blood-soaked turquoise housedress was being cut off by a nurse while a medical team hurried alongside. Only one of her sturdy black shoes remained on her feet. Another nurse stepped in front of Judy and Jerry when they tried to follow the gurney.

"No admittance beyond here. I'm sorry. You'll have to wait over there." She pointed to a waiting area. "Are you family?" she asked.

"Yes," Judy blurted. "Yes, we are. When can we see her? How is she?"

"We'll let you know as soon as we can," the nurse replied, her voice strict with practiced patience. "Meanwhile, there's paperwork you need to take care of at the desk over there. And be sure one of you stays in this waiting area until the doctor comes out with a report. I can't tell you more than that. I'm sorry." She turned away and walked with brisk steps through the swinging doors that had swallowed Margaret.

"We're not family—" Jerry began.

"Well, we will be now!" Judy interrupted, her voice shrill. "She doesn't have anybody else. Only Lila. I'm gonna say I'm her daughter. I have to take care of Margaret. For Lila."

The intensity burning in her eyes silenced Jerry. He ran his fingers through his hair and settled his lanky body onto a bench. He let out a sigh and turned to Judy. "Okay, okay. Let's do the paperwork then, I guess," he agreed, reluctance and worry clouding his face. "But it's not right, Jude."

"Well, there's no other way. I don't care! Margaret needs us and I'm gonna do it!" Judy marched over and spoke to the nurse behind the counter. She returned a few minutes later, tossed her bulging denim purse down, flopped into the chair next to Jerry, and settled the clipboard across her knees. She shoved the cuffs of her sweatshirt up, scuffed her tennis shoes into a comfortable position, and began filling out the top page.

"Do you know what to say? Do you know her medical history... Does she have insurance—" Jerry started.

"I don't know!" Judy snapped without looking up. "But I have to do this. I'll put in everything I know and I'll make up the rest if I have to."

Judy ignored her husband, and began filling in the blanks, absentmindedly brushing back the wisps of dark hair that fell across her eyes, and swiping her sweaty hands on her jeans while she struggled with the form.

Jerry settled down beside her with a sigh.

When she'd filled in what she could, Judy rushed the forms back over to the desk, then came back and crumpled onto Jerry's lap. "I'm so scared. I wish I knew where Lila was. We need to call her," she murmured, huddling against him for comfort. He drew an arm across her shoulders, bringing her close.

Judy nestled into him. "I bet it was Lou. Damn it. How could anybody hurt Margaret? She's just a harmless old lady. There was so much blood..."

Tears spilled from her eyes as pent-up sobs racked her body. Jerry tried to gather Judy tighter into his arms, but she shrugged out of the embrace and turned her tear-streaked face toward him. "Margaret was telling me she just got a letter from Lila. We need that letter. There's probably a return address on it. I have to get in touch with Lila and tell her about this. Can you go back over to Margaret's and get the letter? Maybe it shows where it was mailed from…" She paused, "Will you please go get it, Honey?"

"Sure, Baby. I'll be right back." He gave Judy a quick hug and hurried out of the hospital.

Time dragged while Judy waited for his return. Restless, she ran her hands down her thighs and frowned at the blood stains drying on her pant legs. She looked toward the swinging doors anxiously, wishing a doctor would come through and tell her Margaret would be all right.

When Jerry strode through the doors a long half-hour later, Judy saw by his worried frown that he didn't have good news.

"The police have the house cordoned off," he explained, voice tight, face beaded with sweat. He plopped down beside her. "They say it's a crime scene. They're looking for signs of burglary. They wouldn't let me in, even when I told them I'm the one who called them about Margaret. They took our names and phone number. They said they need to talk to both of us as soon as possible. I have a detective's card here."

Jerry draped an arm around Judy's shoulder and looked into her anxious face. "I told them about Lou,

43

and asked 'em to look for the letter or the envelope, but they couldn't find anything. No letter. No envelope. I told them it was in Margaret's hand during the call with you. But the only mail they could find was on the end table by her rocker, and it was all from a few days ago." His face reddened. "It had to be that asshole Lou."

Judy cuddled into Jerry's arms, sobbing against his shoulder. Her head snapped up when a doctor stepped through the swinging doors. "Family of Mrs. Margaret Geerdes?" he inquired, looking around. He tucked the end of his stethoscope into the pocket of his white coat, brushed a hand through the tight waves of his silver hair, and faced Judy and Jerry.

"Yes, here," Judy replied, jumping up and dabbing at her tears with a damp wadded tissue. Jerry rose to stand beside her.

"Your mother's not awake yet," the doctor reported, his eyes solemn. "Her right arm is broken in two places, with gashes that were pretty deep. We stitched those up and set the arm. Her throat was badly cut. She was lucky; whoever did it missed the jugular and just sliced some…"

Judy shrieked, "What? Someone cut her throat?" She crumpled against Jerry, gulping back a shocked breath.

The doctor nodded, blue eyes sympathetic behind his glasses. He straightened his shoulders and continued in a clipped, professional tone. "Apparently. Of course, we don't know exactly what

44

happened. That's for the authorities to determine. She's a very lucky woman. It looks to us like she survived a brutal attack. Her necklace, a big, beaded thing, must have got tangled up in the blade and is probably what prevented the wound from being deeper."

At Judy's horrified expression, he gave a small smile. "We have a great team—she'll be getting the best of care. We're doing all we can for her, but I don't expect her to regain consciousness until tomorrow, at the earliest. She's heavily sedated and won't come out of it for at least twelve more hours and she needs to remain in intensive care. She's not aware or awake and we don't have her completely stabilized yet."

"Can we see her?" Judy interrupted.

He shrugged. "She won't even know you're here if you go in to see her now. You might as well go home. Leave your number at the desk, and we'll call you if anything develops before morning. It's best for you to go home and get some rest." He moved the stethoscope from his pocket, hung it around his neck and gave a sigh. "Do you have any questions?"

Judy's voice was weak. "I need to see her. Please?"

The doctor paused, concern evident in the set of his mouth.

"Will she be all right?" Judy asked.

The doctor straightened his shoulders and continued in a clipped, professional tone. "The situation is still life-threatening, but most likely she'll recover. She's not young, so it'll take a while. There could be complications. But she seems to be in generally good health and that's in her favor."

"Can we see her now? Just for a minute?" Judy begged.

"Okay then, but just for a minute. Follow me." He pushed his hands into his pockets, turned, and disappeared through the swinging doors, Judy scurrying at his heels.

Judy blanched at the multiple wires and IV lines leading into the white blankets covering Margaret's frail form. Monitors beeped and screens glowed in the eerie greenish light of the room. Only the upper half of Margaret's deathly pale face was visible above thick gauzy bandages that wound around her neck and up her chin. She looked so small, so vulnerable. It was hard to tell if Margaret was even breathing. Judy tried to gulp back the tears that began to pour down her cheeks, and fled.

Judy wept on the way home, snuggled against Jerry in the cab of the truck. Even though it was after ten when they got there, Jerry agreed that a call to the detective who'd given him his card was a good idea.

He dialed the number and exchanged a few words, then hung up. "The desk clerk says he's off duty 'til morning," Jerry reported. "I left an urgent message for a return call as soon as possible. Even asked them to call him at home."

But the phone didn't ring at all until the next morning. It woke them from fitful, exhausted sleep when it finally jangled at eight. After listening to Jerry's first few words, the detective on the other end of the line insisted that both Jerry and Judy report to the downtown station at once.

"He said his name is Detective David Adams and he'll be waiting for us at the front counter," Jerry said. "He said we need to move on this."

They scrambled into clean clothes and headed downtown.

Detective Adams was waiting to meet them as promised, his intense brown eyes, short cropped dark hair, and black suit with a silver tie projecting experience and authority. It took less than an hour and several cups of coffee in paper cups to pass on all the information they had. The detective agreed that Lou was likely Margaret's assailant and that Lila, wherever she was, was in danger.

"Can you think of anywhere Mrs. Peterson might have gone?" he asked. "Anywhere at all? Any place she talked about lately? Friends or family in another city?"

When Judy and Jerry shook their heads, he went on. "We'll get an alert out for the car she took and its license plate number, but it would help if we had even a general idea of what direction she might have headed."

Jerry and Judy shook their heads again.

Jerry spoke first, "Sorry. She didn't say a word to her mother or us about leaving. We were sure surprised when she disappeared. It's not like her to just leave like that."

"At first, we weren't even sure she left on her own," Judy interrupted. "She didn't answer the phone that day, and we talk every day, so I got pretty worried. It wasn't like Lila not to answer the phone 'cuz she was always home. Then when her husband showed up at our house the next day, he was in a rage. He was just crazy. Yelled that we better tell him where his car and his wife and his money were. That's when we figured out she'd taken off by herself. It must have been pretty bad for her to leave like that. Not even to tell me or her mother. She's really close to her mom."

When Judy paused, Jerry cut in, "That letter Margaret had in her hand probably answered a lot of questions, but it's gone."

"We'll keep looking for it, but he probably has it. How's Mrs. Geerdes doing?" the detective asked.

"She was still in intensive care when we left last night," Jerry replied. "They expect her to survive, but we need to get over to the hospital as soon as we're done here."

The detective stood, "Stay in close touch. You're key witnesses, and you're all we have for now. If you think of anything, anything at all, that might give us a clue, call me right away. Day or night. I'll tell the front desk to put all calls from you through to me no matter what the hour. We've already put a guard at

the victim's hospital room. We have to get this guy
before he hurts somebody else."

Chapter 6

LILA GREW MORE aware of Whittier's silence every day. The background hum of traffic, sirens, planes, and voices that had been a part of her St. Paul neighborhood had been replaced by the muffled sounds of ocean waves lapping the shore, the faint splash of the waterfall, the soft sigh of wind, rain, and snow. Even the cries of birds were muted by the frigid air. Snow seemed to swallow all sound, especially at night. Stars sparkling against a deep, black sky provided a display unlike any Lila had ever seen. The peacefulness of her new home seeped deep into her being while she settled into life at the Hodge, becoming more eager every day to get her own apartment furnished and livable. The moment Paul stepped through the door at Nan's in the morning for a cup of coffee, his presence filled the apartment with a sense of warmth and well-being. It felt empty when he left.

Paul helped Lila carry an abandoned bed frame and nearly new mattress into her still-bare apartment and Nan rustled up pots and pans, curtains, and a floor lamp left behind by others. Lila looked forward to a trip to Anchorage to buy bedding, food, and the other essentials she'd need so she could move into her place.

Paul also began stopping by the store every evening, and stayed until Lila closed up for the night. She was always glad to see him and became aware of his presence the instant he walked in the door, as if they were connected by an invisible current. She felt his gaze on her while she wiped tables and waited on customers, and basked in his obvious admiration.

Every night, after Lila banged the cash register drawer shut, she and Paul walked side by side back to the Hodge. Crisp night air surrounded the pair as they strolled through the autumn darkness, accompanied by Whittier's relentless wind, the lapping of waves in the bay and the faint rushing of the waterfall behind the Hodge.

Lila brushed out her hair and applied her favorite cherry-colored lipstick each morning. She patted blush onto her cheekbones and drew on eyeliner more liberally than she'd ever done in her life, hoping Paul would notice.

There had been wolf whistles, winks and blatant flirting from other boys and men ever since she reached her teens. Mom teased Lila about getting Grandma Logan's "chest" and warned her about

51

asking for trouble if she wore skimpy or revealing clothing. Lila's skinny legs had turned shapely just after her fourteenth birthday, drawing more stares, especially when she wore a mini skirt or Bermuda shorts. Since she'd been taller than most boys her age, and very bashful, Lila had been content to spend her spare time on homework, with Judy, and helping Mom with her house cleaning clients. Spending Saturdays vacuuming, dusting, and shining up bathrooms at Mom's side brought a sense of satisfaction to Lila. Since Mom had to provide everything for the two of them since becoming a widow, parties and afternoons at the pool didn't seem as important as helping bring income into the home. Lila felt proud to be a partner to Mom, and what she was missing with dating and friends hadn't mattered.

Flattered by Paul's attention and comforted by Nan's friendship, Lila gradually lost some of the intense homesickness of the first weeks in Whittier and the constant worry about being followed. She began to think of Paul first thing when she awoke in the morning and last thing before falling asleep. Walks home at the end of the day, sharing coffee in the morning, his caring eyes, her own growing determination to be strong, all helped nudge thoughts of danger from her mind.

Lila was finishing up the breakfast dishes when Nan opened the door to Paul's knock.

He stepped inside with a bright smile, his eyes seeking Lila's. "Hey, you two, how about a walk instead of coffee today? Let's get some fresh air. It's already over forty this morning and the sun's out. There won't be many days like this again until spring and I don't have to work until one today. Wanna go?"

Nan looked up from her coffee cup and shook her head. "Nope. Not me. You know I don't go tramping around outside unless I have to."

"Lila?" Paul asked, a trace of shyness in his voice.

"Ummm… Sure," Lila replied, her heart beginning to skip. "I'd like to check out that big abandoned building with all the broken-out windows." The idea of a walk with Paul and the chance to satisfy her curiosity about the empty building sounded good.

When Lila followed Paul out the front door a few minutes later, the cold nipped her cheeks, and she gulped the unfamiliar, frigid, ocean-scented air. Screeching gulls rode the wind above them like drunken revelers. She stumbled a bit on the ruts of the gravel parking lot that had been hardened to frosty roughness by traces of snow that blew in wind-swept whorls across the ground. She hadn't brought her boots along from Minnesota and would have to buy some before the snow came.

"I've only been in there once before, when I first came to Whittier," Paul explained as they walked toward the hulking gray building. "I've always liked history, so after I read about it, I had to check it out for myself. It's called the Buckner Building, after an Army general. I think it housed almost a thousand soldiers in the forties right before World War II. Don't all those little windows look almost like they could be prison cells?"

Lila nodded. "Yeah. Why did they build such a big military base here anyway?"

"Well, the government expected Alaska to be on the front lines for an invasion from Japan. It was supposed to be a lookout or fortress, kind of a first line of defense, if I remember right. But the invasion never happened, so they pulled out a little at a time during the years after the war. The building's falling to ruin now. Nobody can afford to buy it and fix it up. It's just too big."

"You mean it just sits here? Nobody uses it at all?" Lila asked.

"Yeah, it sits here falling apart more every year. There are still seats in the old theatre and you can see where the dining hall was. And all the soldiers' rooms—they're like little concrete cells. There was a gym and a post office and a bowling alley and a shooting range. They even had their own jail."

He led the way into the dimness beyond a dark, gaping entrance door, and reached back for Lila's hand. His felt warm and strong as he guided her along a dim corridor.

"Careful," Paul warned. "Step way over these pieces of broken glass and sheet rock." He turned to steady her. "It's dark in here. We should've brought a flashlight."

"It's spooky," Lila whispered.

They wandered the drafty, littered concrete corridors. Jagged pieces of glass crunched beneath their feet and they had to step over fragments of moldy sheet rock, broken boards and half-frozen puddles. Cement stairwells at the ends of the building, lit by windows open to the air, led from one floor to another. They stood on the stage of the theatre, looking out at the maroon, fabric-covered seats. Some were ripped, some had begun to mold, but some toward the middle of the huge, shadowy room looked like they were just waiting for someone to sit down and enjoy the show.

"Look at this!" Lila exclaimed when they stepped over a pile of broken concrete into the cavernous white-tiled kitchen. She ran her hand along the rusted stoves and corroded stainless steel counters that slanted toward dirt-streaked, shattered tiles littering the floor. Splintered benches in the adjoining dining hall tottered beside broken-down wooden tables that must have served hundreds of soldiers at a time. Lila imagined the place filled with men in uniform, the place humming with their voices, the aroma of cooking filling the air.

"So many soldiers must have lived here," she marveled.

"I guess there were a thousand men here at its peak," Paul answered. "It sure must have been boring, don't you think? They had their duties and training, I suppose, and some kinds of entertainment, but it was before television and there was just no place they could ever go."

"You sure know a lot about this place," Lila remarked.

"Yeah," Paul replied. "History was my favorite subject in high school. My Dad's from Russia, so I've learned a lot about his country, too."

She turned to Paul, curious. Maybe that explained his accent. "Russian? Your Dad's Russian?"

"Yeah. He was part of a commercial fishing boat crew from Russia that got shipwrecked off the western coast of Alaska in forty-one. The Bering Sea is really treacherous. Rescuers brought the men to shore and that's where he met my mother. He never went back home."

Lila had never known anybody with Russian heritage. She studied Paul for a moment, and then asked, "How did you get here and meet Nan?"

"Oh, I was lucky to get on with the railroad after high school." His voice faltered and his eyes took on a faraway cast. He shook his head as if to clear it and went on. "I didn't know anybody when they sent me here five years ago, but somebody in the lobby of the Hodge told me to go see Nan, and we sorta hit it off from there. She cooked me dinner my first night and found me an empty apartment to stay in for a few days 'til I could get my own. I was going through a pretty tough time then, and…well…anyway… she's been my friend ever since."

He paused, his gaze again drifting far off, then rustled his shoulders and met Lila's eyes. "I like Nan. She takes care of herself and anybody else she cares about. But she seems kinda lonely, sort of lost and sad sometimes. I don't know why." His face grew puzzled, eyebrows drawing together. "I think she was married a long time ago, but she never talks about it. She's a little rough around the edges, but that's just Nan. She's good-hearted."

"Yeah, she does seem really nice," Lila agreed. "And I've noticed that lost look on her face a couple of times, too. I wonder what's it's about."

She shivered, pulled her coat close around her shoulders, and turned back to the deserted room before them. "I bet it was really cold in here in the winter. It's all concrete block walls and cement floors. It's freezing in here, and it's just such a huge building!"

"Yeah," Paul agreed. Then, with a mischievous grin, he added, "They say bears hibernate in the basement every winter now. People have seen them coming in and out—"

Lila's squeal cut his sentence short. She pulled her hand from his and in seconds, they were scrambling for the entrance, Lila leading the way. They burst into the open to a darkening sky and wind howling with a high-pitched wail. Icy pellets of snow whipped their faces as they ran hand-in-hand for the Hodge, stumbling through the ruts, laughing into the wind.

Chapter 7

AN ASTRINGENT, AMMONIA-LIKE smell greeted Judy and Jerry as the entry doors of Midway Hospital whispered open before them. The ICU upstairs hummed with the constant, low murmur of voices; beeping, buzzing, and gurgling sounds; and the sharp air hung even heavier here, as if fresh air never made its way that far into the interior of the building.

The couple hustled to Margaret's side, finding her motionless, pale, and frail-looking beneath the blankets covering her to the muffler-like bandage around her throat. Wisps of silvery hair, mashed back from her forehead, disappeared beneath the gauze wrapped around her head like an unsightly turban. An IV tube snaked from its hanger into one thin arm.

Judy's face blanched at the sight of Margaret looking so small and old, and so broken. They hovered by her side for almost an hour, but there was no response to their gentle words, and no return squeeze when they held her hand. They drove home in silence, hearts heavy, shocked at the turn of events. Jerry called his brothers when they got home, and all decided Jerry and Judy, for their own security, should temporarily move in with brother, Greg, since there was no telling what Lou would do.

It was a difficult day for Judy, moving necessities out of the house over to Greg's, worrying about Margaret, desperately wishing for a way to reach Lila, and fighting a growing fear of Lou. She tried to settle down, but it was hard to feel comfortable in someone else's home.

THE NEXT WEEK passed with no sign of Lou, no change in Margaret's condition, and no clues found by the police. It was as if Lou had vanished right along with Lila. Since Lou had failed to show up for work since the day of Margaret's attack, Detective Adams assured Jerry and Judy that he was their prime suspect in the case. All agreed he'd most likely left town right after the attack on Margaret, probably on a search for Lila. There wasn't the slightest clue to his whereabouts, and no trace of the letter from Lila had been found.

On the eighth day after the attack, while sitting by Margaret's side during her daily visit to the hospital, Judy spoke gentle words. "Hi, Margaret. It's Judy. Time to wake up. Can you hear me?"

Margaret's eyelids flickered open to Judy's delight, and focused on her.

"Margaret, can you hear me?" Judy repeated, leaping up when Margaret mouthed a weak reply. Judy dashed to the nurses' station down the hall. "Come quick, she's awake!" she cried.

Medical personnel crowded the room within minutes. Judy gulped sobs of relief when Margaret responded to the commotion by whispering a few words and struggling to sit up. After seeing that Margaret was still awake an hour later, and even able to take a few sips of water through a straw, Judy agreed with the nurse's recommendation that she go home to allow Margaret to rest.

"We'll talk tomorrow," she said, bending over the bed to give her a careful half hug. "You rest now. I'll be here bright and early in the morning. You'll feel even better and we can talk more then."

Margaret settled back on her pillow, her eyes filled with questions. A stern nurse stepped forward, adjusted a valve on the IV, and directed Judy toward the door.

Judy couldn't wait to tell Jerry. Judy and Jerry called Detective Adams immediately with the news that Margaret was awake.

Margaret had made what her nurse described as "remarkable improvement" by the next day. She'd even been able to sit shakily on the side of her bed for a few minutes, so the doctor left word allowing the police to interview her the next day. Judy sat at Margaret's bedside and explained the events of the past week. Margaret listened intently and lifted her chin at the details, and although her face was pale, her eyes glowed with resolve.

MARGARET WAS PROPPED up in bed, eager to answer questions, when Detective Adams and his partner arrived the next morning.

"I remember getting Lila's letter... And calling Judy," Margaret whispered in a barely audible, hoarse voice. Her neck was wrapped in heavy white bandages, her right arm in a cast. "But I had to answer that...that awful pounding...at the door."

She paused for a painful swallow and her gaze drifted off. "Yes, it was Lou there. He pushed his way in... He was acting crazy. He wanted to know...where Lila was and...right that very minute. I was...I was just shocked. His eyes...they looked wild."

She tried to swallow again. Judy hurried over and held a glass and straw to Margaret's lips. Margaret sipped, then took a shaky breath. "He didn't believe me...when I said I didn't know...I remember him...coming toward me...then that's all."

Her demeanor wavered and a sob caught in her throat. Judy slipped onto the edge of the bed, and put a comforting arm around her shoulders. "There...there. You're safe. Lou's long gone."

Margaret regained her composure, clutched Judy's hand and turned back to the detective. "What else do you...need to know?" she whispered.

"Did Lou take the letter from Lila?" he asked.

Margaret thought for a moment. "I don't know… I can't recall… Have you found it? Did you get in touch…with my daughter?" Her voice became weaker with each word, then broke, and her face paled. "Is my Lila okay?"

"As far as we know, she is. We'll fill you in more tomorrow on everything. That's enough for today," the detective announced, the tone of his voice leaving no room for argument.

Although all were desperate to learn if Margaret remembered any details of the return address on Lila's envelope, the detective honored the doctor's order to let Margaret lead conversations, and not push her in any way if she appeared tired. He slipped out and Judy helped Margaret settle back into bed where she dropped off into sleep at once.

MARGARET HAD RALLIED by the next afternoon. She was sitting up in bed, the bandage had been removed from her head, and her hair had been shampooed and fluffed into its usual white curls. The dressing around her throat had been replaced by one allowing her to move her head side to side, and the IV had been removed from her arm. Her blue eyes crinkled over a smile when she saw Judy.

Detective Adams got right to it as soon as he arrived. "Do you remember if the envelope had a return address?"

63

"Hmmm…" Margaret whispered hoarsely. "Yes, I do believe it was a Montana address. Yes, now I remember… I recall it because I was really puzzled. You see, we don't know…a single soul in Montana. Never even been there… I remember wondering why Lila would be mailing something from Montana… She's never been there, I'm certain of that."

"Think hard about the name of the town in Montana. Any sense of what it was? Any clue you can give us?" Detective Adams prodded.

Margaret furrowed her brow. "Not exactly… Maybe it'll come to me. Something about a wild animal… A wolf maybe? Yeah, that's it… there was a wolf in the name of the town. But I can't quite recall…" she paused in frustration and held out her hand for her water, beckoning to Judy.

Judy hurried to hold the straw to Margaret's lips, elated. They now had a clue about the town where Lila had mailed her letter.

The detective quickly ended the interview. "A security guard will remain posted outside the hospital room door," he assured Margaret while he shrugged into his jacket. "Since you've provided a positive ID of your attacker, you're considered an endangered witness and are entitled to this protection until we locate the suspect. We're quite sure Mr. Peterson is long gone from the St. Paul area, but I insist that a guard be kept in place, just in case."

The women sighed with relief as he nearly sprinted out the door. However, Judy's relief was matched by alarm, picturing Lou somewhere in Montana, hot on Lila's trail.

Chapter 8

ON A BRISK October morning on the first of October, a dark-haired man stood on the shoulder of Highway 10 heading west out of the Twin Cities of Minneapolis and St. Paul, his thumb outstretched and his shoes smudged with traces of blood he'd been unable to completely wipe away. One hand obsessively patted his pocket, checking his wallet and the torn envelope it held. He was soon settled into the cab of an eighteen-wheeler barreling northwest out of St. Paul.

THREE THOUSAND MILES away, that same morning, Lila watched from Nan's apartment as the sky darkened, the fury of the wind increased and a watery sun tried to poke through scraps of clouds skittering across the mountain tops. Pellets of wind-driven sleet began to hurtle against the window, pecking it like gravel. A gusty wind whipped white-tipped waves across the waters of Whittier's harbor, causing moored boats to jostle against each other, the wharf, and their lines. Gulls cried shrilly as they were buffeted over the seascape. Nan had been right yesterday when she predicted a storm. It was Lila's first Whittier blizzard only two weeks after arriving in town, and it looked like it would be a very cold walk to the store in this worsening weather.

By mid-afternoon, Lila had to fight her way through sleet and a raging wind that nearly stole her breath. The wind bit through her light jacket, whipped her hair across her face, and her fingers tingled with cold even though they were in her pockets.

She opened the door and pushed her way into the warmth of the store, where old Tom greeted her. "Looks like the first big one of the season's here," he wheezed. "Close up early. When it gets like this, everybody goes home, and hunkers down 'til it's over. Sometimes for days. I'm headin' outta here right quick now 'fore it gets worse. Can't take the cold. Gits right inta my bones, an' it's too blamed hard to breathe. Gotta bit a' heart trouble, ya know." His shallow, rasping breath rattled in his chest. "This is gonna be a bad one. Wrap up here by five or so. Kick anybody out who's still hangin' around."

Lila nodded, blew on her stiff fingers, and wiped her watering eyes. Such a raw, piercing wind made her anxious to get into Anchorage for a warmer jacket. Maybe Paul would take her soon.

She puttered around, polishing the counter, straightening canned goods on the shelves, counting the money in the cash register. Nobody was in the store, and nobody came in during the next few hours. There was no sign of activity outside other than the blowing snow. An eerie feeling crept over Lila; it felt like being alone in a ghost town. As she crouched to dust a shelf, she jumped at the sound of the door banging open.

Paul burst in, bringing with him a blast of icy air. "Hey, Lila, let's go. Everything's closing up early. I'll give you a ride home. My truck's running right outside."

Lila was only too happy to follow him into the cozy cab of his pickup. When they parked in the Hodge's lot, Lila's thoughts turned again to her mother. "Paul, thanks a lot for coming to get me. And, well…well…I have a favor to ask."

The warmth in his eyes encouraged her to continue, "No problem picking you up. Nobody should be out in this. I was going home anyway to get something to eat. What's the favor?"

Lila hesitated, but anxiety overcame her reluctance to ask more of him. "Do you know of any way I can call my mother? She has to be really worried about me by now. Is there a phone somewhere around here that's set up so the number can't be traced?" She glanced at Paul, uncertain." I just have to talk to her. I have to see if she got my letter and knows I'm okay."

Paul halted his pull on the door handle and turned to her, face pinched with concern. "Not many people here have their own phones, Lila. I don't, either. Actually, Whittier's phone system isn't very reliable. Sometimes in bad weather, there's no service at all for days at a time if the power lines get blown down or iced over. Once, a couple of winters ago, the town didn't have power or phones for a whole week." He grinned at Lila's expression. "The weather was so bad crews couldn't get in. Even the tunnel was closed."

After a moment of thought, he went on, "But, we might be able to use the phone at the railroad office. It's something employees are allowed to do. They keep a record of long-distance calls, and then we pay back the ones that are ours. Kind of a benefit of the job. A call from that phone could be traced, I suppose, but at least your name wouldn't be on any records." He paused and met Lila's eyes. "I can ask."

"Thank you," Lila replied with a grateful smile. "And thanks again for coming to pick me up. It's nasty out there. Will it get much worse?"

"Yeah. It looks like the first real blizzard. Do me a favor, don't go out in it by yourself."

They scrambled out of Paul's truck and scurried through stinging snow up the steps and into the lobby. When the elevator stopped at Nan's floor, Paul got out and walked her to the door.

Lila turned to Paul with her hand on the doorknob. "Nan's so good about letting me stay until I get things set up in my own apartment. But she might not be here right now. She said she'd be helping down in the library room these next few days." She hesitated, feeling bashful. "You have to go back to work, right? Want me to make you a sandwich to take along?"

"Sure," Paul answered, sounding pleased, his eyes brightening. "I do have to drive back over to the office for an hour or so to file the paperwork and lock things up." He followed her into the apartment and sat watching her work at the kitchen counter.

"Mustard?" At his response, Lila spread mustard before folding tinfoil around the ham sandwich. She handed it to him, feeling unexpected intimacy in the action. Making a lunch was something wives did for their husbands.

Paul took the sandwich with an awkward, "Thanks. Should I stop back and let you know if we can make the phone call?"

"Sure. That would be great," Lila answered.

He gave her another grin before letting himself out the door. As it closed, she was already looking forward to his return. She busied herself, washing up the dishes, sorting her belongings for the move into her apartment, making frequent trips to the window to watch for Paul's truck.

PAUL ANNOUNCED AS soon as he returned, "Good news. My boss said he won't mind if we call Minnesota as long as I make sure the charges get paid. So, let's do it."

Lila's heart leapt. "Yes! Oh, yes! When can we call?"

"Tomorrow morning? I could pick you up early, unless the weather's too bad. It's later back in the Midwest, isn't it? So if I pick you up around nine, it'd be about noon there, right?"

Lila smiled, thrilled. She'd get to talk to her mother tomorrow and maybe Judy, too.

She stopped Paul with a touch on the arm when he turned to leave and met his gaze. "Paul. Well…thank you. You've been so good to me. Thank you so much for everything."

He smiled, then reached for Lila, drawing her into his arms and pulling her close. She felt his heart thundering as hard as hers was. He stared into her eyes while he lowered his face. His lips, warm and firm, touched hers with tenderness. His tentativeness vanished when she began to return his gentle pressure, and the kiss deepened.

All at once, Lila realized what she was doing, pulled back, and pushed herself out of Paul's arms. She took a deep breath, heart fluttering, overcome by shame, and stammered, "I'm… I'm…married."

Paul's face flushed and his voice thickened with emotion. "Your husband, that's who you're running from, right?"

"Yes," Lila said, relieved to finally be able to tell him.

Paul leaned away to look at her with earnest eyes. "Nan told me someone almost killed you. That was him, right?" He tugged her back into his embrace. "Don't worry. We won't let that creep near you."

Lila nearly cried with relief at his words. She pulled back to look him in the face. "Thank you with all my heart, Paul. You don't know how much that means to me..."

"You don't know how much *you* mean to me," Paul murmured, his voice low with tenderness. "Ever since I first saw you, I haven't been able to get you out of my mind." He paused. "You're tough. And so beautiful," he added, his words carrying a caress.

"Thank you, Paul. You've made all the difference in my life since I got here. I'm glad...well, I'm glad..." Her voice faltered.

They pulled apart, locked into each other's eyes after the heartfelt words, Lila stepped back, shaken, mind whirling while Paul's pleased smile accompanied him out the door.

Chapter 9

NOBODY IN WHITTIER KNEW that the theft of a plain blue sedan from an elderly couple at a gas station in northern Montana had been reported to the authorities. Or that by the time the bulletin spread across the state, their car had already passed through Canadian customs and was being driven hard, recklessly, north toward Alaska.

BY THE TIME Paul knocked at Nan's door the next morning, Lila had been up and dressed for hours, too excited about the call home to sleep any later. She felt the heat of a blush creep over her face when she met Paul's gaze. He blushed, too. No words were spoken about the kiss the day before. They shared toast with raspberry jam, whispering to avoid waking Nan, and then drove through blowing snow to the railroad hut at the mouth of the tunnel. Lila hardly felt the bitter wind that clawed at her face as they scuffed through snowdrifts to the office door.

Inside, a young man with "Bob" sewed on his shirt jumped up from his desk. He was sandy-haired, with genial blue eyes that flashed with mischief. "You must be Lila," he exclaimed with a big grin. His eyes skimmed her head to toe before she could answer, and turning to Paul, he grinned approval. He gave a smirk, stuffed his uniform cap over his hair and headed out the office door, leaving them alone.

"Ready?" Paul asked, an embarrassed look stealing over his face.

Lila nodded, momentarily flustered by Bob's reaction to the introduction, but her thoughts were too focused on the call to mind. It would be so good to hear her mother's voice.

It seemed to take forever for Paul to spin the numbers on the bulky black rotary phone. He handed the receiver to Lila as soon as he finished dialing, but there was no ring at the other end. Instead, staccato static filled Lila's ear. She handed the phone to Paul.

"That's weird. I've never heard a sound like that before," he said. "Let's try again." But, once more, all they heard was static.

Her mother had that same number ever since Lila could remember. There'd never been a problem before. "Well, let's try Judy's number then," Lila suggested, her brows knit with concern.

Paul handed the phone to Lila, and this time it rang as usual and was picked up.

Lila gave a squeak of excitement at the sound of Judy's voice before blurting out, "Judy! Hi! It's me!"

"Lila! Thank God!" Judy cried. "Oh, Lila, where are you? We've been trying to get in touch you. It's your mom. She's been hurt. She's in the hospital." She stopped for a quick breath and rattled on. "I'm so glad you called!"

Lila crumpled to her knees onto the wooden floor at Judy's agonized words. Paul rushed to her side and knelt, putting his arms around her. "What—" he began, but Lila shushed him.

She tipped the receiver so he could hear, too, and he leaned in. "What, Judy? What happened? Mom's hurt? She's in the hospital?" Lila could barely get the words out. Her throat had grown dry, and her heart began thudding. She leaned into Paul.

Judy's trembling voice came over the line. "She'll be all right, Lila. She's been in the hospital since it happened. It was Lou. She got a letter from you and just when she was reading it to me over the phone, Lou got in her door and...well...and...he...it's her throat and her arm that are cut the worst."

"What?" Lila screamed. "What did he do?"

Lila grew light-headed while Judy's familiar voice, tight with pain, explained what had happened.

Finally, Judy finished with a plaintive, "Where are you? Can you come home right away? It's been so terrible!"

Lila managed to gasp, "I'm in Alaska."

Judy's shriek pierced their ears. "What? How in the dickens did you get there? Alaska! Good Lord, Lila!"

"I had to run from Lou, Judy. But, about Mom. Tell me about Mom. Is there a number where I can call her? What hospital?" She broke down into heaving sobs. The receiver fell from her hands. "Oh, this is all because of me. Oh, Mom!"

Paul grabbed the phone. "Judy? This is her friend, Paul. I heard most of what you told her. My God! Someone hurt her mother?"

"Who are you again?" Judy's high-pitched voice came over the phone. "We've all been worried sick about Lila. Just worried sick."

"I'm Paul, her neighbor. You sure her mother's gonna be all right?"

"It happened about ten days ago," Judy answered. "Now her mom's getting better every day. She should get out of the hospital next week. Me and my husband will keep her at our house when she gets out. It looks like Lila's husband did it and he's disappeared as far as anybody here can tell. He has to be a real sonofabitch to hurt an old lady like that. The police have a nationwide, all-points bulletin out for him as a suspect in an attempted murder. They're pretty sure he's left the state."

Judy stopped for a minute, then continued, "We weren't sure where Lila was, and we were so afraid he'd hurt her, too. I am so glad she's finally called and that she's fine. But, it looks like Lou might have the letter Lila sent to her mother. We know there was a return address on the envelope, somewhere in Montana. We aren't sure why."

Paul drew a sobbing Lila tighter against him. "I can't believe Lou put her mother in the hospital. And he might have an address for Lila, you say?"

Lila snatched the phone from Paul's hand "I have to talk to Mom. I have to talk to her. Now! Where do I call?"

"Just a minute. I have the number in my purse here. It's Midway Hospital, five six zero fifty fifty, room two ten. I'll have to get over there and answer the phone in her room and hold it up to her ear. She can't answer it herself. Visiting hours go 'til three, I think. Phone calls, too, so we only have a couple of hours. But give me time to get there. Can you call again in twenty minutes?"

"Yeah. Oh, Judy, thank you. I should have been there. I can't believe this happened. Are you sure Mom's all right?"

"Yeah, it looks like she'll be fine. I'll fill you in more the next time we talk. But right now, let me drive over to the hospital so you can call there, okay?"

"Yeah. Yeah. I'll call the hospital number in twenty minutes. Five six zero, fifty fifty. Room two ten?"

"Yup."

It was the longest twenty minutes of Lila's life. She and Paul sat facing each other across the desk in

77

agonized silence, watching the clock, their hands entwined.

Finally, Paul stirred. "Well, that's twenty. Let's give it another minute or two to make sure she's in the room. Then I'll dial."

Judy answered on the first ring. "Lila? I'm here."

"Oh, Judy! Put Mom on. Please, put her on!"

Margaret's faint, croaky voice was barely audible. "Sweetheart? Is…is…that…you?"

"Yes, Mom, it's me. I'm so sorry. I should've been there. I have to come home right away."

"No….no…Sweetheart. Don't…." after a gurgled swallow, her voice faded.

"Lila? It's Judy again. It's hard for her to talk. But she's smiling. It's the first time she's smiled since…well, since…I can tell she's happy to hear your voice. It was a good thing, this call."

Judy's voice, tinny and distant, babbled on. "She's really brightened up. Can I tell her where you are? Can you call again? Maybe tomorrow? Same time? We shouldn't overdo it right now. Just so she knows you're somewhere safe, that's all that matters right now." Judy paused. "Lila, she's gonna be fine. She has some color in her cheeks, and her voice is getting better. The doctor makes rounds every morning about ten. I can be here and talk to him tomorrow. Then I'll fill you in when you call back again, okay?"

Lila replied with reluctance, "Yeah. Thanks, Jude. Tell Mom I love her very much, will you? Tell her I'll talk to you both tomorrow and that I'm fine."

"Sure. I am so glad you called! And thank God you're safe. We were plumb crazy, not knowing. But, anyway, enough for today. Be sure to call tomorrow! Do you have a number I can write down?"

"I'll have to find out," Lila promised. "I'm using someone's office phone, so I don't know the number right now. Please tell Mom I love her, and I'll be thinking of her every minute 'til we talk again."

"Don't worry. She's tough, you know. And hearing from you will help most of all."

"Yeah. I can't thank you enough, Judy. You're the best friend I could ever have."

"I know," Judy replied. Lila could hear the familiar grin in Judy's voice before the line cut off.

She turned to Paul. "Well," he said, his voice somber. "I'd say you're running from a maniac. I better remind all the guys just how dangerous he is. We can't let him through the tunnel."

"He's had the letter with the Montana return address for over a week now..." Lila whispered.

They looked at each other, eyes wide. Lila clutched both hands to her mouth and cried out, "Dee and Chuck! That couple I stayed overnight with in Montana! Their return address was on the envelope Mom had. What if Lou tracked 'em down? What if he's been there? Oh, no!"

Paul dropped her hand, snatched up the phone and dialed the operator. "Get me the Alaska State Troopers. Quick. This is an emergency!" he barked into the receiver.

He reported the information about the likely danger to Dee and Chuck to the officer who answered. He hung up after being assured that the information would be transmitted to Montana authorities as soon as possible. He and Lila stared at each other in silence.

Chapter 10

NAN LISTENED TO the day's developments and tried to reassure Lila that her mother would be fine. But the halibut and potatoes she fried for supper might as well have been made of cardboard. Lila stared blankly at the TV screen, her mind drawn to an image of her mother, bandaged up, lying helpless in a hospital bed. Lila's face felt hot, her eyes dry and scratchy, and it was hard to swallow around the burning lump in her throat.

Wracked by worry, she found it hard to get to sleep that night, but finally drifted off to thoughts of her mother and Judy, imagining them back at home. There was Mom on a Sunday morning, standing at the stove flipping French toast, the aroma of frying bacon filtering through the house. The flowered curtains at the kitchen window, the deep green of the giant white pine at the corner of the yard, and their voices, filled her dreams. And Judy, with her new pixie haircut, tipping back one of the Hamm's beers she loved, a cigarette poised in her fingers like a movie star. Memories of home soothed Lila, and she slipped into sleep.

The next morning, knocking and a muffled, "Nan, are you awake?" woke Lila.

She sat up, immediately doubled over by the waves of nausea that seemed to have become more intense these past few mornings. She gagged, then took deep, shaky breaths until the pangs subsided and she could slide out of bed. She tugged her robe on and joined Nan, who was unlocking the door. One look at Paul's white face and Lila knew something was wrong.

"What?" she cried. "Is it Mom?!"

"No. There's no word from Judy. It's not that."

Paul stepped inside and pulled the door shut behind him. He hesitated, grimacing. "It's… It's… Montana. They had my office number on record from when I called the troopers. Paul sucked in a deep breath. "I drove over here on my break, as soon as I could get away. It's bad, Lila…"

Lila gasped. Her mind raced.

Not Chuck and Dee!

"What happened?"

"There was a fire. About a week ago. Somebody torched their house. Chuck and Dee were working at their café when it happened. They ran over but their house burned to the ground right before their eyes. Chuck tried to get some stuff out and his arms got burned so he's in the hospital in Williston."

"Oh, no! Their house? He torched their house? They must have lost everything. Oh, this is all my fault!" Lila cried out in disbelief.

Paul hesitated for a moment. Lila couldn't speak. She felt Nan's arm slip around her shoulders as he went on. "The sheriff said they have a suspect. A dark-haired stranger had been nosing around Wolf Point earlier that day. He went all over town, trying to get information on his missing wife, insisting she'd been there. Some old man at the counter in the café finally told him to get lost, that if Dee and Chuck helped people out, it was their own damn business. They think the names must have tipped the guy off."

Paul heaved a sigh and shook his head. "They decided he nosed around enough to figure out who Chuck and Dee were and which house was theirs. It's a real small town, only forty people or so. They assume Lou searched their house before he set the fire. Dee wanted to make sure you were informed that their address book was on the kitchen counter by the phone. He probably took it. Your Whittier address was in it."

She pulled away from Nan and sank onto a kitchen chair, burying her head in her hands. "So he knows where I am now. I'll never get away from him!" Her words tumbled. "Look what he did to Mom, and Chuck and Dee. It's all my fault what happened to them." She wiped away tears. "I wish I'd never met him. I'm so afraid now."

Huge sobs racked her body. Paul strode over and put his arms around her. Nan hovered, patting Lila's back.

Soon, Paul pulled back. "Lila, that settles it! We have to keep him out of Whittier. We'll do whatever it takes." He pulled a picture out of his breast pocket, the picture Lila had given Paul the day she arrived at the Whittier tunnel. "This is all I need. You can tell me about everything when you feel ready."

"But, don't you need…but—" Lila began.

Paul laid a comforting hand on her cheek. "Lila, it's okay. We're dealing with a monster here. I can see why you're so afraid." He drew back, stood to his full height, and declared, "The guys and I have total control of the tunnel. And as long as we have his picture, he won't get through. Sometimes, we have to kind of take the law into our own hands. We've done it before. I promise you we'll keep him out, no matter what the rules say. Nobody ever checks up on us— we're not really very important business to the railroad. And we say whatever we need to in our reports. I'll do this for you."

With a great sigh of relief, Lila reached into her purse. "Okay. Here's another picture. He's the tall one on the right with the dark hair and the pack of cigarettes rolled up in his shirt sleeve."

Paul studied the new picture for a long moment, then stuffed it into his pocket, his face darkening.

Chapter 11

"HOW DID YOU meet that couple in Montana? Dee and Chuck?" Paul asked as Lila sipped the hot chocolate Nan assured her would calm her down.

"I met them in a little town called Wolf Point. It was the night after I left Minnesota, I'd driven like crazy and I was so scared, I couldn't think straight. I just kept going up through Fargo, and all the way across North Dakota. The only thing I stopped for was gas. All of a sudden, I noticed a little bit of pink and gold in the rear view mirror and saw the sun rising behind me. I'd driven all night and didn't even know it. It felt like I was waking up from a dream or something when I noticed a sign for the Montana border."

After another sip, she went on. "When I got to Glendive, the little town was just waking up and I pulled into the Standard station. The coffee smelled good when I came out of the restroom, so I got a cup, even though I don't usually drink it. I thought it might help me stay awake. I sat in the car for a moment before pulling out, sipping my coffee. The dashboard clock showed that Lou'd been home from work for more than six hours by that time. I was sure he would've called my mother's house when he made it back to the apartment, even though it would have been in the middle of the night. I knew he'd have been at Judy's door by then, too, demanding information."

Lila's voice rose. "I was so worried! What if he didn't believe them when they said they didn't know where I was? I didn't dare call because Lou has an uncle at the phone company who might help him check phone records. I felt pretty tired, but I knew I had to get a little farther north toward Canada, and try to get across the border as fast as I could. I figured Lou would never look for me in Canada. That was the only plan I could think of. So, I decided to head off the highway to Wolf Point, because it looked pretty close to the border and was so small it might not get noticed if someone was searching for me."

She paused, a faraway look filling her eyes. "The next few hours of driving that morning were really hard. My head kept dropping forward and my eyes were so dry. I was glad for the bright sun through the passenger's side window and I opened it to let the cool air blow in. I turned the radio as loud as it would go and sang along to every song I knew the words to. But I knew I'd have to stop soon. That straight, flat highway just went on and on, and I was beyond tired."

"You drove all night?" Nan asked with a shake of her head. She sucked a deep draft of her fresh cigarette and blew the smoke toward the ceiling.

Lila nodded and told them how cottony morning mist had been lingering along the two blocks of Wolf Point's deserted, dirt-packed main street. "It was scary. Kind of like a ghost town or something. But right there on Main Street was the Sunshine Café. The lights were on and the place looked ordinary and safe. I was starving by then, too. The cafe was empty except for an old man in a dirty black baseball cap sipping coffee at the counter. He seemed lost in his own early morning world and didn't seem to really notice me."

"The waitress came a second after I slid into a booth," Lila said. "She had a nice smile, and she hung around my booth, kind of curious, you know. When I ordered the Sunrise Special, she said it was a good choice, if someone's real hungry. I told her I was." She went on at Paul's encouraging look. "I was so tired I could hardly hold my head up."

She sighed at the memory, and told them how she'd dug into the pancakes, eggs and ham, and two slices of toast perched along the edge of the plate. The waitress had appeared again, a pitcher of water in her hand, just as Lila was finishing the last bite of breakfast. Her chestnut hair was caught in a low, messy bun along the back of her neck, her blue eyes crinkled into a web of wrinkles when she smiled, and she'd tugged at the slightly stained apron tied off center around her waist.

"When she handed me the check, she told me her name was Dee," Lila recalled. "Then she said, 'You're by yourself, aren't you, young lady? You're not from around here, and I can see you're tired. I can spot a gal in trouble a mile away. You're one of 'em, right?'"

Lila looked over at Nan. "I couldn't stop the tears. Dee pushed an extra napkin across the table, slid into the other side of the booth and waited. When she said, 'Okay, Honey, what's up?' I just melted."

Paul gestured for her to go on, his look steady and comforting.

Nan shook her head, stubbed out her cigarette, then flicked the lighter hanging on a leather cord around her neck. She sucked in a deep breath to light a new one, huffed a cloud of smoke toward the living room and returned her gaze toward Lila. "What else?"

Lila went on, "Dee told me her husband, Chuck, was cooking in the kitchen and that they owned the café. Kind of to reassure me, I guess. So, I told her I was running from someone. But all of a sudden, I couldn't keep the words coming. My lips felt numb and my tongue wouldn't work right. Dee got up and went over to talk to her husband. She came back and said 'Here's what's gonna happen. Our house is across the alley out back. You're coming with me to get a good nap. You're not going anywhere 'til after you've had some rest. Only after that, we'll let you get back on the road. And that's that.'" Lila gave a small smile at the memory.

"It sounded good because I was so tired," she explained. "I know it seems crazy to just go with her like that, but I guess I wasn't thinking straight. Dee told me to get my purse and jacket and come with her. She said she wanted me to tell her what was up on the way over to their house. So I told her my story. Maybe I shouldn't have trusted strangers like that, but Dee was so nice and I've never felt so tired. My neck was hurting pretty bad by then, too, so I just did what she told me to. She let me sleep in their daughter's old room."

The next thing Lila knew, she heard voices murmuring, and had to squint against dawn's sunlight streaming through the window. To her amazement, she'd slept all that day and through the next night. She'd pulled on her clothes and entered the kitchen where Dee and Chuck turned toward her with worried looks.

"They asked if I always slept so long and if I was rested enough to continue. Then they told me about a woman they'd heard about who found refuge in Whittier, Alaska, for over ten years. I didn't have any other plan, so it sounded good. Dee had already packed me three sandwiches and an apple and brownies, almost like they knew I'd agree. Chuck said the roads should be safe and dry through the Canadian Rockies all the way to Alaska for another month or so. They thought Whittier was my best chance."

"So that's how you heard about Whittier?" Paul asked. He shook his head, wonder playing across his face. "From strangers? And you just went?"

She turned to Paul. "Yeah. I almost can't believe I did it. But I was scared and I didn't have any other plan. So before I knew it, I was following Chuck's pickup out of Wolf Point on little country roads. He stopped after about fifteen minutes and opened the bars of an old rusty gate. He told me that locals used this back road to avoid the official border stations checking northbound traffic on major highways crossing the Canadian border. He said customs officials knew about the gate, but they looked the other way since the offenders were their friends and neighbors just traveling back and forth. I couldn't believe my luck. I could get across the border into Canada without a trace!"

She paused, remembering. "Chuck said to be sure to stay on that same road until I hit Route 18, then turn north on it through Kildeer, and the signs for Regina and Saskatoon would show up right after that and get me onto the Alcan Highway. Then he warned me to be careful and made me promise not to pick up any hitchhikers. He gave me some envelopes Dee had addressed and stamped so I'd be sure to write as soon as I made it to Whittier. And he told me to write to my mother as soon as I could, too. He said I could send my letters to them first and they'd forward them on to Mom so the return address and postmark wouldn't be Whittier. He gave me their phone number and said I could call anytime, collect if I needed to."

"So you just drove all the way across the Canadian Rockies and half of Alaska alone? Based on the advice of strangers?" Paul asked, wide-eyed.

"Yeah. What else could I do?"

"What was it like, all those days driving by yourself? How'd you do it?" Nan asked, her face filled with awe, curiosity shining from her eyes.

Lila took a shuddering breath.

"What?" Paul asked as the silence lengthened. "What are you thinking about?"

"Lou," she answered. "While I was driving, I had visions of my husband behind the wheel of a pickup. I could see his face, and his voice haunted me, 'My little darlin'. Thought you could get away from old Lou, huh?' It was a really lonely quiet drive because there was no radio reception that far into Canada, so I kept imagining his voice." She trembled.

Paul moved his hand over hers, "That sonofabitch will never get into Whittier, I promise you. You're safe here." He touched her cheek with a gentle hand. "God," he murmured. "My, God, Lila."

Chapter 12

BY THE END of October, Lila had begun to learn the names and faces of some of the other residents of the Hodge. Although many scurried down corridors with the briefest of acknowledgments as if human interaction were undesirable, a few introduced themselves when passing in the corridors or sharing the elevator. She met others through Nan and Paul, but Lila couldn't keep the names and faces straight quite yet. Everyone pretty much kept to themselves, anyway.

Whittier life was definitely not like life back home. Puzzled by these people who lived so closely together, yet so separately, she wanted to learn more about them—what they did all day, why they were in Whittier, how long they'd been here, where they'd come from. Everyone guarded personal information, though, as if needing to keep their distance. It was all so strange.

Nan remained evasive about her background, too, occasionally letting a few hints drop, then laughing off Lila's questions with silly answers. All Lila had managed to learn so far was that Nan had come to Whittier from Seattle about twenty years earlier and had once been married. Nan directed conversations away from herself so deftly that Lila soon realized prying wasn't an option.

At the end of Lila's fourth week in Whittier, Paul offered to take her into Anchorage the next day for the essentials she needed. Tom agreed to let her have the day off, and Lila looked forward to the trip, not only for the shopping, but for the chance to spend an entire day with Paul. Neither had mentioned the spontaneous kiss the week before.

LILA AWOKE EARLIER than usual after a night of fitful sleep, filled with anticipation. She tried on three tops before deciding on a navy blue sweater that, even though faded, highlighted the blueness of her eyes. She'd had been ready and waiting for an hour by the time Paul knocked on Nan's door at eight-thirty. There had been only a twinge of nausea this morning, to Lila's relief, and the coffee Nan perked in the old tin coffee pot on the stove tasted good for a change. Lila felt nearly giddy with anticipation by the time Paul arrived. She couldn't wait to get on the highway.

Paul walked to the passenger side of his truck and opened the door for Lila, and her heart melted. Lou had never opened a door for her. Paul's truck was immaculate. He'd probably done that just for this trip, and she felt flattered and special.

They rode in silence to the mouth of the tunnel where the train sat chugging its smoky plume into the sky. It was a short wait in line behind the three other cars waiting ahead of them to load onto flatcars for the nine o'clock tunnel opening. The railroad workers on duty noticed Paul's truck and gave waves of acknowledgement.

"It feels funny not to be out there with the guys," Paul said. "I hardly ever take a day off on Tuesdays or Saturdays when the train goes through. This is the first Saturday I've had off since I can remember. It's nice."

He turned to Lila, smiled, then reached over and covered her hand with his. She didn't dare look at him. He kept his warm hand over hers during the loading of vehicles onto the flatcars, all the way through the tunnel, and across the Portage Valley. Neither spoke, as if to do so would break a spell.

Paul removed his hand from hers when they turned onto the Seward Highway and began heading north to Anchorage. He put both hands on the wheel and turned toward her with a cheerful grin. When his eyes lowered to linger on her lips, she knew he was thinking about the kiss, just as she was. Lila smiled back at him. Lou's face flashed before her and a rush of anxiety coursed through her. She ignored it. There was no room in her thoughts for him today.

Paul pointed out sights as they drove. The waters of the Turnagain Arm of Cook Inlet followed along the highway on the left as they passed Beluga Point, a rocky, forested spear of land sticking out into the larger body of water. A group of white Dall sheep cavorted on the steep cliffs above Bird Ridge, taking Lila's breath away. They stopped for pancakes and spears of spicy reindeer sausage at Paul's favorite highway café just before reaching the Anchorage city limits.

Paul knew right where to go for everything when they reached the city. The Northern Commercial Department store downtown had almost everything Lila needed. Diagonal parking spaces along Fifth Avenue were crammed with Rambler station wagons, Cadillacs with big fins and fancy hood ornaments, sedans and a variety of pickup trucks. Many of the vehicles had dogs in the passenger seats, licking the glass, barking at passersby, and watching the activity of the city sidewalks. Paul pointed out a pickup with a long bed holding a dozen little homemade wooden compartments, each with a curious canine nose peeking out from wisps of straw.

"Dog teams," he said in a matter-of-fact tone, at Lila's questioning look. "That's how mushers haul their teams around."

"Mushers?"

"Yeah, dog sleds. The guys who drive dog sleds are called mushers."

The sidewalks bustled with people bundled against the chilly late October air. Almost all wore hats of fur or colorful knitted wool. The bulky, scarred wooden doors of the numerous bars swung open and shut constantly. Window displays featured furs, gold jewelry, ivory carvings and custom-made fur and leather coats and footwear decorated with intricate beading, furry trim, and dangling feathers. This world was so different from St. Paul. Even the air had a distinct smell, permeated by the salty scent of ocean from the huge docks and port forming the western border of the downtown area. Lila sniffed the slightly fishy, piercing odor that nobody else seemed to notice.

Paul and Lila shopped side by side at the huge Red Owl Grocery, chatting, and left with overflowing carts. In answer to her question about the cardboard cartons of canned goods, bottles and dry goods that filled many shelves, Paul explained, "Oh, that stuff goes to the Bush. People buy in quantity, still all boxed up, because it's easier to transport by air if it stays packaged up in its original boxes. The day the plane lands in a Bush village with the delivery is kind of like a celebration."

Lila's day was spent in wonder, not only at the uniqueness of Anchorage, but at getting to know a little more about Paul and being so close to him for a whole day. They talked constantly about everything and anything. Several times, Lila noticed people staring at her, their looks unfriendly, almost hostile.

She'd turned to see if something or somebody was behind her, but couldn't figure out what was causing it. One old woman actually pursed her lips and shook her head at Lila with a frown. Although Lila was puzzled, the sights and sounds, the shopping, the nearness of Paul, all allowed her to push it from her mind.

They loaded their purchases into his pickup and headed out of Anchorage in plenty of time to make the tunnel for the six-thirty train back into Whittier. Paul drove quietly, as if not wanting to distract Lila from the spectacular scenery. She grew ever more stunned by the beauty surrounding them on the hour's drive back south to the Portage Valley cutoff. Monstrous sharp mountains rose in white-tipped splendor across the wide, calm inlet bordering the highway, shadowy clouds lazing above them in a sky blushing rosy and gold with the setting sun. Huge, rugged cliffs with rushing waterfalls of various sizes formed a wall along the other side of the twisting two-lane highway. There was a clarity and crispness to the air unlike anything Lila had ever felt. This was nothing like the city streets of Minnesota. She glanced over at Paul, admiring his profile and his strong hands on the wheel.

He sensed her look and turned to her, smiling. "Pretty nice, huh?"

"I've never seen anything so beautiful," Lila replied. "Alaska's just incredible."

She absorbed the beauty, feeling peace seep into her bones, not only from the scenery but from having Paul next to her. It had been a long time since she felt secure and content like this. Maybe the police had caught Lou by now. Maybe he was actually out of her life. Maybe… But she didn't dare let herself hope more. Lou's face came to mind; the memory of his voice chilled her. She gave a little shrug, hoping Paul wouldn't notice, then forced her mind back to the present. Lou wasn't going to intrude on this wonderful day.

Lila felt like a veteran this time through the tunnel as the sweating walls and darkness swallowed them. It felt comforting to be with Paul during the first quiet moments in the eerie darkness, and she hoped he'd hold her hand again. So when Paul again laid his hand over hers, it felt natural, and she grasped his in return. It was a large hand, bigger than Lou's, stronger, warmer. A fleeting thought of how it might feel elsewhere caused Lila to blush, and she turned her burning face away in embarrassment even though Paul couldn't see her in the poor light.

Over the muted clacking of the train's wheels, Paul filled her in on details of the tunnel's construction and statistics, and the eight minutes in the darkness flew by until they reached daylight once more. It felt good to be bringing back most of the things she needed to get settled into her own place at last.

Paul helped her carry her purchases up to her apartment and then lingered until the new sheets and blankets were on the bed, the shower curtain hung, and the groceries put away. He seemed reluctant to leave when there was nothing left to do, and Lila didn't want him to go. But it was nearly nine o'clock by then and both were worn out.

Paul finally picked up his jacket from the orange crate table by the door. "Well, see you then," he began. "You going to stay here tonight?"

"Yeah. It's so nice to be here in my very own place. I can't wait to sleep in my bed on the new sheets. And have my own bathroom in the morning. See you tomorrow? Coffee at Nan's?"

Paul nodded. "Sure. I'll stop up there now and tell her you're staying here tonight so she doesn't worry."

"Thanks, Paul. See you in the morning then."

They stood awkwardly at the door, not quite touching through the growing heat between them. Paul took a sudden step toward Lila, pulled her against him and murmured, "I don't wanna leave."

Lila turned her face to him, and his lips covered hers in a tentative kiss. He tasted fresh, of sun and wind and the outdoors and his mouth begged hers to meet his. She lost herself to the tender, warm kiss consuming them. Paul cradled her cheeks between his hands, then moved to caress the waves of hair hanging down her back, his lips never leaving hers. His hands slid over the dip of her waist, then lingered, possessing her hips. A fever grew between them until both pulled back at the same instant, breathing hard.

Lila stepped back, troubled.

I'm married. What am I doing?

She'd only known this man for a month and knew very little about him. She'd let his hands roam her face and hair and shoulders, and lower. She felt shaky from the kiss. Paul noticed her shiver and reached out to steady her. When she drew further back, his eyes grew puzzled.

"Paul, you better go. I...I...well, thank you so much for all you did for me today. The ride to Anchorage, the shopping, the meals... It was really nice..." She hesitated, "You better go."

Paul stammered, "I...I know. I'll see you in the morning, right?" His admiring eyes never left hers, but she was sure she saw a fleeting shadow of puzzlement flash through them.

"Sure," she murmured. "Tomorrow, then."

With an abrupt movement, Paul turned and closed the door behind him. Lila clicked the lock and licked her lips, loving the taste Paul had left on them. Her lips felt swollen, full of him. She turned to her new little home, drank a glass of milk, changed into her nightgown, slid between the cool fresh sheets, and this night didn't think of Judy or her mother, or Lou, before falling asleep. Savoring the day, immersed in memories of the kiss and the warmth of Paul's hands, she drifted off.

Chapter 13

LILA WOKE THE next morning, delighted to be in her own place, feeling a new sense of security knowing that Lou's picture was most likely already posted at the tunnel entrance. She couldn't wait to ask Paul if he'd help her call her mother again as soon as possible.

Paul was already upstairs at Nan's when she got there, cradling an almost empty coffee cup. He leapt to his feet when Lila entered the apartment, then hesitated as if realizing he couldn't just grab her like he wanted to, not in front of Nan. Nan looked from one to the other, and a tiny, knowing smile crept across her face.

"You two had a good trip to town yesterday, Paul tells me. Get everything you needed?" she directed the question to Lila.

Lila dragged her gaze from Paul's. "Yeah, I got pretty much everything on my list and I have all of it put away already. Curtains, towels, pillows, sheets and a bedspread, a tablecloth, that kind of stuff. And groceries. It already feels a little like home down there now. When can you come and see?"

"You work today?" Nan asked.

"Yup. At noon. So, should we go down now?"

"Sure," Nan answered. "Comin' along, Paul?" She patted her pocket for her pack of cigarettes.

Lila felt a sense of pride while Nan and Paul looked around her snug home. She was glad she'd made her bed and hung her nightgown on the hook inside the closet.

Nan expressed approval. "Good job, Dearie. Looks real comfy." She mumbled something about having to get back upstairs, and invited them both for coffee the next morning. They barely answered and hardly heard the door shut behind her.

Paul drew Lila into his arms the instant Nan was gone, pulling her tight and close against him. She welcomed his tongue when he began to explore her mouth, wantonly matching his every move. She molded herself against his body, not caring about his obvious reaction to the embrace.

When he finally pulled back, Lila stepped away, too. She took a deep breath, overcome with sudden shame, and stammered, "I'm… I'm…married."

"I know," Paul replied. His face grew flushed, his voice thick with emotion. "Believe me, I know. I'm well aware of that. You're never going back to him, though" He tugged her back into his embrace. "He'll never touch you again!" Paul hugged her tighter. "I

102

won't let him near you, I promise. You don't have to worry anymore. We'll help the police get him. You can get a divorce and then it'll all be over."

Lila's tension melted deep within her at his reassuring words. She believed him. She smiled back into his earnest eyes, "Thanks Paul. I can't believe how safe I feel."

Paul his voice soft and low, replied, "I haven't been able to get you out of my mind. I fell right into your eyes. I'd never seen any that blue. They remind me of the stained glass windows in a church. You had me from that first look..." He paused. "You're in my heart now," he added, his words carrying a caress.

Lila had never felt so adored. "Me, too," was all she could manage in reply.

After a few more long seconds looking into each other's eyes after the heartfelt words, they pulled apart. Lila shook her head and stepped back a little more, mind whirling, shaken by the intensity of the last few minutes. Paul closed the door behind him after a lingering look.

Lila leaned against the door, feeling content and protected. It was now the end of October and Lou hadn't found her yet. Maybe he never would. Maybe there was hope. She finally had her own apartment, her own home, a job. Maybe she'd actually reached a safe haven. Snuggled beneath her new blankets that night, drifting toward sleep, Lila mulled over what little she knew about Paul. She vowed to ask him about himself as soon as the time seemed right. What had Paul meant when he said he'd gone through a hard time before he came to Whittier? At that, a flash of trepidation overcame her. Paul hadn't been very forthcoming with personal information. Was he being secretive? Would he turn out to be like Lou and change into someone she didn't know? Misgivings tickled at her sense of security. Doubt grew. Paul seemed nice, caring, and was so attentive, but she really didn't know him at all. It was time to change that. She had to ask him, too, if he'd noticed the strange unfriendly looks people had given her in Anchorage.

In an effort to shove her worry about Lou to the back of her mind during the following days, Lila put in long, busy hours at the store, and continued settling into her new home. Her days at work were easier now that the shelves were clean and the groceries and other sundries organized. It was satisfying to serve drinks and beer in glasses that sparkled, and after hours of scrubbing, the character and warmth of the wood floors glowed. The old green cash register had given up its secrets, yielding more easily to her pecks on the stubborn keys. Some of the regulars seemed to come in more often than when Lila started, so she felt she was becoming a part of the community when they included her in their chatter and bantering.

She and Nan roamed abandoned apartments in the Hodge, locating an unblemished brown leather sofa that must have been too bulky for someone to take along when they moved out. They'd scavenged a small wooden kitchen table with two matching chairs, a smattering of kitchenware, and several ancient but clean orange crates to use as end tables.

A closeness developed between Nan and Lila during these weeks, replacing part of the homesickness that often nudged its way into Lila's thoughts. Nan filled Lila in with scraps of gossip about everyone and everything in Whittier, and seemed glad for Lila's company. Lila couldn't figure out why Nan fended off questions about herself, but decided that would come when Nan was ready to share it.

"What about Paul? What do you know about him?" Lila asked Nan as they made chocolate chip cookies together at Nan's.

Nan reached for an ash tray and rustled for her lighter, buying time for her answer. "Well, he's had a pretty full life already. And his own troubles. But you better ask him yourself, Dearie." She turned away and shoved the mixing bowl into the sink, scrubbing too hard, dismissing the conversation.

Lila's curiosity grew at this and she decided to do just that. She knew too little about the man she'd been spending so much time with.

Although Lila's days were busy, she had to fight off a longing for her mother and Judy, as well as the familiar sights and sounds of Minnesota. This homesickness surprised her with its intensity. She'd never been farther from home than the evergreen bordered highway on the way to and from Duluth, and her Dad or Mom had always been behind the wheel on those Sunday drives.

It was comforting to imagine Mama's trim, white stucco house tucked back from the stately oak and elm trees that bordered the sidewalks of St. Paul neighborhoods. She visualized the canopy of blazing orange, gold, and crimson leaves that sheltered the streets at this time of year, and the flitting birds feasting on bright red mountain ash berries. The streets and yards would be swarming with kids, bikes, and junior high boys tossing footballs, their muted shouts part of the sounds of autumn. And while lingering dusk claimed the daylight, the air would hang heavy with the tang of burning leaves, one of Lila's favorite smells. Mom would have to take off the screens and put up the storm windows without her this year. Maybe the Anderson twins next door would help. It was all Lou's fault that she was now so far from all that had been her only home. And always, a sharp pang of fear interrupted her thoughts of home when she wondered what Lou was doing and where he was. Was he close? Had he traced her? Had he made it to Alaska?

To distract herself on these nights, so far from the life she'd always known, Lila finally let herself think about Dad, too. What had been an ember of resentment toward Lou began to burn brighter now, when she realized her father wouldn't have wanted her to just take all this without fighting back. It had

106

been fourteen years since the heart attack that took him so unexpectedly. Lila had found it easier until now to deal with the grief and emptiness if she didn't allow herself to think about him. But here, far from home and loved ones, feeling so alone at night, she allowed herself to indulge in the memories she usually pushed away.

She could still bring Dad's face and voice to mind, and remembered how his khaki uniform smelled of lumber when he walked in the door after work at the mill. She recalled the glow between him and Mom, as if the two of them had their own special world. It had always made her feel warm when Dad grabbed Mom for a whirl around the living room to the music of the *Lawrence Welk Show* on Sunday nights.

Dad would have known what to do about Lou. But he was gone and she had to be tough. She'd realized very soon after the funeral that she'd have to take care of herself and not cause any worries for Mom. The flickering flame of grief for Dad she'd always fought to keep buried deep in her heart flared on these nights far from home. There was so much she wished she could tell him. How different it would be if he were here to help her. She resolved to be strong, like he'd expect her to be.

It always comforted her to think about Judy, too. Judy, with her bright smile, her quick chatter, her ever-changing haircuts, and the flirty miniskirts that made guys stop and stare. An admiring group of fellow dancers often gathered around when she and

Jerry did the Twist, fascinated at Judy's energy and skill as she gyrated to the rhythms of Chubby Checker and Elvis. When Judy did the Limbo at school dances, everybody crowded around to watch, amazed at how far she could bend backwards and still maintain her balance while shuffling under the bar. Judy's split level house had been like a second home to Lila and the twin bed in Judy's room like Lila's own after the many sleepovers. Judy's mother made the best spaghetti and cinnamon rolls in the world, and her dad, with his teasing manner, always made Lila feel welcome in their home. He'd even walked her down the aisle. Lila often felt herself sliding into sleep with a small smile, almost smelling the cinnamon rolls, remembering her friend's sparkling brown eyes and feisty spirit.

It cheered Lila, too, to think about the plans she and Judy were making to take a class together at the University of Minnesota. Judy wanted to be a teacher and Jerry was supportive. But Lila had been certain Lou would protest about the plan because he liked her to be at home during the day. She'd planned to tell him that their apartment building manager had agreed to let her take over the cleaning of the halls and entry and laundry room of the building. It would bring in a hundred dollars a month, more than enough to cover tuition and books for a single class. Lila had been waiting for the right time to tell Lou but it hadn't come yet. Her dream of owning a business, though, remained her secret. She thought back to her plans to take math and accounting and business courses, and then start a string of walk-in beauty shops in the Twin Cities. The details had been all worked out in her head, and she enjoyed going over them as she drifted toward sleep.

In the stillness of dark nights in Whittier, Lila finally began to wonder why she'd allowed Lou's dominance to overpower her during their marriage, and why she'd allowed him to drag her into this insane mess. What had been an ember of resentment toward Lou began to burn brighter. She resented the sharp fear that interrupted her thoughts of home when she wondered what Lou was doing and where he was. It was time to resist the trouble and fear Louis Edward Peterson had brought to her life. Maybe it was time to get a gun and learn how to use it. And it was past time to call the Minnesota police and tell them what she'd witnessed.

Chapter 14

LILA AWAKENED LATE to a dazzling morning and wandered, a glass of Tang in her hand, to the living room window. Sparkling sunlight reflected off the water, the wharf bustled with activity and a few commercial fishing boats were already headed out of the bay, leaving fluffy white trails in their wake. Gulls squawked and whirled, sailing the wind currents. It felt good to be in her own home, one she was able to provide for herself, and in such a beautiful place.

The twinge of nausea that followed a sip of juice stopped her short. Why hadn't this morning queasiness gone away now that she was safe? Suddenly, she blanched and her breath caught. When had she had her last period? Realization slammed into her, almost driving her to her knees. She blinked away a searing whiteness behind her eyes.

Pregnant? I couldn't be. But then…

It was November first already. If it had happened on that Fourth of July weekend when she'd been afraid to tell Lou she was out of birth control pills until the pharmacy opened after the holiday, the pregnancy would be more than three months along now, maybe even close to four. The trouble with Lou and the escape to Alaska had dominated her mind during the past couple of months, so she'd attributed her nausea to stress and fear from all that. But she'd had no periods during August, September and October and hadn't even realized it. Feeling the fullness of her breasts straining against her bra and realizing how tight her clothing had felt at the waist lately, she stumbled to the sofa and sank down, hardly able to breathe. There was no denying it. She was pregnant.

Lila sat her glass of juice on the coffee table with trembling hands.

Pregnant? A baby? What will I do? How could I have not known?

Her mind skittered. She was going to be a mother. Alone. On her own. With Lou's child.

With a sudden, crushing realization, she knew she'd have to tell Paul. He deserved to know. Their relationship had definitely moved beyond being just friends. What if it changed things—her having someone else's child? He might be upset that she hadn't told him before. He might think she'd been purposely deceiving him. Maybe she'd lose him. She'd asked Lou many times about having a baby, but he'd always gone into a huff and told her to wait

111

until they could afford it. Now a baby was real. And she had to tell Paul.

She tingled at the memory of Paul's kisses and the overpowering response of her body. Lou had never kissed her like that. His kisses had been dry and brief, obvious now as only a prelude to what he was really after. She was realizing more and more with each passing day what a rotten husband Lou had been.

Lou had been a real catch, according to her girlfriends. She remembered how they envied her when Lou started paying attention to her. It had been flattering since he unofficially led the gang of older guys he hung around with. He was handsome like Elvis, almost six feet tall with black hair and smoky blue eyes. His jeans rode low on his hips—he didn't walk, he sauntered. Lou patrolled the streets in the gleaming red convertible he'd owned then. Its polished chrome could blind you in the sunlight and the wire spoke wheels were the envy of all the guys. Every girl wished she could be in Lila's place next to Lou, the wind caressing her hair. The roaring lion hood ornament spoke—"Watch out! Here I come!"

Lou had landed a job at the Ford auto plant as soon as he turned eighteen, a good union job on the assembly line, with benefits, so he always had more cash to pull from his wallet than the rest of the guys he hung around with. He'd been a catch, alright. He even had his own apartment.

Lila recalled the first time he noticed her, and still remembered his first words to her, "Love your hair, Kid."

Surprising herself, she'd tossed the golden waves over her shoulder, stood all of her five feet eight inches tall, and shot right back at him, "Yours, too." It wasn't like her to flirt like that; she'd always been so shy, but the words just flew out of her mouth.

Lila had returned his gaze boldly when he paused to look her up and down with an approving stare. She felt uncharacteristically daring, confident in the tight jeans she knew fit her just right. Lou had studied her for long moments, given her a long, insolent look, then winked and smiled his lazy smile before turning away.

It wasn't long before Lou began seeking her out whenever they were in the same place, and they were a couple before she knew it. Lila had never had a real boyfriend before, but she decided he didn't have to know that. So she matched every move of his lips and tongue the first time he kissed her, determined to show him she knew what she was doing. Lila remembered how shocked she'd been when he pulled back, panting, and without a word, put the car in gear and headed to a park on the outskirts of the city. She hadn't known what to expect, but when his kiss heated up right away and he'd reached under her blouse there in the deserted parking lot, she realized she was in over her head. He'd been annoyed at her refusal to go further, but took her home when she asked, driving in silence, brooding, oozing displeasure. But he called the next morning, sounding just as usual.

Mom had described him as "cocky" the first time Lou picked her up for a date, and Lila had to agree. And Lou and Judy had never really hit it off, but since a newly-engaged Judy was busy arranging her wedding to Jerry, and then setting up her new house, it didn't become an issue. After Lila's wedding, it wasn't long before Judy began coming around to the apartment only when Lou was gone to work.

Lila wondered now if she'd ever really loved Lou. Maybe she'd simply been in love with the idea of moving into an apartment, having a husband, and being a wife. She remembered the first months of marriage, when Lou spent more time with her than with Artie and his other buddies. They'd sleep late after his night shift, make unhurried love when they woke up, go out for breakfast at the Embers across the street on Sunday mornings, and talk about everything. She'd loved their life together.

Their one-bedroom apartment in suburban St. Paul had been cozy, even though it was "garden level," which really meant the basement of the building. The tiny paneled bedroom opening directly off the living room had grown so crammed with Lou's bowling trophies, stacks of old *Playboy* magazines, shoes, and tangled sports gear that only a skinny path led to Lila's side of the bed on the far wall. It had been a long time since she'd been

114

pampered in Ruby's chair at the Cut and Curl. She thought about the clothing she'd brought with her as a new bride, now faded and worn, and how there'd never been any money to replace it. She didn't even know how much Lou's salary was, only that there wasn't ever enough for her to have spending money for herself.

Now that she really thought about it, though, he'd always had plenty to slide over the bar at Spruce Grove, sometimes even hundred-dollar bills. She didn't know how much the fancy slipcovers and rims and other upgrades and gadgets for his cars cost, but it must have been a lot because none of it looked cheap. Then there were beer and cigarettes, that top of the line bowling ball and case, new shoes for work, jackets, and going out with all the friends who liked to hang around him, too. It didn't make sense how much money he spent if they didn't have any. Now she realized how strange it had been that he constantly assured her he'd never be poor again like he was when he was a kid, no matter what it took.

The dark good looks that had attracted Lila suddenly seemed menacing, revolting, ugly. A shiver overtook her. How could she have been so blind and where was he now?

She didn't realize before now how their life had gradually changed, as if Lou grew more tired of her every month. Lou spent his days with his friends and seemed to prefer their company to hers by the time their first year together had ended. And by then, he hardly ever took her anywhere, and answered her, as if annoyed, when she initiated conversation. Lou turned to her in bed often, but after the first few passionate months, Lila always felt as if something were missing. But she'd decided it was how things were when people grew used to each other, since Lou seemed satisfied.

Lila hadn't recognized until now just how barren and cold the relationship had become over the two years they'd been married. Maybe she'd never loved Lou at all. Maybe she'd just been in love with the idea of being a wife. She shook off the memories and took another drink of her juice, but couldn't help wondering what Lou was doing and if she would ever have to see him again, and how long would she have to keep hiding.

An unusual feeling of power overcame her.

I'll do whatever it takes to get Lou out of my life. If Dad was alive, he'd help me, but I have to take care of this myself. That's what he'd want me to do. I'll go to the police. I won't live like this forever. Lou'll be surprised when he finds out I'm not going to be his scared "little darlin" anymore. I have to take care of this, for the baby's sake, too.

Oh, how she missed Judy and Mom, and life back home. How would they react when she told them about the pregnancy? At the same time, she realized how much she liked having Paul in her life. Her mind returned to Paul's kiss and the feel of his body pressed close against hers, how his hands had caressed her face and hair so tenderly. A prickle of desire rippled through her. She shivered it away, then wandered to the kitchen, poured some Rice Krispies and milk into a bowl, returned to the living room window and munched them standing up.

Her thoughts skittered between the baby and home and Paul while she enjoyed the view across the bay She felt a growing curiosity about Paul. What was his family like? How old was he? How long did he plan to stay in Whittier? She realized that their chatter so far had been mostly about her, and about other things. She needed to know about him, lots more about him. And she needed to let him know she was pregnant. And Nan, too. And Mom and Judy. She turned from the window, breathless.

A baby coming. What will I do?

She shook her head and walked to the bedroom. It felt good to dress in the new long-sleeved denim blouse with white lace trim that Paul had helped her pick out in Anchorage. But the waistband of her jeans was so tight that the top snap wouldn't close. Of course, the queasy stomach and the hazy cloud of fatigue that so often crept over her were signs of pregnancy. That was why she'd been so tired on the long drive, too. It hadn't been only due to the stress of the murder, the difficult drive, or the upheaval in her life. She was pregnant. Why hadn't she realized it before this?

Lila made her bed in a daze, working automatically, smoothing the covers. An odd feeling of light-heartedness, almost trance-like, nudged aside the stunning awareness of her pregnancy. The baby she'd wished for was a reality. Despite her anxiety, it had been a long time since she'd felt cheerful and happy like this.

Paul was already at Nan's when she got upstairs. Lila smiled a hello, fighting the tendrils of anxiety teasing the corners of her mind. How would he feel about the pregnancy? It could ruin everything. She squared her shoulders. He had to be told. And soon.

Nan waved a cigarette in Lila's direction in greeting and shrugged into a sweater. "I have to go help down at the library room again. Just lock up when ya leave."

The instant the door closed behind her, Paul rose and drew Lila into his arms without a word. She felt his heart pounding as hard as hers was, turned her face to him, and waited. He waited, too, through the heat that burned between them. When he leaned down and covered her mouth with his, she wanted his lips to stay on hers forever. A fever grew between them until both pulled back at the same instant, gasping.

Lila stumbled back when they finally pulled apart, overcome by sudden guilt, the pregnancy heavy on her mind. She drew a deep breath and stammered, "I… I can't do this, you know."

"I know," Paul replied. His face flushed deep red and his voice came as a growl. "Believe me, I know. I meant it when I said you're never going back to him."

Lila nearly cried with relief at his words. "Yes, I know. Thanks so much, Paul. You don't know how much that means to me..."

Paul answered, his voice low. "You just don't know how you make me feel. You make me so happy."

They took a few more long seconds looking into each other's' eyes almost shyly after the heartfelt words. Lila shook her head and stepped back further, shaken by the intensity of the last few minutes. Her mind whirled.

Who is Paul, really? What about the baby? Where's Lou?

She took a step back, troubled, overcome by guilt. She was married. What was she doing? She felt shaky from the kiss, and, noticing her tremble, Paul reached out to steady her. He looked at her with a question in his eyes.

"Paul, I. I...I...well... Thank you so much for all you've done for me. The ride to Anchorage, the shopping, calling Mom..." She hesitated. "You better go."

Lila could tell he was as shaken as she was. His admiring eyes never left hers, but she was sure she saw hurt flash through the warmth there.

Paul paused and stammered, "Well... I have some stuff to do before work, so I guess I'll head out. See you this afternoon, right?"

"Sure," she murmured. "Later, then."

Paul turned with an abrupt movement and pulled the door shut behind him. Lila clicked the lock and licked her lips, savoring the taste Paul had left on them. Her lips again felt swollen, loved, full of him.

Chapter 15

RUMBLING CLOUDS DARKENED steadily, obscuring a lemony sun, and freezing snow pecked at Lila's cheeks during her walk to work that afternoon. She bent her head into it, glad it was such a short distance compared to walking the six blocks to school on bitter winter mornings in Minnesota.

As soon as Lila walked in, Tom smoothed his rumpled shirt sleeves and stuffed them into an oversized, crusty, army green parka.

"Close up right quick again today," he ordered. "Everything's already shuttin' down 'cuz of another storm comin' in hard. Everybody's headin' for home. Close up real quick." He jammed a black fur-lined hat over his scraggly hair, tied the ear flaps beneath his chin, and scurried off for the Hodge, head sunk deep into his collar against the wind.

Paul burst through the door a half hour later. "Lila, lock up. I'll give you a ride. You shouldn't be out in this. Another big one's starting. C'mon, let's get outa here."

Even the few steps from the door to the warm truck chilled Lila to the bone as Whittier's damp wind shrieked around them. Paul noticed her shivering and suggested, "Let's stop at my apartment when we get to the building. I have something for you."

When Paul let her in the door of his apartment, Lila realized it was the first time she'd seen where he lived. His apartment's floor plan matched hers, and the view was the same although it was a few floors below hers and on the other end of the building. This apartment had a very lived-in feeling compared to her place. A striking black blanket with a bold red geometric pattern caught her eye where it was displayed on the wall behind a black leather sofa. A wooden stool sat behind a tripod with a telescope pointed through the big front window. Newspapers lay in a neat pile on the coffee table.

Paul noticed her looking at the telescope. "Everybody has 'em. We watch the boats and even see wildlife across on the mountain slopes. We spy on each other, too." He grinned, a fleeting, sheepish look crossing his face.

Lila looked toward the tidy kitchen. A dish drainer in the sink held a single, clear glass plate and a few pieces of silverware. The stove top was as clean as her mother's always was. A set of white porcelain canisters lined the counter beside the refrigerator. A clean cast iron frying pan sat on the stove, two apples and half a loaf of bread lay on top of the refrigerator. The square, red Formica kitchen table with four matching chairs was polished clean. She was glad to see that he was a neat person.

A blond wood console TV faced the sofa in the living room, and a stereo system half-filled the shelves of a high oak bookcase next to it. The bottom level of the bookcase held albums, stacked upright side by side. It pleased her to learn that he liked music and she wondered what albums he had. Lila turned to find Paul watching her. She smiled, and he grinned back.

"Well, this is it," he said. "Been home for almost five years now."

Sudden chagrin overcame her. She didn't know what had brought him to Whittier, where he came from, or hardly anything about his family. The whole time she'd been here, she'd been thinking only of herself and her own troubles and her own life. He'd been so nice, so caring, so supportive. She hadn't even asked him a thing about himself. How self-centered she'd been! And now she had to tell him about the baby.

"Well, aren't you curious about what I have for you?" Paul asked, his eyes dancing with eagerness.

"Sure," Lila answered. "What is it?"

An angry burst of wind rattled the window, diverting their attention for a moment. Thick, driving snow had caused the harbor to disappear, the world outside reduced to whiteness. Lila looked at Paul in alarm.

"Nothing to worry about. This building can withstand anything. We're okay," Paul reassured her. "C'mere."

He walked to the closet by the front door, reached in and drew out a long, royal blue jacket, its cuffs and oversized hood trimmed with shining brown fur. Stripes of bright red, white and yellow embroidery zigzagged along the bottom border of the jacket, ran alongside both sides of the zipper, and trimmed the cuffs. The inside was lined with soft, gray fur. It was the most beautiful coat Lila had ever seen.

"Here, try it on," Paul urged, holding it open toward her.

Lila moved to him and Paul slid the coat closed around her. It felt luxurious, cozy and warm, like wearing a cloud. Its silky fur ruff tickled her face and wrists. Paul pulled the hood up close around her face with great care and tipped her face toward him. A look of immense sadness passed over his eyes before he bent his head in an attempt to hide it.

Lila, enveloped in the parka, managed to reach out to him. She touched his arm. "What is it?" When he didn't respond, she tried again, "What, Paul?"

Tears were slipping down his cheeks when he managed to look up at her. He swiped at them with a helpless shrug.

"What is it, Paul?" Lila asked again. She waited, puzzled and concerned, while Paul pulled himself together enough to speak.

"Let's go in the kitchen. Here. I'll help you out of that," he managed to mumble in a broken voice.

He helped Lila slip out of the parka and hung it back in the closet. With a final pat to the jacket, he closed the door and walked toward the kitchen. Lila followed and sat down across from him at the table. She waited, sensing he needed time to gather his words.

"Well," he began, his face now splotched with red, his voice unsteady. "Well...you need a good coat for this Whittier weather. The parka—I want you to have it." He paused, then continued after a deep breath. "It was my wife's..."

A thin smile crossed Paul's face at her gasp. "It's...okay, I'm not married. Not now, anyway. She died..." his voice broke.

Lila sat, stunned.

"It was five years ago. The baby didn't make it, either," he murmured, gulping hard.

Lila felt frozen, shocked that he'd been married and had lost a child. Her gaze fixed on his face.

Paul took another deep breath before continuing. He looked away, almost as if he'd forgotten that Lila was sitting across from him. "We were living in our village, Alukiak. Hilli and I were both Yup'ik, but we were of different villages. We knew each other when we were students at Mount Edgecombe, that's the government high school in Sitka. We got married two days after we graduated." He gulped hard. "The baby was our first one, a girl..."

He stammered a bit and his voice caught. "Something happened at four months. Hilli was just starting to really look pregnant. The day it happened, she got bad real fast. There was a blizzard with zero visibility and eighty-mile-an-hour winds so nobody could fly us out of Alukiak to the hospital in Anchorage. We had a midwife in the village and she'd delivered most of the people who lived there, but Hilli's condition was so sudden and so severe that she'd never run into it before and she didn't know what to do. Our phone service was out, too. They said later that only being in a hospital might have been able to save her. But maybe not even that would've been enough. Something about blood pressure, toxemia, a freak thing with damage to the blood vessels that happens to only a few women."

Paul choked back tears, his face contorted with agony. "First, she got a bad headache. Then she had a seizure. She went into a coma that same night. She died in my arms on the second day. Everybody in the whole village gathered and cried. My mother was crushed. It would have been her first grandchild. She loved Hilli like a daughter."

Paul stopped, and looked at Lila. The sadness and grief in his eyes tore at her heart. She stood, walked over to him, and pulled his head and shoulders against her side. He reached around and buried his

126

head against her hip while sobs overtook him. They stayed that way for a long time, until Paul quieted and pulled away. He walked to the sofa and motioned her over beside him.

His eyes and face were red and puffy when he looked up at her. "Been a while since I did that," he said, his voice somber.

"I'm so sorry, so very sorry," Lila murmured. "The parka? It was hers?"

"Yeah," Paul replied. "It's a genuine parky. My grandmother made it for Hilli, but she never even got to wear it through a whole winter. I kept it—I just never could let it go."

Lila was touched beyond belief. The parka was such a precious thing to Paul, and he'd offered it to her. Her heart melted. He'd lost his wife and baby. The village? What did he mean—he grew up in the village?

Suddenly, it made sense. The unique burnished cinnamon eyes, the rugged features beneath dark brows, the unusual, lilting accent. Of course! He was part Native Alaskan, an Eskimo. Lila was shocked at her failure to put this all together before. How self-absorbed she'd been all this time. Paul had a whole life she knew nothing about.

Paul pushed back from her embrace and shook his head, pulling himself upright. "Hungry? Should we go to your place?" he asked, trying to sound normal.

Lila shook her head. "I'll stay here with you," she said. "I'm so sorry, Paul. So sorry about Hilli and the baby, and everything."

They reached for each other at the same moment and Paul leaned into her across the sofa. She held him close until he gave a puppy-like jerk and slid into sleep. When his even breathing told her he was sleeping soundly, she slipped out from under him.

Chapter 16

PAUL'S KNOCK AWAKENED Lila the next morning. He held the parka out to her when she opened the door, and she slid into his embrace, still groggy with sleep, the thick jacket crushed between them. Neither spoke. She dressed quickly and Paul tucked her into the parka before they struggled through blowing snow out to his idling truck. Lila nestled into the parka and cozy cab for the few minutes it took them to reach the railroad office.

This time the call to Minnesota went better. Margaret's voice sounded stronger and her words clearer. She and Lila talked for a few minutes and then Judy came on the line.

"I've been wondering. How did you take care of things for Mom at the hospital?" Lila asked. "When you first got there?"

"Well, we did what we had to."

"But tell me. What happened when she got to the hospital? How did—"

All right, here's what we did," Judy interrupted. "We followed the ambulance and ran in the emergency door while they were carrying her in. The receptionist made us stay in a waiting area 'til a nurse came out. When she asked if we were family, I lied. Said I was the daughter so she gave me paperwork."

Judy hesitated for a moment until Lila reassured her. "Judy, you did just right."

Judy continued, her tone now more certain. "Jerry scolded me for lying, but I told him we had to be your mom's family for now. She didn't have anybody else. So I had to take care of her."

"How did you know what to write? How did you know her medical history? If she had insurance?"

"I didn't know any of it!" Judy replied. "I put in everything I thought I knew, and made up the rest as best I could. I knew it was wrong, but I didn't know what else to do."

She paused, as if waiting to be challenged, but went on when Lila didn't say anything. "We were sure it'd been Lou by then. I was just so mad. How could anybody hurt your mother?"

When she again sounded unsure, Lila replied, "Judy, thanks for what you did. And thanks for all you're doing for Mom now, too. You're the best friend anybody could ever have. You know that, don't you?"

"Yup." The grin in her voice came through.

"I know I should call the police in St. Paul and tell them what I saw Lou do," Lila said. "But I'm afraid to. Maybe they'll make me go back there, and nobody knows where Lou is, so that scares me. I think you shouldn't know anything about what happened, or exactly where I am yet. So it would be better if you don't even ask, okay? I'm pretty sure if Lou shows up at your door again he'll be able to tell if either of you lie to him."

"Yeah, I guess so," Judy agreed. "We have Detective Adams' phone number. Maybe you should just call him directly when you feel ready. Want it?" She read the number off.

Lila hung up. Things were under control back home, her mother was improving, and Margaret, upon her release from the hospital, had moved in with Judy and Jerry. Lila tucked the detective's number into her purse with a sigh of relief.

Paul drove Lila back to the eerie, silent, white cocoon of her apartment while the snow continued its steady fall. Lila chopped onions and cheese for an omelet and Paul twisted the radio dial, hoping for an update on the storm. But all he could get was static. The TV screen was as snowy as the world outside. They edged around each other, restless and distracted, intensely aware of how much closer Paul's revelations of the night before had brought them. They picked at their omelets. Conversation floundered. Their gazes met, darted apart, met again.

Paul fidgeted and finally spoke, his voice hesitant. "Lila, Judy gave you a detective's number, right? So the authorities in Minnesota must consider that you're running from to be a crime. It was something Lou did, wasn't it?"

"Yeah," Lila murmured. "Yeah, it was."

Well...umm..." He halted as if he wanted to say more while a grimace played across his face. He avoided her gaze.

Her heart began to flutter. "What?" she asked. "There's something you're not telling me, isn't there? What else?"

"Well, actually, Lou does know where you are—"

"*What?* What do you mean?" Lila leaped up and faced Paul, her face ashen. "What are you talking about?"

After a deep breath, Paul replied, his tone laden with reluctance, "Well, he was here..."

Lila blanched and clutched her throat. Familiar, crushing panic raged through her. "Here? When?" she croaked. "When was Lou here? Lou knows where I am? No!" Her knees went weak and she took a stumbling step backward.

Paul sprang up and gathered her into his arms. "It was about two weeks ago. He tried to get through the tunnel but we turned him away every time, no matter what he did. Then he got in trouble with the law in Anchorage. When they arrested him, they discovered a felony warrant for him in Minnesota. So the troopers sent an escort with him on a one-way flight back there. He's out of Alaska, and he won't be allowed back in."

While Paul spoke, shivers of cold fear sliced deep within Lila and she began trembling. At that, Paul pulled her close again, wrapping his arms around her protectively. She sensed his reluctance to go on.

"Go ahead. Tell me all of it." It would be better to know than to imagine what else had happened.

"Well, okay," Paul said. He pushed Lila back a little and searched her eyes. She stared at him wordlessly until he continued, his voice faltering. "Well... Lou tried every way he could think of to get through the tunnel. He failed at disguising himself, and tried to bribe three different railroad employees. He tried to pick the lock on the tunnel, and tried to break through the metal doors at night with an ax. He was caught trying to sneak in on foot alongside the flatcars, too. Tunnel staff had to start searching the trunks and back seats of all vehicles."

He dropped his head, still avoiding Lila's eyes. "Lou kind of melted into the underground of downtown Anchorage while he was here. You know, those sleazy bars and cheap hotels and the late night life. Finally, he had a drunken confrontation with police outside a bar and that was when they discovered the warrant and put him on a plane." Paul's voice faltered. "But he slipped...he slipped away after he was turned over to security at the airport in Minneapolis. He's...he's sort of disappeared."

Lila bolted out of his arms and turned to him, wide-eyed. "He escaped? Nobody knows where he

133

is? And he knows I'm here in Whittier?" She shook her head and blinked hard to clear the shimmer of white light behind her eyes. "He got away? He's out there somewhere?" Her hands balled into fists.

Paul took a step toward her, but stopped at the look on her face. He spread his hands. "I'm sorry, Lila. I'm sorry I didn't tell you he was here. I thought you'd worry too much. And we handled it like I promised you we would. He didn't get through the tunnel. We're still searching every trunk and back seat and watching for him."

Lila's legs wobbled and she wrenched herself back against the table, stumbling to regain her footing. "Why didn't anybody tell me? Why didn't I know?"

"It was my decision," Paul answered, his face now grave and pale. "I didn't want to worry you then. You were just settling in here, starting to feel like the Hodge and your apartment were home. You were finally feeling safe. I decided we should wait to tell you..." he looked at Lila with growing indecision in his eyes. "Are you mad? I thought it was the right thing to do. To protect you right then."

Lila sank onto the sofa.

Paul was only trying to protect me. He discovered Lou was here and he didn't want to worry me.

She should be angry that he hadn't told her, but she couldn't be.

"Well...okay then," she began. "I guess you're right. I would've been so scared if I knew he was near."

While Paul explained a few more of the details about Lou's persistence in trying to get through the tunnel, Lila's heart began racing, and the familiar terror returned in full force. Lou had tracked her down. She wasn't surprised. She'd always been certain he'd find her, and was now more positive than ever that even with everyone on alert and law enforcement in Anchorage watching out for him, Lou would figure out a way to come back and get her.

After a few more minutes absorbing the news, she agreed with Paul that she needed to call the police in Minnesota so they'd know what she'd witnessed. But what if they wanted her to come back there to be interviewed or testify? Could she travel being pregnant? It would probably take most of the money she had for a plane ticket. She couldn't drive all that way again, not when expecting. And what if Lou was there and found out she'd come home? Who would protect her back there? It seemed too dangerous to risk going back. But maybe if she told them about Lou's best friend, Artie, participating in the murder, that might help them find him.

She tried to push the dilemma from her mind. Her stomach clenched every time she thought of Lou and what might happen if she had to go back. Calling the police seemed so dangerous. It could ruin this life she was just settling into.

"Lila, what happened anyway?" Paul asked. "What's this all about? What did Lou do?" He sat back down and settled in across from her. "I think it'll

135

help if you can tell me what happened." Paul's eyes darkened with sympathy. He motioned her to sit across the table from him and reached over to cradle her hands between his. "I'd like to know what made you run."

Lila thought for a moment. She sighed, and looked at Paul for reassurance. When he nodded encouragement, she took a shaky breath and began. "Well, we went to the Spruce Grove Club every Saturday night because Lou's friends were always there. I didn't like the club that much—loud bands, cigarette smoke, people getting really drunk. And there were always fights. But we never went anyplace else, so I went along with Lou just to get to go somewhere. Mostly, I watched him play pool and listened to the music."

Paul gave a small smile and an incline of his head. "Go on."

Lila gulped away the tightness in her throat. "It happened the Saturday night before I ran. I was going out to our car in the parking lot to get my sweater when I heard something at the far edge of the lot. When I saw it was Lou and his best friend, Artie, kicking a man and whacking his head with a tire iron, I couldn't believe my eyes."

The past became real while Lila talked. Even in the dark, she'd seen a spreading patch of blood on the ground, and the sickening thud of the blows had forced up bile to her throat.

"Lou and his friend, Artie, the two of them at once, were beating a guy who was curled up on the ground. Who could do that? And why? Lou could be kind of mean sometimes but he was always sorry after. This was something different!"

Paul stood up, moved behind her and placed his hands on her shoulders while she continued. "My God, Lila!"

Lila leaned back into him. "I turned and started to run as soon as I realized what I was seeing. But I tripped and fell on my knees on the gravel. I couldn't help making kind of a little croak—it hurt. Lou whirled around when he heard it. We stared at each other across the lot before I got up and ran back into the club. I was so shocked I could hardly breathe."

She told Paul how Lou had slid nonchalantly onto the stool beside her when he and Artie sauntered back into the club ten minutes later. And how he'd wrapped his arm around her waist a little too tightly, hurting her.

"I couldn't move away and I didn't dare look at him. On the drive home in Artie's car, nobody said a word the whole way. Lou acted as if it hadn't happened. But the knot in my stomach told me what I saw was real. I stayed awake most of that night, trying to get the horrible sight out of my mind. And trying to comprehend that Lou and Artie had actually done that."

She shuddered. "The next morning, Lou said he'd kill Mom first, and then me, if I ever told anyone what I saw. He said he knew where Judy lived, too," she murmured, eyes distant. Her voice rose. "The murder was the big story on the news the next day. And all the next week. They didn't have any suspects or clues. Just a man who had been left to die in the parking lot of the Spruce Grove Club."

She told how the next morning, finally dozing off after a long night of disbelief and shock at what she'd witnessed, she hadn't heard Lou mumble at her to get him some water. A second later, she was jolted into wakefulness by a hard poke to the ribs.

"Didn't you hear me? Get some water. Now!" Lou had barked.

Lila bolted awake, clutching her burning side in amazement. She'd slipped off her side of the bed and scurried to the kitchen for a glass of water.

"Lou drained it, held it out, and told me to get him a cold can of Fresca this time. And that he was hungry so I should cook him some breakfast. He kept saying 'And you didn't see nothin' last night, my little darlin' Got it? You saw nothin'! Nothin'!"

"Lou brought me roses when he came back from getting cigarettes later that morning," Lila reported, eyes focused far away. "That was a first. While I was putting them in a vase, he yelled at me and told me again I better keep my mouth shut about what I saw the night before or I'd be sorry. He said I had no right to squeal on him because I was his wife." She shivered. "He kept asking, 'Understand, my little darlin?' Lou always called me 'my little darlin' when he was feeling sorry or wanted sex, but that morning his tone scared me to death."

Her voice hushed, she went on to tell how, after that Saturday night, Lou harangued her and threatened her with a similar fate if she'd dared breathe a word to anyone about what she'd seen. The blood-red roses on the coffee table made her nearly sick every time she looked at them and their cloying smell made her gag. And after that night, he didn't let her out of his sight except when he was at work and called to check on her every time he had a break. She grew unable to sleep for more than a few hours at a time—the image filled her dreams. And she never knew when Lou would pull her close, even in front of other people, and mutter through closed lips, "You saw nothin', Lila. Nothin'. I ever suspect you been talking about it, you're dead, too. Got it, my little darlin'?"

Lost in memories, she didn't notice Paul's face flush when she told how those same three muttered words, "my little darlin'" always finished Lou's lovemaking after the murder, too, though it could no longer be called lovemaking. Every morning, as soon as they awoke, Lou would roll over, pin her beneath him and pound himself into her, as if to demonstrate his control. Then, during the day, he'd act so nice that she wondered if she was going crazy. He'd compliment her on the cooking, grab at her rear when she passed by his chair, nuzzle her neck while she did the dishes. And always the murmurs, "Good chow, my little darlin'. I'm lucky to have such a good wife." He behaved as if everything was normal, but it had given Lila chills every time he touched her.

She turned agonized eyes to Paul. "Then that morning when he tried to strangle me, I thought I was going to die. I guess I didn't answer fast enough when he wanted me to promise out loud that I'd never tell what I saw. He grabbed me when I was walking by him to the refrigerator and threw me down on the kitchen floor so hard it knocked the wind out of me. Then he jumped on top of me. I couldn't get my breath at all. When he squeezed his hands around my throat, everything went black. Then, all at once, he pushed off me and I heard the kitchen door slam, like from far away. I must have stayed on the floor a long time. Finally, I could breathe again, and I managed to get up. My neck was already hurting and it was really bruised by that night."

She swallowed a sob, "I knew then that the man I was married to was crazy. I didn't know him at all anymore. After the morning when he choked me, I was sure I had to get away right then. So, I ran that same night. And I know he'll finish the job if he finds me. I have nightmares about it. I thought if I could figure out a way to disappear, he'd leave Mom and Judy alone if they actually didn't know where I was."

At this Paul's hands tightened on her shoulders. Lila leaned back into him and swiped at her tears.

140

Paul dropped his hands and stomped a few paces away, his face now crimson. He turned back and slammed into the chair across from her, breathing through lips twisted into an angry grimace. "My God, Lila. My God! You saw him murder someone? And then he threatened you and almost strangled you?" He reached across and enclosed her hands between his again. "What else?"

She explained how the fifty dollars Lou handed her every Wednesday after he cashed his paycheck came with a stern admonition to not spend it all on her grocery shopping the next night. Thursday nights were the only time she had something to drive. He took the car to work otherwise, leaving her stranded at the apartment.

Paul shook his head while she told how shocked she'd been to find all that money in Lou's wallet while he was in the shower the night she'd run. Earlier, he'd tossed the usual fifty dollars onto the kitchen counter with a curt "Here." so Lila had been pretty sure he wouldn't look in his wallet again before he left for work.

"How come he had all that money stuffed in his billfold if we were so poor?" Lila asked. "There was a little over twelve hundred dollars. I was just shocked to see that much because whenever I asked about money, Lou always said we couldn't afford it."

Her voice trembled. "When I took the money I was so scared I could feel my heart thundering in my neck. I could hardly breathe. There was so much of it and I felt like I was stealing from him. After he'd choked me that morning, I didn't dare think about what he'd do to me if he discovered I'd been in his billfold and taken all that cash."

Concern and anger on chased each other across Paul's face. Lila let her shoulders relax in relief. He knew everything now, and he cared about her. Then, vexation and bitterness and a flare of resentment began to burn. What a mess Lou had made of her life. Why had she ever married him? And now he'd almost killed Mom.

"I need to call that detective in St. Paul and tell him what I saw, don't I?" she asked, bitterness creeping through her words. "I can't just let him get away with all this." It was time to do something more than just running away, time to take some action to protect herself and Mom and Judy. Do something. Not just sit here being a victim. "He'll be trying to get into Whittier again. I know he will. I have to report what I saw so they can catch him."

Paul took a deep breath, then answered, his voice firm. "Yes, you should report it. The police in Minnesota need all the help they can get. The sooner they get him, the better. And you can be sure we won't let him into Whittier, Lila. Don't worry. We will *not* let him through the tunnel."

Lila wanted to believe him, but she knew Lou was dangerous, crazy, and clever beyond anything Paul or anyone else knew. There was no doubt Lou would figure out a way to get to her. After a few minutes, the flicker of anger flared again to compete with her agony. She had to fight back, had to be strong.

She sighed. "You're right. I'll call."

Paul smiled approval, looked over at the cottony whiteness outside the living room window, and shoved his chair back a little. "How about going to my place and listening to some albums? Not much else we can do in this weather, I guess." He was trying to distract her, ease her mind.

"Yeah, sure."

Paul rose and drew her into his arms. "It's going to be all right, Lila. You're safe." His lips dropped toward hers. The kiss was gentle, but when it began to change, Lila pulled away.

I can't do this. I'm pregnant and he doesn't know. I just can't do this.

Paul backed away in confusion. "What?"

"Maybe you better go instead."

With a perplexed look, Paul strode to the closet and pulled out his jacket. "Okay, but...well, okay."

As soon as the door closed, Lila turned to the sink. Fretting, she finished washing the dishes and stacked them in the drainer. The baby would be starting its fourth month now if it had happened on the Fourth of July weekend like she suspected. Lila drew a deep, anxious breath. She had to tell Paul soon. He deserved to know. But what if it changed things—her having someone else's child? He might be upset that she hadn't told him before. Maybe he wouldn't want the embarrassment of being associated with a pregnant woman with no husband around. Or he might be afraid to get involved after losing his own baby.

Chapter 17

LILA REMAINED TROUBLED while she got ready for work, trying to accept that Lou had been in Alaska and she hadn't known about it.

When she stepped outside to walk to work, the wind had died, no more snow was falling, and a circle of blue sky peeked through clouds high across the bay. She shuffled through the drifts, glad for the bulky, white rubber Bunny Boots Paul had assured her were the best for Alaska weather. She burrowed into the parka. It was time to tell Paul about the pregnancy. She'd do it tonight.

The day dragged for Lila. By noon, the incessant roaring of the plow outside the store windows had become annoying, and a nagging throb built behind her eyes with every hour. There was little to do since hardly anybody could be out and around until the snow was cleared away.

Lila felt too ornery and headachy to stay any longer in the dim store by five o'clock. Not a single customer had come in all day and it was already dark as night outside. She banged the cash register drawer shut, slammed the store's heavy wooden door behind her, and set out for the Hodge. She trudged through the snow, feet crunching across the rough ridges left by the plow, eager to get to the sanctuary of her apartment. Tom would surely understand if she'd left early because of a headache. And Paul would figure out she'd gone home when he came by later and found the store closed.

But when Lila pushed open the door to her apartment, the rich smell of meat and gravy took her by surprise.

Paul greeted her as he turned from the stove, his eyes shining. "Hi! You came home early! I got off early, too. No trains tomorrow because of the snow. I could tell you were pretty upset last night after telling me about what happened with Lou." His smile crinkled up to his eyes. "So I wanted to surprise you. I was just getting some moose stew going before I went over to pick you up. I had this moose meat in my freezer and thought you might like to taste moose…" he chattered on, and turned back to the pot he was stirring on the stove.

Lila stood still, taken aback.

Paul laid down the big wooden spoon, turned from the stove, and started toward her. "Here, let me help you out of that. You look so beautiful in the parka with your cheeks all rosy." He stopped at the sight of Lila's face. "What's the matter? What's wrong?" he asked.

"I guess I don't feel so good. Kinda have a headache."

Her guilt intensified when Paul rushed to her side and began helping her out of the coat. "Here, let me help you." His voice carried worry he clearly tried to hide.

Lila whirled away from him, jerking her arms from the sleeves. She yanked the rest of the parka off, tossed it over a kitchen chair, and turned to him. "There's something I have to tell you, Paul. Something I should've told you before."

Paul remained where he was, brows knit in puzzlement. Lila couldn't look him in the eyes. She turned her back to him and walked toward the living room window. "I'm pregnant," she announced, just loud enough for him to hear. "I'm having a baby. From Lou. I'm in my fourth month."

There was silence behind her. Lila held her breath for what seemed like forever, waiting for a response. She didn't dare turn around. She heard a scuffling sound, then gasped at the sound of the apartment door closing. He was gone. Without a word.

Chapter 18

THAT NIGHT WHILE Lila worried about Paul, she had no way of knowing that an ornery dark-haired man in a basement apartment in Minneapolis had emptied another bottle of beer and tossed it toward the wastebasket. The clatter startled Artie's old dog, who'd been dozing in the middle of the tiny living room. She leaped to her feet in confusion, stumbling against Lou's outstretched leg. Lou landed a solid kick to the dog's middle, and the animal slunk away to lay on a rug by the door.

When Artie returned from his job late that afternoon, Lou staggered to his feet.

"We're gonna go out and cruise Hennepin Avenue as soon as it gets dark. My billfold's too damn thin again and we're almost out of beer. I need money."

Fearful of being turned in for his part in the murder and even more fearful of what Lou could do to him, Artie grudgingly agreed. He drove Lou to the sleazy section of downtown Minneapolis where Lou instructed him to wait with the engine idling.

Artie sat waiting, fuming, helpless, wishing he had the nerve to just speed away. Speed away from Lou, who'd dominated him since they met in seventh grade and discovered they lived only a block from each other. There had been random and unexpected hard punches to Artie's shoulder ever since the day they met, along with supposedly friendly slaps to his face that stung a lot, and too many hungry days at school because Lou took his lunch money. Lou had helped himself to Artie's best marbles and baseball cards, too. Artie was the one who lugged boards for tree houses, talked his mother out of extra cookies, delivered notes to girls in junior high, rounded up the cats they tormented in the woods bordering the park.

He'd always felt helpless and bullied, especially since he was so skinny and had developed deep, pitted scars across his cheeks from the acne that plagued him. He hated having to wear glasses, but couldn't see at all without them. He wished for thick black waves like Lou's instead of his stick-straight, mud-brown hair. And even though they dressed alike in tight jeans, short-sleeved white T-shirts, pointed black shoes, and leather jackets, Artie knew he wasn't like Lou. He tried to imitate Lou's swagger and attitude, but when girls glanced at him, their eyes slid right on by, as if he didn't exist.

So Artie sat in his car on Hennepin Avenue, filled with resentment, waiting for his only friend. He hated having to use his car to take Lou around, hated sharing the apartment he paid for, resented buying food and beer and having to pay for gas. But it had always been that way. Lou had been bigger, stronger, and in control. And Lou was always after more money, saying there was no way he was going to live his life being poor like his folks. So he bought expensive beer, bourbon by the quart, nice clothing from the men's shops downtown, two hundred-dollar shoes. His cars were decked out with every fancy accessory possible. Lou complained bitterly about Lila stealing his Galaxie, and gloated about what he'd do to her to make her sorry for that.

Artie felt trapped and angry that his friend's hold on him was deeper than ever since Lou had dragged him into the murder. And then, along with most of the people who knew Lou, he'd had to go downtown to be interviewed after Lou had been identified as Lila's mother's attacker. Thankfully, by that time, Lou had already disappeared, and there was no mention of any connection to the murder at Spruce Grove. Artie was sure Lou had left on a search for Lila, but at least he hadn't had to lie when he told the detectives that he didn't know where Lou was.

He sank deeper into his car seat, shuddering as always at the memory of that night outside the club. He knew it had gone bad because the man refused to hand over his wallet there in the parking lot. Artie still couldn't believe what should have been one of their simple robberies had ended in murder. Earlier, inside the club, Lou had noticed the man's fat wallet full of cash, and ordered Artie to keep an eye on the guy until he left. When he did, they'd followed him to the parking lot and confronted him while he was unlocking his truck. The man burst free, to their surprise, and kicked Lou hard right between the legs. Artie had never seen anything like the rage that overcame Lou, who bellowed in pain, bent over, clutching himself for a moment, and then reared back up, seething, his face purple with pain and rage.

He'd reached in and grabbed the jacket of the man who was scrambling into his truck, frantically trying to pull the door shut. Lou kicked the door half off its hinges in fury and yanked the man out, throwing him to his knees on the gravel. Artie had watched in disbelief while Lou kicked the man in the face and side again and again while he tried in vain to regain his feet. It had been like watching a madman on a rampage.

And when Lou roared, "Git in here, Artie!" Artie had instinctively rushed in.

The rest was a blur, a frenzy, a spasm of madness. Lou's eruption of violence was unlike anything Artie had ever seen. He tried not to think about the tire iron Lou had picked up after it clattered from beneath the man's truck seat. Artie always felt a little sick remembering the terrible sounds. It had all happened so fast. Before Artie even had a chance to think, the man was lying motionless, a puddle of blood slowly spreading beneath his head. Artie remembered the greed on Lou's face when he grabbed the man's billfold from his pocket and tore out the wad of bills, his face gleeful. But Lou hadn't seemed bothered, he'd even remembered to follow his strategy of stuffing fifty dollars or so back into the wallet and returning it to the victim's pocket so the police would think the crime was something other than a robbery.

Artie had followed Lou back into the club and watched in disbelief while Lou slid onto a stool beside Lila and put his arm around her, drawing her close, as if nothing had happened. By the time the three of them left a half hour later, Artie hadn't been able to stop shivering, and felt sick. The lights of oncoming traffic on the drive home glared into his dry eyes and he felt like he was in a dream.

He'd been trying ever since to push the murder from his memory. But he couldn't keep the images away, especially at night when he was trying to sleep. His dreams were haunted. He woke up many nights sweating, gasping, frantically hoping it was only a dream.

It had been so senseless. So horrible. A man was dead because of them.

The news had been full of the brutal murder of a young man who had apparently been in the wrong place at the wrong time. Nobody could come up with a motive for the murder, and there were no suspects. But Artie knew. Artie shuddered and looked out the car window, desperately wishing Lou would get back. He sunk into the driver's seat, hiding from the blinking neon of Hennepin Avenue.

"I wish I could disappear. I wish I'd never met Lou Peterson. The bastard," he muttered. "And poor Lila. She was so sweet and she was always nice to me. I wonder where she is. I hope she's okay."

Artie started when Lou burst back into the passenger's seat with a wallet clutched in his hand. "Outta here!" he shouted, hurling himself in and slamming the door. "A thousand bucks this time, I bet!" he crowed. He grabbed the bills, shoved them into his pocket and gave Artie a hard whack to the shoulder. "Let's go! Quick! I kicked that guy pretty hard, but he jumped right back up. Here, toss the wallet out the window. I got most of the cash. Look at these hundred dollar bills! No wonder he tried so hard to fight back! Put your foot to the floor, man! Get outta here!"

Chapter 19

THE EVENING ALONE dragged. Lila tried a few bites of the moose stew Paul had been making, but found she could hardly swallow, so she put it in a bowl, covered it with tin foil and set it in the refrigerator. Paul had been making supper for her. He'd been taking care of her. And now he was gone. He'd left without a word when she told him. This is what she'd been afraid would happen.

Lila read the same meaningless sentences over and over before finally tossing her magazine aside and going off to bed. It felt empty and cold beneath the covers, and she had a hard time falling asleep. She dozed through the night, awakening as the pale, gray light of morning finally filtered its way through the bedroom curtains.

Lila dressed, listless and tired. It was important to eat, for the baby, so she forced down a few bites of tasteless cereal. Had she lost Paul by telling him she was pregnant? She listened for the sound of his knock all morning, then left the still, lonely apartment early for work.

Lila's thoughts remained in turmoil all afternoon, and her mood grew bleaker with each passing hour. She forgot to give change to a customer who handed her a twenty dollar bill for a single beer, and slouched, despondent, on the stool behind the counter instead of cleaning or stocking shelves. Anyone who talked to her was an interruption, a nuisance, a bother, an annoyance in the long and difficult day.

She waited, hoping for the sound of Paul's truck as the evening waned. At closing time, she walked home alone in the wintry darkness, despondent, parka unfastened, welcoming the cold that seeped like freezing water into her bones.

Her silent apartment felt hollow. She wandered, aimless and discontented, between the dark living room window and the kitchen. She caught a reflection of herself in the blackness of the window, surprised at the droop of her shoulders, and wondered what Dad would think if he saw her like this. He wouldn't want her to be overcome by it. He'd expect her to be tough. To take care of herself and be strong.

Dad would know this was all Lou's fault. I guess I was young and dumb to marry Lou, but Dad wouldn't let him get away with ruining my life like this.

She strode to the bathroom and yanked the bathtub faucets on full force. A nice hot bath, that would help. Then it would be time to make a call to the police in Minnesota and tell them what she'd witnessed. Give them all the information she could to help them put Lou where he belonged. No matter the risk, no matter how it disrupted her life, it was the right thing to do. If they hadn't found him by now, they needed her help. She'd tell them Artie was involved, too. Maybe that would be the thing that would allow them to track Lou down and she wouldn't actually have to go back there herself. But poor Artie. He was such a nice guy and her action could ruin his life.

After a soothing soak and the renewed resolve about calling the police, Lila felt better. But time still dragged and she felt an unceasing loneliness for Paul. She toyed with the idea of going down and knocking on his door, but couldn't bring herself to do it. If he came back to her, it had to be because he wanted to, not because she'd asked him. He was so kind that he'd probably agree to stay friends if she asked, but she didn't want to do that to him. He had to want to be with her, like it had been.

Maybe she should go up to see Nan. But Nan would surely recognize her troubled state. She didn't want to explain this to Nan. Paul and Nan were friends. This wasn't a burden she should put into that relationship.

She puttered around the apartment, an ear cocked for any sound at the door, but none came. By bedtime, all the laundry had been folded, the dishes put away, the dusting and sweeping done, and the bathroom scrubbed until it shone. Lila had left the door ajar even when in the bathroom so she could hear if there was a knock, but she heard nothing. She curled up on the couch with the same magazine as the night before. Again, the words wouldn't register.

Her mind returned over and over to Paul's voice, his clean, masculine scent, the feel of his lips on hers. How he'd protected her and kept his word about keeping Lou out of Whittier. How he cared. And he'd given her the parka that meant so much to him. Lila longed for him and missed him more than she ever would have thought possible. She got up, opened the closet, and buried her face in the parka to drink in the scent.

A glimmer of resolution grew within her. She wouldn't let it end this way. She'd get dressed and go down to his apartment. At least she could let him know how sorry she was for not telling him about the baby earlier. And she needed to thank him for helping her get settled, and especially for protecting her from Lou. He deserved that. She'd tell him she understood if he didn't want to see her anymore. But it seemed like he truly cared about her, so he should still be able to care, even if she was pregnant. No, that was too much to ask of him. Her thoughts whirled.

Feeling really alone for the first time since reaching Whittier, sudden terror that Lou might be trying to get to her again resurfaced. What if Paul wasn't around to protect her anymore? A feeling of dread overcame her, and her insides lurched with familiar panic. Trembling and unable to stifle the sob that had been building in her throat, Lila gave in to fear and grief, and felt hot tears fill her eyes.

At that moment, she heard a sound outside her apartment door. Was somebody there? Had Lou found her? Then there was a definite knock. She swiped at her eyes, heart pounding, and crossed to the door, afraid to open it.

"Lila? Lila, are you in there?"

It was Paul. Lila wiped her cheeks dry, cleared her throat, flipped the lock aside and flung open the door. Paul's heavy blue jacket, still zipped up, gave off a whiff of cold outside air. A dusting of snow lay on his shoulders. He fumbled a blue and gold stocking cap from his head, revealing the mussed brown curls Lila found so appealing. They stared at each other.

Paul strode into the apartment and without a word gathered Lila into his arms. He smothered her against his frigid, stiff coat so tightly she could hardly breathe. She wiggled her arms free and hugged him back as hard as she could. They clung to each other in silence.

Paul pulled away at last. He managed to kick the door shut behind them without completely releasing her. "I've been out walking. And thinking," he said. "I'm sorry. Sorry about how I acted. I was just so surprised about a baby. I...well. It's a lot to take in, it's all right, my darling."

Lila felt chills at the words "my darling." Her heart raced at the memory of Lou's cruel version of Paul's tender words. When Lou said it, it didn't sound like this. She grew lightheaded and stumbled backward.

"What is it? What's wrong?" Paul asked.

"Nothing. Nothing," Lila replied, trying to regain her composure. "It's just that…that…well, I was afraid you wouldn't come back. I'm sorry I didn't tell you right away that I was expecting, but I didn't realize it until just the other day. With all the other stuff happening, I didn't think about and, well, I was afraid you wouldn't want me when you found out." She sniffled and wiped her sleeve across her nose. "And, well…well… Lou used to call me his little darlin', so, when you said it just now, I had sort of a flashback. It was awful the way he said it to me. But…" Lila felt herself babbling and tried to stop. "I, I'm so glad you're here."

Paul reached out and gathered her back into his embrace. "Hey, it's all right. I'm glad to be back, too."

He gave Lila a gentle push back so he could see her face. "I can't believe all this time you've been pregnant. And you drove from Minnesota by yourself! You just struck out on your own. You got a job and a place to live, handled everything." His eyes widened in admiration. "Does Lou know about this baby?"

Lila shook her head. "No. I didn't figure it out myself until the other day."

159

"Whew!" Paul took a breath. "Does your mother know?"

Again, Lila shook her head.

"Well," Paul said." We better tell her she's gonna be a grandma, don't you think?" His face lit. "We're having a baby!"

Lila's anxiety vanished at his words. Her legs grew unsteady as relief flooded through her. She pulled away from Paul and tugged him along with her to the living room.

A long sigh escaped her as they settled on the sofa. "You're not upset? Not mad?"

"No, I'm not mad," Paul answered, his eyes shining. "I'm happy. I'm going to be with you on this. We'll have this baby, and it'll be ours. I'll help you with the baby, and with Lou. And no matter what it takes, we'll get that divorce so you're free."

Paul rose and faced her, his face lit with emotion. "I love you, Lila, and I want to spend the rest of my life with you and our children." He dropped to a knee. "As soon as we can get you free of Lou, will you marry me?"

He grinned, hopeful and expectant. Lila gulped. He wasn't mad. He wanted to marry her. He wanted the baby. But a sudden and troubling sense of trepidation overcame her at the thought of marriage. Lou had been attentive and loving before they got married, such a catch, so nice. But he'd changed, and it hadn't taken long for her to feel like he didn't really care about her. Then after what happened, he was a different person, hostile and frightening. She couldn't believe she'd been married to someone who could kill. And despite the way she felt about Paul, she'd only known him such a short time.

She lifted her eyes to Paul. "Oh, Paul. I love you, too. But I need some time. I'm still married. And I...I..."

Paul reached over and pulled her close against him, interrupting, "Take all the time you need. I'll wait 'til you feel ready. We'll find a lawyer in Anchorage who can help us figure out how to get divorced from someone in another state. And we'll tell the authorities in Minnesota everything you know so they can get that son of a bitch." Spots of red dotted his cheeks and his eyes burned with resolve.

At Lila's nod, he went on. "I want us to spend the rest of our lives together. This baby will be the start of our family. I'll take care of you both." He patted her stomach, unable to hide his excitement and happiness.

Lila captured his strong, warm hands, guiding them against her belly, feeling love connect all three of them. "I love you, Paul," she murmured.

"I love you more," he answered.

Suddenly giddy, they couldn't move fast enough. Paul's lips never left hers while he half carried her toward the bedroom. They stumbled through the trail of their clothing and fell, still clinging together, onto her bed.

They pressed their naked bodies together for the first time, holding tight, exploring the fit. Paul grew more tender with each passing moment. He covered her with his smooth, strong body, keeping her tucked beneath him. He cradled her face between his hands, giving her eyelids and cheeks featherlike kisses. Her ear tingled with his hot breath as he whispered, "I love you so much, Lila." When he buried his face in her neck, nuzzling, she squirmed against him, unable to stifle tiny squeals of pleasure. He returned again and again to her lips until their mouths held no secrets and their breath became one.

The response to his lips and hands burned deep within her. His breath grew hot and ragged while he moved completely over her, heavy, now possessive. She loved the feeling of having him on top of her, wanted to stay beneath him forever, to always be this warm and loved. She hungered for his lips whenever he moved them from hers, losing herself to the strange, wild craving. Her hands swept his back and lower, causing him to moan. She tickled her tongue into his ear, giggling at his shudder. She pushed against him, trying to get even closer, loving the feel of his chest and legs molded against hers, pinning her to the bed. When she wriggled beneath him, he gave a low moan and began nudging her legs apart. She opened to him without hesitation and matched his every thrust.

He panted, strong arms braced on either side of her head. His voice rumbled from low in his throat.

"You feel so good." He dropped his lips to her breasts, flicking his tongue from one to the other, tugging each one deep into his mouth. He groaned, the sound humming against her skin. When she gave a mewl, he stiffened, gasped, and made one final wild thrust. She convulsed at the same time, astounded at the involuntary spasms that shook her. Paul shuddered above her, then collapsed, burrowing his head into her shoulder. He settled on top of her, breathing ragged. His warm weight was all she knew, all she wanted, her shelter from the world.

They didn't notice the rest of the evening pass. They made love, lost in each other, unmindful of passing time, exploring, until both lay spent and satisfied. At last, deep in the night, half tangled in the sheets, they gave in to exhaustion. Lila slid into sleep with Paul curled behind her. She slept deeply, secure and warm, cradled in the arms of the man she loved.

Lila rolled over in the faint morning light to Paul's face only inches from hers and lay still, admiring him. He breathed through slightly parted lips. His lashes lay dark and full against cheeks flushed with sleep. The shiny curls she loved spread across the pillow like some crazy hat. His chest gleamed beneath a fuzz of caramel-colored hair, and the wrinkled sheet lay twisted around his hips. When Lila reached out to tuck a wayward curl back into place behind his ear, her touch woke him. No words were necessary as they smiled into each other's eyes.

Paul rolled toward her and, taking her face between his hands, kissed her deeply and murmured, "It's great to wake up with you in my arms."

They molded themselves together again, leisurely fitting their bodies together, then dozed until the late morning light pouring through the window onto their faces woke them. They rose and showered and dressed, not shy, not embarrassed, enjoying the newness of the intimacy they shared.

Contentment seeped deep into Lila's very being at Paul's loving actions and words. She decided she'd marry him. There was no doubt left after last night's lovemaking. Paul's gentle caresses and his attentiveness to Lila's enjoyment of their lovemaking was a stark contrast to Lou's selfish, cold-hearted focus on just satisfying his own physical release. In Paul's arms, Lila had felt cherished and safe. So, while pouring coffee at the breakfast table, she leaned over and murmured close to his ear, "I've had enough time to think about it. My answer is yes."

Paul froze for a second, then his face brightened and he grinned, joy shining from his eyes. He pushed back his chair and leaped up to hug her. "You'll never be sorry," he whispered into her hair. "I'll show you what a real husband is like." His hands dropped to cup her behind and he pulled her hard against him. "Just wait."

She stood at the window after breakfast, watching him leave for work, wishing she never had to let him out of her sight. Great mounds of snow covered

164

everything below, muffling sound. Cars in the Hodge parking lot wore giant white mushroom caps, and snow had drifted across both sets of the building's entry steps, completely burying them. Cheerful residents were emerging from the building, working together, shovels and brooms sending snow flying as they dug themselves out. Children scampered among them, tossing handfuls of snow, tumbling through the drifts, their joyful, tinny shrieks thinned by distance. Everyone wore hats—bulky fur hats with ear flaps flopping, thick wool stocking caps pulled low over foreheads, jaunty, bright, pointed knit caps with colorful, dangling tassels.

Mountain peaks and slopes in all directions, heaped with pristine snow, glowed through the gray daylight. Whittier's decrepit orange snowplow chugged around the parking areas and roads, spitting stinky, dark smoke. It slowly widened paths and roads through the drifts, pushing more snow into the huge ridges forming tall white borders for the town.

From her snug apartment window high above it all, Lila watched Paul help clear the far set of steps, then shovel a path to his truck. He balanced his coffee cup on the hood of his truck while he brushed snow from the windows, then looked up and gave her a wave before he climbed in. How she loved that man. Her heart leaped at the thought of spending her life with him.

They knocked on Nan's door the next morning, unable to hide grins, excited to tell her about their plans and the baby.

"Hey, you two," Nan greeted them, sweeping the door wide and gesturing them in. She stepped back and flicked the stub of a cigarette into the ash tray on the kitchen counter. "Kinda lonely around here in the mornings now."

She smiled, then noticed their faces. Her eyebrows pinched together and her lips pursed. "You two look...well, funny. What's up?"

Paul spoke, "We're going to get married. Well, as soon as we can...after..."

He was interrupted by Nan's hoot. "Well, by God! Happy to hear it. I knew somethin' was up between you two. Ever since that first ride through the tunnel. I could tell. Just gotta git rid of that asshole husband first, huh?"

"There's more," Lila said, unable to hide a smile. "I'm pregnant. About half way now. My husband's."

Nan's brown eyes crinkled over a huge grin. "I know. Saw it on ya it right away. Knew it could only be one thing. Wondered when you'd tell me."

Nan's eyes darted from one to the other. But Lila caught a flash of an odd expression before Nan abruptly turned away. It looked like Nan had tried to hide a flicker of sadness or grief. But why? What would make Nan look like that and turn away so fast?

"What, Nan? What is it?"

But Nan didn't answer. She turned back to them a moment later, her face arranged almost back to normal. "Nothin', Dearie," she answered, her tone evasive. "Nothin' at all. I'm just so tickled for the both of ya." But there was something other than happiness on her face.

Chapter 20

LILA AND PAUL slept entwined in Lila's bed every night after that, snuggled close, enraptured and content. Even though her mother and most of society would not approve of such behavior, a curious detachment and willfulness about this uncharacteristic lack of morals settled over Lila. Whether it was Whittier or Alaska or Paul or circumstances, Lila gave in to a surprising lack of conscience about her willingness to live this way of life. Feeling oddly cavalier and light-hearted, Lila grew ever more satisfied with her Alaskan refuge while the long dark days of November passed.

The routine trips to Anchorage she and Paul made provided more and more touches that made her apartment truly a home. After one trip, as they passed the rippling waters of an oncoming tide in the inlet along the highway heading back to Whittier, Lila asked, "Paul? Do you ever notice the way people look at us sometimes in Anchorage?"

Paul kept his gaze on the road, not acknowledging her question.

"Paul? Do I imagine it? Or do some people give us dirty looks? Why would that be?"

Paul's posture became rigid as Lila spoke and his knuckles grew white on the steering wheel.

"Paul?"

"It's nothing," he finally replied, still staring at the road ahead. His tone was oddly cold, one Lila had never heard before. He remained silent as the miles passed, and Lila felt rebuffed.

What's wrong with him?

Soon, daylight gave way to the early blackness of night typical of this time of year and Lila's attention was drawn to the sparkling snow surrounding the road and mountainsides. It looked as if millions of diamond specks had been scattered across the ground and over the branches of the frost-covered trees.

She turned to Paul in awe. "What's that twinkly snow? It's beautiful. I've noticed it before, but never like it is today. It's like fairy dust or something. What is it, anyway?"

Paul shook his shoulders loose and answered, his voice now normal. He finally looked at her. "Oh, that's what we call diamond dust. It's ice crystals, kind of like prisms, reflecting light. On cold, dark nights, if conditions are just right, the landscape glitters like this. Pretty, huh?"

Lila nodded, delighted by the spectacular sight. Pearly moonlight reflecting off the inky waters of the bay added to her high spirits when they drove out of the tunnel. Paul's odd behavior after her question about the people in Anchorage was forgotten. Spruce and willows glittering with diamond dust climbed the mountain slopes surrounding Whittier, further enchanting her. While she and Paul stood outside the truck in the parking lot admiring the fairyland around them, Lila twirled until Paul grabbed her and they collapsed against each other and fell sideways into a high, soft snow drift, laughing with delight. Lila could never remember feeling happier.

HER SPIRITS GREW even higher when they told Mom about the baby on the next Sunday morning's call.

Mom, after a long stunned silence, asked incredulously, "A baby, Lila? You're expecting? I'm to be a grandmother? But… What….when…why didn't?"

They heard Judy squeal in the background. "Lila! What? You're gonna have a baby? What in the? When?"

The phone got passed back and forth between Margaret and Judy until everyone knew every detail. The joy in Mom's voice warmed Lila's heart. Paul beamed from the other side of the desk while Judy's shrieks came through the receiver.

"She's a loud one," he observed.

"Yeah, Judy's kinda wild and crazy," Lila explained after she hung up the phone. "She's been my best friend forever. We did everything together since we were just little. Slept over at each other's house, walked to school together every day, took swimming lessons, rode our bikes. She says she loves the taste of Hamm's beer made in St. Paul, but I can't stand it. I don't think I could have a better friend."

Lila paused, smiling and remembering. "She's cute, too. Petite. Just got one of those new pixie haircuts with the feathery bangs and edges. Wears her pants too tight, Mom says. Mom thinks Judy's a hoot." Lila sighed. "I sure miss her. I can't wait for you to meet her. And Mom, too."

The following days passed uneventfully until the afternoon Paul burst into the store. "The President's been shot!" he yelled. "He's dead! The President's dead!"

Paul and Lila rushed to the lobby of the Hodge, where residents had gathered in a tight, silent knot around a wooden console TV someone had carried out and placed in the corner. The following hours of odd and somber silence were broken only by hushed sobs of anguish while the news unfolded over the rest of the day. No one spoke. No one even looked at anyone else.

People wandered away to their own apartments as night deepened, their faces grave and pale. Lila and Paul gripped hands in the elevator, shaken, glad for each other's presence. They lay awake, side-by-side in shocked silence, late into the night. Whittier remained grim the next day, gray and quiet, in mourning.

That mood still lingered on Thanksgiving morning when Lila awoke to her first holiday ever away from family. An almost overwhelming sense of homesickness and nostalgia set in as soon as she opened her eyes. But when Paul took her to his office for a holiday call to Minnesota, the familiar voices of Judy and her mother made things easier.

Nan's Thanksgiving dinner included stuffing made with oysters and walnuts, sweet potatoes smothered in melted marshmallows, and cranberry relish with orange peel—all new dishes to Lila. Paul contributed an appetizer of moose sausage swimming in barbeque sauce, and Lila baked the frozen pumpkin pie she'd picked up during the last trip to Anchorage.

Nobody was surprised when Nan's next door neighbor, Agnes, knocked on the door, apparently drawn by the aromas filtering into the hallway. Nan, anticipating this, had already set a place at the table for the tiny, hunched old woman. Agnes wore large pearl earrings, a matching strand at her neck, and a gray linen dress that draped to her ankles. Wisps of white hair trailed onto her neck from the thin braid wrapping her head. She ate with dainty movements, and said a gracious, "Thank you very much. It was most delicious," before slipping out the door as soon as she finished eating.

"That's not unusual 'round here," Nan explained with a good-natured shrug. "Agnes keeps pretty much to herself. Only comes over when the spirit moves her."

"Or at the smell of good cooking," Paul retorted, and grinned. He pushed his chair back from the table and patted his stomach.

Nan chuckled. "Rumor has it Agnes is filthy rich." She sat back from the table, too, and drew a deep drag of a freshly-lit cigarette. "They say she's in Whittier hidin' out from her three kids, who've been tryin' to get at her money for years now. I've heard 'em at her door a coupla times over the years, but she never opens up for 'em."

She paused to tap ashes into the ashtray, "Her son wandered around town for a few days one summer 'bout five years back. Tried to get somebody to help him get into his Ma's place, but nobody gave him the time of day. She didn't come out, not at all, while the guy was in town."

She took another drag on her cigarette, blew a perfect smoke ring toward the ceiling and continued, "It's not our business. If Agnes wants help, we know she'll ask. And we'll be there for her. When she's ready to let us in on what's goin' on with her family, she'll tell us. 'Til then, we'll leave her alone." As an afterthought, she added, "Her kids musta really pissed her off."

She turned away to the kitchen, but not before Lila caught a flash of deep melancholy pass over her face.

"Nan?" Lila asked in concern.

Nan didn't answer, instead ducking her head and evading Lila's gaze when she turned back to the table. She drew hard on a cigarette, and with forced cheerfulness continued. "Agnes is kinda the watchdog for the whole building. Just sits down in the lobby by herself most mornings watchin' people come and go. Other'n that, we don't see much of her at all."

Lila, rebuffed and puzzled by Nan's fleeting expression and evasiveness, sensed that Nan was uneasy. "Well, how does she get food and other stuff she needs?"

Paul answered this time. "Oh, she sends a detailed order down to the railroad office with one of the kids from the building about once a month. It's always on thick white stationery with her name engraved along the top in gold. And there's a matching envelope with a hundred-dollar bill in it. We hand it off to whoever of us is going into Anchorage next, and they shop for her. Then we give her the change when we bring it to her door. She always insists on giving that person a five dollar bill in appreciation. I've done it lots of times."

"Me, too," Nan added. "She doesn't need much."

Lila listened in fascination.

This is such a strange place. They look out for each other, but everyone has privacy, too. Paul was right when he said Whittier wasn't like any other town in America.

She studied Nan's face while they talked, wondering about the apparent sadness she'd

174

witnessed so often before, but Nan continued to avoid her gaze, busying herself with the meal.

Old Tom had also joined them for the Thanksgiving dinner. He talked, seeming glad for an audience, while they lingered at the table letting dinner settle. He basked in their rapt attention to his memories of commercial fishing on the Bering Sea in his early years. When Lila had trouble imagining huge nets bulging with thousands of thrashing salmon, he invited them down to his apartment to look at pictures.

"When ya come down, I'll get them pictures out so you can see what I'm talkin' about," he enthused, scrabbling a finger around the bristly beard covering his lips.

Nan turned a secretive, eager face to Lila, as if to say, *"Yes! Let's get a look at his apartment!"*

Tom rambled on in his raspy voice, "Hey, I got pictures ya just won't believe. Fishin' was somethin' in them days, all right. We lived right on them boats for days, 'til the holds were too full to cram any more fish in 'em. Hell, we almost sank from the weight more'n once." He looked around at the attentive faces. "Pay was damn good, too. That's how I saved up to buy the store. Tough life. Dangerous as hell. Coupla' good men bought it out there. Damn..." His voice trailed off.

He shook his head and patted his beard, covering his mouth in mock embarrassment. "Whoops, 'scuse the language, ladies."

Lila and Paul were back in Lila's apartment by late afternoon, still full of turkey dinner. They stretched out side-by-side on the sofa and talked lazily while wind-blown snowflakes melted against the window.

"I bet Mom's still doing dishes at Judy's right now," Lila smiled. "She can never walk out of a kitchen until everything's done. Even the burners on the stove have to be shined, and the sink scrubbed out." After a pause, she added, "This is the first time I haven't been with her on a holiday. But, I get to be with you and that's just as good." She nuzzled Paul's neck. "What would you usually be doing on Thanksgiving?"

"I'd be back in Alukiak," Paul explained. "But it's really nice to be here with you and not have to do the traveling. It's pretty tough to get there this time of the year. It's really dangerous traveling in the winter in interior Alaska. We can only get there by dog sled from Willow and it's a long haul, at least a whole day. Or, we have to fly in. But flights only go into the village on certain days—depends on the wind and weather. One Thanksgiving, I got stranded there for eight days 'til we could be flown out. Terrible blizzard. Even the dog teams and their straw beds had to be moved into the arctic entries on the houses. It was impossible to go anywhere. It sure was a good visit with everyone, though, and it always feels good to be home. Then I always go back again only a few weeks later for Christmas."

He turned to Lila, his voice hesitant, almost bashful. "I'd like to take you there. Maybe for Christmas? My mom and dad and grandmother want to meet you."

She swallowed her surprise. He'd talked to his family about her already. And he wanted to take her home for Christmas.

"Sure, I'd like to meet them, too. When do you talk to them, anyway?"

"Well, I call from the office when I can," Paul replied. "And sometimes I use the shortwave there, too. There's a receiver in the village but I can only get through to it at certain times. Whoever answers talks to me for a while, and then they go get my parents. Actually, anybody who answers is considered my family. Pretty much the whole village raises kids together, no matter whose they are. It's a shared thing in our culture, bringing up young ones. When kids are little, they eat and sleep wherever they are at meal time or bedtime. It's like I had a bunch of aunts and uncles, and their homes were mine all the while I was growing up. I had to mind all my 'uncles' just as much as my dad. I want you to meet all of them. And my sister, Tatiana."

He hesitated. "I hope you'll like the food. Even though planes deliver ham and turkeys and everything, it's usually just our traditional dishes at holidays." He grinned. "I remember the first time the plane brought pizzas. Nobody knew what they were or how to cook them. The whole village gathered at my aunt's kitchen while she tried to fry one. After we figured it out, though, there were always a few cases of frozen pizza on every plane."

"What else did you like?" Lila asked.

"Oh, peaches. Canned peaches. They were my favorite thing. And everybody always wanted oranges and apples and lettuce. Dad orders tins of sardines and jars of pickled herring because he says they're a taste of his homeland. Mom and the other women get their spices, like cinnamon and vanilla, and my sister and the other kids love any kind of candy."

Lila listened in fascination while Paul talked about his home. How different it was from her life in Minnesota. A flash of Lou's face intruded at the thought of home, and she gave a little shudder.

"Hey!" Paul said. "You were a million miles away just now. What were you thinking about?"

Lila turned to him. "Oh—sorry. I was thinking about going with you for Christmas. Then I started thinking about home, and about Lou. I know I have to call the police in Minnesota. But I can't get past worrying that they'll make me go back there. Do you think it would help if I tell about Artie being in on it? Maybe send an anonymous letter? Maybe they could find him easier, and he could lead them to Lou. Those two were always together. Artie was quiet and shy and really nice to me, but I saw him kicking the guy, too."

Paul answered. "Yeah, let's do a letter. You have to do something. If you eventually have to go back, I'll go with you. That jerk will never touch a hair on your head or he'll have to deal with me."

"I guess you're right," Lila answered. Why couldn't they just catch Lou without her? She should let them know about Artie's involvement. Then maybe he'd be the one Lou would blame. She could send an anonymous letter. She couldn't just keep this secret any longer, not while Lou was on the loose. Mom and Judy were still in danger. Dad would want her to do what was responsible and right. Yeah, a letter—that was the thing to do.

She scribbled a note about the murder, included Artie's name, and copied the detective's address off the business card onto an envelope. Dropping it in the outgoing mail slot in the lobby the next morning lightened her heart. Maybe this would do it.

Chapter 21

PAUL WAS UNUSUALLY talkative the next evening. Lila knew he was trying to keep her mind off Lou. To her surprise, she became enthralled while Paul explained why he hadn't told her much about his family. It was fascinating to hear that his people don't talk about themselves because they believe it's rude. Instead, they focus on keeping harmony in the whole group, so if an individual has a grievance, he asks someone else to intervene for him to avoid direct confrontation.

"Our culture doesn't indulge in negative talk because they believe words are so powerful that complaining out loud will cause the speaker to become negative himself," Paul explained. "And storytelling is really important. They don't have TV yet in the village. I wonder how that will be for them when they get it and can watch stories from the Outside."

Paul rattled off words in his own language with a proud smile, and then explained. "That was the dialect of our area. The elders try to teach us because they don't want the language to die. My grandmother doesn't speak any English at all. But the only time I ever speak Yup'ik is when I'm with them. It's unique to our people. They think words lose their spirit when translated into English."

He paused for Lila's acknowledgement. "Maybe they're right. I understand the stories better in our own words than in English."

He waited again and when Lila remained silent, went on. "I can't wait for you to meet them all. But, you know, it'll be really different for you. I guess my dad adjusted to village life right away, and just found his place with my mother. He hasn't ever wanted to leave."

When Lila dipped her head in understanding, he continued, "I don't look like the other kids in the village because of him, so I've had an easier time in the outside world than most of the guys I grew up with. I'm only one of the few from Alukiak to ever finish high school. Hilli did, too. Everyone was so proud of us." A shadow of grief passed across his face.

Lila stood and reached for him, enveloping him in her arms.

He returned the embrace before sitting back down, and went on. "I moved to Anchorage after Hilli died and lived with my aunt and uncle for a few months while I did the railroad training. Before I left Alukiak, Dad told me to always walk with my head high. I didn't know why he told me that until the first time I got spit at and called 'Eskimo.' I got called it a lot when I got to the city. And the looks. Man! In Anchorage, people give me the dirtiest looks for no reason. At first, I didn't know what I'd done, but then I got it. Pretty quick."

He paused, sounding reluctant to go on, but at Lila's sympathetic look, he continued. "It still happens. And it's still pretty hard to take. The best word I can use to describe it is disdain. I sure know why my father told me to walk with my head high. He knew I'd run into it as soon as I left the village. But I guess there wasn't any way he could really explain it to me. I don't know what words he could have used to tell me what it would be like to be spit at in a parking lot. And to have people kind of draw away from me in the grocery store like they don't want to be near me. And to have somebody mutter 'dirty Eskimo' when I walk by. I see the bums on the streets—most of 'em are pretty rough-looking, and most are Eskimos. Some people treat me like I'm one of them."

Lila swallowed hard. So that explained the looks in Anchorage. It was prejudice. Against her for being with an Eskimo. Paul had to deal with it all the time. No wonder he hadn't been able to answer her that night in the truck. What an impossible thing to explain.

Paul choked through the roughness in his throat and continued, "I got hired on with the railroad right after...after...Hilli... It was a lucky break to get such a good job. I'm not sure how it happened. Maybe my father pulled some strings—he has a few contacts through his shipmates who stayed on in Alaska and got on with the railroad. I needed to get away..."

At Lila's troubled gaze, Paul continued, "But it's better here in Whittier. People know me for who I am. I think it helped that Nan accepted me right away. I guess that's why I like living in Whittier. Nobody judges me or looks down on me. Everyone accepts me, and I feel comfortable here. It wasn't like that in Anchorage..." his voice dropped.

His eyes took on a faraway look before he shook his head and added without meeting Lila's eyes, "I like my job, too. I've been pretty happy here. And now I have you."

Lila swallowed hard to hide a gulp of sympathy. "Oh, Paul..." she began. But he didn't seem to hear her.

Paul turned to Lila. "I can't believe I've talked so much about myself! I usually don't do this."

Lila reached for him, and wrapped her arms around him. She'd never loved him as much as she did at that moment. What a different life he'd had. She now had an understanding of the odd, disapproving, hostile looks she'd received in Anchorage. Now it was clear.

She drew him tighter to her and burrowed her face into his neck. He was such a strong man. A good person. He'd been putting up with this and never even mentioned it. Now he was sharing a vulnerability, and he was willing to take her back to his home and family, to see where he grew up, what had made him who he was. She couldn't wait to meet his family and become one of them. They had to be good people. There was no doubt this was the man she'd share her life with. She would take care of this man and do all she could to help make his life the best possible.

Chapter 22

"WHY'D YOU EVER marry Lou?" Paul asked over Sunday breakfast the next morning. "Why him?"

Lila took a sip of her juice, startled at the abruptness of the question. "You really want to know?"

"Yeah. Whatever made you marry a jerk like that anyway?"

"Oh, well, the first time Lou kissed me, I met his lips with every bit of passion I could. I didn't want him to think I didn't know what I was doing, but I really didn't. I guess I did okay, and he liked it."

Paul made a small choking sound before nodding for Lila to go ahead.

"After a few months of kissing and petting in the front seat of his car, he begged me to move in with him. He kept begging me, 'Just for a little while. Let's try it out. Please, my little darlin'."

Lila grimaced. "Moving out of Mom's house right after graduation from high school into a place of my own sounded wonderful. Things had been tough for Mom moneywise ever since Dad died, and I thought if I got out on my own, Mom would have fewer expenses."

Lila didn't notice how Paul's face flushed when she described how tempted she'd been to move in with Lou. But she'd refused because she wasn't that kind of girl, and didn't want to bring shame to Mom. So she'd held out until, on a sultry August night when she and Lou were parked at the drive-in movie, only half watching Haley Mills in *The Parent Trap*. After they'd kissed for most of the previous hour and Lou's hands had roamed her lower than ever before, he pressed his hardness against her thigh, whispering in a ragged voice, "Well, then, if you won't move in with me, we better get married."

"That was how he proposed," Lila explained. She added that Lou had grandly given Mom all the money she needed for the wedding, as if trying to show that he would be able to provide for Lila.

"I thought I loved him, too. I was young and dumb. Well, stupid, I guess, now that I think about it. I can see I didn't ever really know him. I guess Lou always got what he wanted. I just never realized it before."

She shook her head, as if to clear it and return to the present. Paul, his face solemn and stony, waited for her to continue. She told him of the only time Lou had taken her to his parents' house, that weekend before the wedding.

"Lou's mother reminded me of a nervous little bird. She didn't even sit down once, the whole time we were there. She was skinny and pale. And really quiet. She hardly said a word, just flitted around, serving Lou's dad and us beer after beer, setting out potato chips and dip. Hustling around like a waitress or something. She seemed keyed into her husband's every wish. They didn't even seem to notice her."

Lila realized for the first time with these words that Lou's father had treated his wife like his servant in their, dim, shabby little house. Why she hadn't recognized before this how unfair and demeaning that was? It had been surprising, too, to see where Lou had grown up—such a small, dilapidated place with worn furniture and a stale odor of years of greasy cooking. The pilled gray sweater his mother wore hung on her like it had been worn a thousand times. His father's thin hair had been slicked back across his skull, and he fiddled with one cigarette after another, tapping them into the overflowing ash tray next to the stained corduroy recliner he never rose from all the while they were there.

She paused and looked at Paul. "I can't believe how dumb I was. What I saw didn't actually register, I guess. I see now that I didn't really even know him. Or his family. He acted real nice on our dates and took me to Porky's Drive In and the A&W and out for breakfast every Sunday. And he had that fancy car with everything on it. He dressed nice and he took me to the drive-in movies once in a while. And

Spruce Grove, of course. He even brought flowers to Mom a couple of times—she was pretty surprised. Judy never really liked him for some reason, but I didn't pay attention."

Paul rose and came to her. He pulled her up to him, nestled her in his arms, and reassured her, "You were young, only eighteen, just out of high school. You didn't know. What else?"

"I didn't really get it until the murder. The night I ran, it was all I could think about. How dumb I'd been."

Lila's thoughts returned to the night she'd left, she took a deep breath, and the words spilled out. Every detail of that night she'd taken off alone for Alaska was fresh in her mind. She told Paul how she'd hit the road less than an hour after she dropped Lou off for his night shift at the Ford auto plant in suburban St. Paul. And how he would have called home to check in with her as he always did on his eight o'clock break. Every Thursday night, he expected her to be home with the groceries by the time he called. He assumed she'd be waiting in the parking lot outside the main gate when he got off at midnight, too. And he'd be hungry for a hot meal when they got home, no matter that it was the middle of the night.

"I hoped Lou would think I just wasn't home yet from the Piggly Wiggly when I didn't answer his call," Lila explained. "That would buy me time. I looked at a map and saw that Fargo was only three hundred miles from St. Paul. I figured if I could make it into North Dakota, it might not be easy for Lou to track me in another state. I hoped I could even make it all the way to Montana before he put out any kind of alarm. That night when I left I drove harder and faster than I ever did in my life."

Paul's face blanched, but he remained silent, his eyes encouraging Lila to go on.

She stifled the catch in her voice and went on. "I was positive Lou would go nuts when he discovered I was gone. I hid all that money at the bottom of my purse. I was really scared carrying that much cash. That money, the car, his sleeping bag, as many clothes as I could stuff in the back seat, a pillow, and the Rand McNally atlas. That's all I took. I was terrified. I'd never done anything like that in my life. I felt like I was in a dream and wasn't actually doing it. Like I was watching myself from behind glass or something. I still can't believe I just took off like that alone. And then ended up here in Alaska, of all places."

Lila shrugged and choked at the memory, telling Paul how she dropped Lou off at work, returned to the apartment, grabbed her things, and just started driving. She'd sped northwest out of St. Paul, headed for Fargo, heart pounding. She remembered pulling into a Shell station when the gas gauge dropped to near empty, slumping down in her seat, hoping nobody would notice or remember her. The teenage attendant, hunkered into his gold and black letterman's jacket against a piercing prairie wind, pumped gas and washed the car's windshield. She'd handed him eight dollars through the window, kept her eyes averted, and said nothing.

"I knew I had to stay anonymous, so no one would remember me later," she said.

Back on the road, when Highway 10 merged into the interstate a short time later, an unexpected feeling of power and strength almost overcame her trepidation. The double lanes of the highway stretched ahead, long and flat, leading to Fargo, and beyond, to safety. She drove at a steady pace, just maintaining the seventy mph speed limit while dusk gave way to the late September night's inky blackness. The road lay empty and dark in front of her, broken only by white and yellow lines and the occasional lights of oncoming traffic shining across the wide flat median of level grass.

How frightened she'd been when a car whizzed up close behind her, its headlights blinding in the rear view mirror. She'd gasped in sudden terror but it veered around her into the left lane and disappeared into the blackness ahead with a flash of tail lights. The round glowing dashboard clock already read twenty after nine.

"I realized that Lou would have already called on his break. Over an hour before and I wasn't there. This was the first time, ever, I hadn't answered when he called. I couldn't believe that I was really running from him."

Lila told Paul how she'd driven west from Fargo as if in a trance. Valley City, Jamestown, another stop for gas. Bismarck, Dickinson. Her eyes remained wide; she had no trouble staying awake, even though many hours passed. Another stop at a gas station. She always paid with cash, avoided eye contact, faded into anonymity; driving on and on into the lonely, star-speckled night.

"I just kept going," she explained.

Paul grimaced. "God, Lila. Do you know how dangerous that was being out there all alone?"

Lila could only shrug. "What else could I do?"

Chapter 23

WHILE THE FIRST few weeks of December passed, Lila's pregnancy became apparent. But nobody said a word about it to her. The reticence of Whittier's residents amazed her. What was one person's business was nobody else's. If they were curious about her, they kept it to themselves. She bought a few inexpensive maternity tops in Anchorage, but was able to keep wearing her slacks and skirts since the elastic waistbands had become stretched out enough to be comfortable. Old Tom gave her a sidelong glance the first time she showed up for work in a maternity top, but said not a word.

"I'll keep working, Tom," Lila assured him when she noticed his look. "I appreciate my job. I need it. I'll be right back to work as soon as I can after the baby comes. Nan said she'll babysit for me, at least at first."

Without turning around, Tom shrugged. "Yup," he said, and returned to stacking beer into the cooler behind the bar.

How lucky to have such an understanding boss. Society expected many women to leave their jobs when pregnancies began to show, but this was Whittier. Lila's mood was further lightened because the anonymous letter with Artie's name had gone out to Detective Adams almost a month ago now. And as far as she and Paul could tell from conversations with Judy and Mom, there had been no activity in the case. So, although Lou's whereabouts were still unknown, Paul thought the threat had grown more remote than at first. But Lila still couldn't shake the fear that Lou would appear someday when she least expected it. He was crazy. Nobody knew him like she did.

Lila's financial condition grew better since there was little she could spend her money on in Whittier. She'd managed to put away a hundred dollars already, even after continuing to furnish the apartment and replenish her meager personal belongings. Worry about paying the hospital bill nagged at the back of her mind, but with what she'd already saved, and what was left from Lou's money, it might be enough. It would be necessary to go to a doctor soon, but how was she going to pay a doctor and the hospital bill, too? Maybe the four hundred left of Lou's money, and the hundred and fifty she'd saved already still wouldn't be enough. If she let Lou's insurance know, he would likely find out about the baby, and where she was, too. So that wasn't an option.

As these worries arose, Lila's heart raced and flashes of terror caused her breath to come too fast when she thought about Lou. She'd been away from him for three months now, but the fear remained as strong as ever. The hope that Lou would be caught any day because of the letter kept her from actually making the call and putting herself at risk.

Those first three months of being pregnant in Minnesota and now another three here meant she was already into her sixth month. So the baby would come about the end of March. At least the worst of winter would be over by then, and the parka would keep her warm as long as it still fit. At the thought of the parka, Lila's anxiety about Lou diminished. Paul had given her that very special gift. She couldn't wait to go home with him for Christmas.

Life settled into a pattern—work every afternoon and early evening, share a late dinner with Paul and sometimes Nan, too. Lila enjoyed the trips to Anchorage every other week, proud to be able to handle money that was her own. She talked to her mother and Judy every Sunday evening and was reassured to hear how well her mother was doing.

Lila fretted frequently about calling the detective in Minnesota, the thoughts chasing each other through her mind. Law enforcement there could force her to go back. But she couldn't go, pregnant like this. Even if Paul said he'd go with her. What if she had to stay there? Then she'd lose her job and apartment here. A plane ticket might take the money she needed for the doctor and hospital. If Lou was still around the Twin Cities and found out she was back, that would increase the danger to Mom and Judy, too. The threat remained so real that she couldn't force herself to make the call. Finally, she and Paul agreed that, if nothing had happened by the time the baby was born, they'd call then, and deal with whatever happened.

Christmas provided a welcome distraction from these worries. She bought Christmas presents, proud to be able to do it with her own money. For her mother, a thick white cardigan sweater with red roses embroidered down the front. For Judy, a set of butter yellow towels that would match her bathroom. The largest and fanciest Christmas card she could find for Dee and Chuck, with a letter tucked inside. In it, she thanked them again for helping her, apologized for the trouble she'd brought to their lives, and asked them to write and let her know how they were doing, especially Chuck's burns.

The problem of what to buy for Paul was solved when she noticed the newest Bob Dylan album featured at the Northern Commercial Department store. She slipped it in among her other purchases without him noticing, certain that he'd enjoy the music and the accompanying psychedelic blue poster with the singer's distinct profile.

195

Paul had begun planning their Christmas trip for December twenty third, with a return date four days later. The tunnel would be closed to trains on Tuesday, Christmas Day, so that would allow them a few extra days to get back before the next train ran, in case of bad weather.

When Paul asked Lila if she would be willing to travel to Alukiak by bush plane, she agreed to make her first plane ride, more eager for the new experience than afraid. To her delight, he planned to take her for a dog sled ride when they got there, too. What would it be like to actually fly in a small plane and ride a dog sled? It seemed like something out of a book or movie. Her enthusiasm and excitement grew daily. With Paul by her side, she had no anxiety about the new experiences she faced.

Two days before they were to leave, the postman delivered a large cardboard box to the Hodge post office for Lila. Inside were brightly wrapped gifts from Minnesota—a soft, light blue flannel nightgown with matching fuzzy slippers from Judy, a navy button front sweater and six pairs of thick white socks from her mother, and a new set of Tupperware nesting bowls. Mom and Judy must have mailed the box a month or so ago for it to make it to Chuck and Dee in Montana and then get forwarded here to Whittier.

A wave of homesickness washed over Lila while she unwrapped the touch of home.

They must have gone to one of those new Tupperware parties. I wish I could have gone with them. I miss them so much right now. Next Christmas, we'll have another family member to buy gifts for. A baby! I'll have to get Mom and the baby together before that, for sure. Mom is so excited about her first grandchild, and I'm so far away. Well, I'll figure it out after the baby is born. Right now, I can't even think about going back to Minnesota with Lou still on the loose. Well, maybe Mama and Judy and Jerry can come up here. That would be nice. We'll see....

With these thoughts of home fresh in her mind, Lila packed for the Christmas trip. Paul told her to bring only a few changes of clothing, since everything else they needed would be there.

Chapter 24

THEY DROVE NORTHEAST out of Anchorage to Merrill Field Airport two days later. Lila chattered nonstop, asking Paul everything she could think of about the upcoming trip and his village. Not once did thoughts of Lou enter her mind on this day.

Her curiosity, and a bit of anxiety she couldn't quite shake about flying in a small plane was lightened when Paul assured her that Alaskans did it all the time since many villages aren't accessible by road. He introduced her to the grizzled pilot in the leather jacket who bustled around examining the plane and checking things off a list. After a curt "Hello" to Lila, the pilot ducked his shaggy head and returned to his list.

Paul helped Lila climb into the cramped front seat of the plane, secured a complex seat belt around her middle and over her shoulders, and clamped a hard, heavy pair of green headphones over her ears before squeezing himself in behind her.

The pilot climbed in, secured his own seat belts, looked around and hollered "All clear!" before turning the key. Lila grabbed both hands onto the dash and watched the propeller's speed increase rapidly until it was an invisible whirl. She started when a tremendous roar thundered through her headphones as the plane roared down the runway, bouncing, bumping, and jerking. Finally, the wheels left the ground and she was pushed back into her seat by the force of the liftoff. Exhilaration replaced any twinges of fear. This was amazing!

Once in the air, she gasped in delight at the scene far below where blue and white mountain ranges spread gloriously in all directions and tiny ribbons of frozen rivers curled among dark evergreen forests. She remained awestruck as the plane roared on through the bright blue canopy of sky stretching endlessly ahead. The roar of the plane made conversation impossible, so she immersed herself in the vast, stunning vista that unfolded below.

The hour until the plane's engine began to slow passed too quickly. Lila held her breath while the pilot pulled and pushed levers on the dash, cranked a handle on the ceiling, stomped pedals, adjusted the throttle, and guided the plane to a bumpy landing on a small airstrip covered in frozen dirt and grass. Nearby, a string of small, gray structures showed dimly in the waning afternoon light.

"This is it!" Paul called. "We're here. This is Alukiak."

Lila strained for a glimpse while Paul helped her down from the plane. Alukiak appeared to be a very small settlement composed of single story, weathered-gray wood buildings with small windows. All were clustered around wooden boardwalks crisscrossing yards and paths of frozen mud and snow. How very different from Whittier.

I can't believe I'm here...in the tundra of interior Alaska! I'm so excited. And kind of scared, too, to meet Paul's family. I wonder if Paul told them about the baby or if they'll ask about it. Especially since I am showing so much. How much has Paul told them about me? And us?

Lila's thoughts tumbled as fur-clad figures poured out of buildings, all faces turned toward the airstrip. Dogs, swirling on tethers in the yards of nearly every house in the village began a tremendous barking and the commotion made communication between her and Paul impossible. Lila shrank back in sudden shyness. Would they like her? Would they accept her? She wasn't one of them.

She tried to calm her worries while several boys rushed out in front of the crowd. Within seconds, Lila found herself engulfed by a bustling group of strangers. She couldn't tell how many people were gathered around her, and the babble of friendly voices drowned out any words from Paul. She glimpsed Paul similarly surrounded beside her, and tried to smile back when he grinned at her.

Paul hurried to her side, took her arm and announced, "This is Lila."

A chorus of "hellos" in English, accompanied by a chatter of words she couldn't understand greeted her. She found herself surrounded by deep brown eyes in curious faces, most peering out from hoods of fur-trimmed parkas. She blushed, self-conscious under the scrutiny, and looked at Paul with a helpless shrug.

"Okay, enough, everyone!" Paul grinned at the crowd. "Let's hear what's new around here. Hey, what'd you get me for Christmas, Mom?" he called.

A woman broke from the front row and rushed to Paul's side. "*Cha-ma*. Welcome home, Son," she smiled, wrapping her arms around him. "You think I'll tell you what's wrapped up for you? Not a chance! You always try to trick me, don't you?"

Her voice was playful, rich and warm, with the same lilt as Paul's. She turned next to Lila and opened her arms. "And welcome to you, too, Lila. *Cha-ma*. I am Georgia. Welcome to Alukiak."

Lila stepped into the short. stout woman's embrace, and returned the hug, feeling awkward. Around them, the crowd murmured. A tall man emerged then, his demeanor shy. He stuck a hand out to Paul, who shook it with warmth.

"*Cha-ma*. Welcome home, Son." The man's quiet voice held a touch of an accent that Lila had never heard before.

"Hello, Father," Paul replied. A big smile split his face as he basked in the attention from his parents.

"This is Lila," he added, pulling Lila toward him. "Lila, this is my father, Sergei."

Sergei's pale blue eyes met Lila's eyes for a brief second and he nodded a short greeting. Then he turned away and called, "Tatiana! Tatiana? Where are you?"

A tall, teenage girl in a parka trimmed with a rich, brown fur emerged from the crowd, her steps reluctant. Her face was so similar to Paul's that Lila caught her breath. Copper eyes exactly like Paul's coolly appraised Lila as Georgia introduced her.

"Lila, this is Paul's sister, Tatiana."

The girl stepped forward, face sullen, and dropped her gaze. The girl didn't like her. This is what Lila had been afraid of.

"Say hello to Lila, Tatiana," Georgia instructed.

A muttered word followed before Tatiana stepped back into the crowd. She quickly slipped away behind a nearby building, taking with her three apparent girlfriends, one of whom met Lila's eyes for a brief moment. Her glance wasn't friendly. Lila noticed Sergei and Georgia exchange a meaningful look. With a shrug, Georgia took Lila's arm and led her toward a house in the middle of the settlement.

"I'll be in as soon as I help tie down the plane," Paul called out as they began walking away. Then he ran and caught up to Lila. "Hey, our greeting's spelled *waqaa*, it's pronounced *cha-ma*. So, if you want to greet anyone, they'd be pleased to hear it from you. If you want to, that is."

He turned back and joined several young men about his age who had begun tying ropes onto grommets on the plane's wings with practiced ease, all the while exchanging friendly banter. Lila looked back to see them punching each other in the shoulders, grinning and beaming. They stole looks at her from the corners of their eyes, unable to hide their frank, young male curiosity. Lila's face grew hot, and she turned back to hurry along with Georgia.

When they entered the house, a tiny, wizened woman pushed herself up from a cushioned rocking chair next to the wood stove in the far corner of the room. She wore a baggy, knee-length dress patterned with miniature red flowers. White and yellow rickrack trimmed the sleeves and hem. Soft-looking fur peeked from the tops of beaded leather slippers that laced up to her knees. Her eyes, so dark they were almost black, peeked from the maze of wrinkles covering her face and sunken cheeks. Tendrils of silver hair escaped from the thin braid hanging halfway down her back.

"This is Paul's grandmother, Amelia," Georgia said.

Lila smiled, and feeling brave, greeted her. "Cha Ma."

The old woman smiled, eyes widening in surprise, then hobbled forward and touched the sleeve of Lila's parka. She turned to Georgia and asked something in words Lila couldn't understand, then sighed with satisfaction. She smiled a crinkled smile at Lila, displaying nubbins of stained brown teeth.

"She made your parky," Georgia explained. "She's happy to see it again."

Touched, Lila replied, "Please tell her I love it. Paul told me she made it, and why. It's beautiful and keeps me nice and warm. Please tell her thank you."

Georgia translated, and soon both women were beaming at Lila.

Chapter 25

THAT EXCHANGE BEGAN the most unusual Christmas of Lila's life. She endured the constant staring at her long, golden curls with good humor, and laughed when a few of the youngsters touched her hair with tentative fingers to see if it was real. Paul must have already explained about the baby and although nobody mentioned her obvious rounded shape, they had to be aware of it. Maybe they wouldn't mention it at all. Maybe they were too polite. Or maybe it just wasn't their way to bring up something like that. They all were hospitable to Lila. All except Tatiana. The teenager's disappearance after being introduced to Lila hadn't been brought up since, and Lila didn't want to be the one to ask about it. She'd find out from Paul about it later. Sergei had remained cool to her. Most likely that reservation was just his personality.

Paul's mother—pretty, with high round cheekbones, dark, shiny hair worn in a fat low ponytail, and laughing brown eyes—was obviously in charge of family life. Georgia bustled around the cozy house, looking comfortable in a blue floral print dress with rickrack trim similar to what the grandmother wore.

Within minutes of their arrival, Georgia settled Paul and Lila into a tiny bedroom at the back of the house that had, like the other rooms in the house, only a thick red flannel blanket for a door. Georgia playfully teased Paul, and their constant, affectionate banter pleased Lila. Paul beamed in his mother's presence and it warmed Lila's heart to see their affection. It was obvious that Paul and his mother adored each other.

The kitchen table, under Georgia's supervision, remained laden with food– chunks of shiny smoked salmon, a unique wooden bowl stacked with green apples, a pile of fragrant homemade buns, and two cakes as well as a few foods Lila couldn't identify at first.

Paul lifted the bowl of apples, a look of pride on his face. "Look at this bowl. Mom made it."

Lila turned to Georgia.

"Yes, my sisters and I make spruce root baskets. It's a traditional craft. Our mother and grandmother taught us when we were small," Georgia said. "We go down the river in a canoe until we spot an upturned spruce that's tipped into the water along a bank. I'm the best swimmer so I'm the one who gets to lean out and cut off the roots with a hunting knife. Sergei always sharpens the knife for me before we leave because it's so dangerous. I've never fallen in luckily. We dry the roots and make thread from the thinnest ones. Then we weave the rest into these bowls like this."

"It's beautiful," Lila said. She ran her fingers over the shellacked, woven fibrous surface.

Georgia pointed to a high shelf over the kitchen shelves. "And those are birch baskets. We make those, too. The diamond design signifies it is of Yup'ik origin. Maybe I can teach you someday."

Lila nodded, enthralled. "Yes, I'd love to learn." She'd been accepted here. A huge sigh escaped. Her heart warmed. She looked at Paul with shining eyes.

I like your family. I like it here.

He gave the biggest smile Lila had ever seen on his face and turned back to the table. "Caribou jerky." He handed her a strip of leather-like meat. "Here. Taste it. We smoke it ourselves."

Lila reached for the stick of dried meat. The first spicy, smoke-flavored bite surprised her with its unique taste, but the more she chewed, the more she liked it. She dipped her head in approval and took another bite, causing the others to grin.

Sergei had grabbed a piece of jerky and settled into a wooden rocker by the front window as soon as he got inside the house. Although he made no effort to speak to her, Lila felt his speculative eyes on her more than once. Sergei had remained reserved toward her so far. Lila hadn't known what to make of Paul's father when he stepped forward from the crowd at the airstrip, shook her hand, and welcomed her with just a tip of his chin. Most likely he was reserving judgment until he knew her better.

What he was thinking, and what did he think of her? How much had Paul told him? What did he think about her pregnancy? She studied him when she could, curious. Sergei was a good foot taller than everyone else around him, with slightly hunched shoulders. His thinning, light brown hair showed specks of gray and the pale blue eyes under sparse brows stood out in his weathered face. The faded, red and black checkered shirt that molded to his spare frame as if he had worn it for years hung over the same dark blue, heavy cotton pants the other men wore. The laced moccasins of tanned hide peeking out from beneath the pants cuffs must be genuine mukluks like Paul had told her he used to wear. Lila had noticed that all the men and boys wore them.

And Tatiana still wasn't around. Lila hoped her visit wouldn't be a cause of trouble in Paul's family.

Lila and Paul shared a supper of moose pot roast, boiled potatoes with gravy, and carrots with his family on their first night. Paul's father seemed to warm a bit to Lila during the meal, but remained reserved. Tatiana didn't show up and nobody mentioned her.

A dozen or so people meandered into the room as the meal was ending. While Lila and Paul helped Georgia clear off the table and start the dishes, "aunts" and "uncles" and little ones came and went through the planked doors of the porch-like arctic entry on the front of the house. Nobody knocked. Visitors briskly stomped snow from their feet before clomping in over the wooden floor without removing their footwear. Tall, intricately beaded, fur-lined animal skin boots, tied snugly with leather thongs in a tight crisscross pattern reached nearly to the knees of people of all ages. Strings of beads hung from the fluffy fur ruffs of the boot tops, swinging and waving with each step. Each pair was unique, and must have been made right here in the village. It appeared that everyone wore this footwear all day whether inside or out.

The visitors settled in apparent comfort, crouching on their haunches along the walls or wherever space was available. They seemed content to leave their parkas and jackets on, too, even though the stove glowed with enough heat to keep the winter cold at bay from the cozy home.

Lively storytelling kept Lila spellbound as the night wore on, especially after Paul whispered that his people believe that writing down words makes them lose their real meaning. He added that stories were believed to be the best way to accurately pass on culture and history. The tales of hunting, wildlife, explorations, ancestors, journeys, legends, and mysteries, each one told by a different person, delighted Lila. She listened intently, gradually becoming accustomed to the strong accents.

She and Paul fell asleep on the narrow bed in his old bedroom that first night, snuggled in each other's arms, whispering after stealthy lovemaking. When Lila had to get up several times in the night, the complete blackness all around her amazed her. No light at all entered through the tiny bedroom window since it was covered by a heavy, latched wooden shutter. The sturdy shutter provided protection from subzero temperatures this time of year, and from marauding bears in the summer, Paul explained to a wide-eyed Lila.

The first time she squatted over what Paul called "the honey bucket" in the corner of the bedroom, she tried not to make any noise while crouching and balancing, but couldn't help giggling. Paul, leaning up on his elbow in the bed, laughed, too, while he pointed a dim flashlight in her direction. He welcomed her back into his warmth beneath the blankets with chuckles.

After reindeer sausage and sourdough pancakes the next morning, Lila headed outside with Paul for her first dog sled ride. With Paul's hand on her elbow to steady her, she settled onto the fur-padded seat of a long, hand-carved wooden dog sled with sidebars fashioned from sturdy branches. Paul tucked thick, bushy, odd-smelling furs around her, creating a comfortable nest.

"What are those little log buildings up on the stilts in the yards?" she called back to him. "I noticed them, too, when I was driving into Alaska. They were everywhere. What are they?"

"They're caches. We keep our meat in them. They're built up high so bears and other animals can't get up there. They're kind of like outdoor freezers."

Lila settled back into her nest on the sled.

Weird. They store their meat outside.

Still curious, she called back to him again. "And what is this sled made of? Did you make it?"

"Well, my dad did. I helped him. It's made of seasoned split birch branches. We lashed it with rawhide instead of bolts so it won't be stiff—it has to have some give for the bumps on the trail. These runners are fourteen feet long and this brake is called the gee pole." He pointed to a metal spike.

Lila turned back to the eleven yapping sled dogs straining in a complex leather harness system in front of the sled, obviously eager to get started. Even though Paul kept the gee pole stuck deep into the snow as he readied the sled, the dogs danced and strained with lifted tails, and vigorous, excited yelps, waiting to take off. The black one with the white feet and face must be the leader since it was placed alone out in front, and the rest were paired side-by-side in the long harness behind him. Some of them looked like wolves. They pranced as if they couldn't get going soon enough. They had so much energy that Lila couldn't help smiling as she watched them try to pull even though the sled was held by the brake. She grew as anxious as they were to get started.

Paul tapped her shoulder, "Ready?"

At Lila's nod, he shouted "Haahhh!" and the sled lurched forward, gaining speed quickly as the dogs tore off with a frenzy of excited barking. The dogs settled at once into the steady run as a finely-tuned team while the sled glided across the frozen ground. Lila peeked back over her shoulder through her hood's fur ruff to see Paul standing behind, legs spread for balance, feet planted on the sled's narrow wooden rear platform. His hands, encased in huge, paw-like leather mittens, gripped the carved wood handle that ran across the back of the sled. Noticing her look, he grinned. Lila returned the smile, then twisted back to snuggle into her comfortable seat on the sled.

The next two hours were a complete wonder. The dogs obviously loved what they were doing as they made a steady and vigorous run through snowy fields and along forested paths. A bright blue winter sky capped the jagged mountains jutting majestically in every direction, defining the distant horizon. The sharp air biting at Lila's nostrils invigorated her. She became aware of the absence of wind when a few flakes of snow drifted onto her lap. It was so much brighter out here in the countryside than in Whittier. There was no wind at all and no birds overhead. She felt herself slide into the beautiful and peaceful scene, almost as if being in a dream.

Every once in a while, Paul tapped her shoulder to point out a landmark or animals in the distance and

Lila responded with a lively wave to let him know she was doing fine. She hardly felt the occasional bumps on the trail as the sled whizzed along over them. The wolverine ruff of her parka's hood fit snugly around her cheeks and chin, and the thick, furry cuffs on the sleeves kept cold air from sneaking up her wrists. An old pair of cable knit mittens that Georgia had let her borrow didn't quite keep the bite of the cold air from her fingers, but Lila hardly noticed.

Before she knew it, an eerie twilight had chased away the afternoon light. Ghostly white birch trees began fading into the deepening mist that was a precursor to Alaska's sudden, dark winter nights. Soon, the dogs began to slow in their traces, and Lila twisted around to look back at Paul, a question in her eyes. In answer, he waved her attention ahead to the horizon where, barely visible, the buildings of Alukiak swam in and out of view through the fog.

Lila rolled off the sled when it stopped and scrambled to her feet, thrilled.

How lucky I am to experience all this. Paul's so good to me.

Chapter 26

LILA HAD BECOME enthralled by the way of life in the village by the time everyone gathered in the tribal house later that day for a Christmas potlatch dinner,

"Potlatch?" she asked when Paul told her of the evening meal.

"Yeah. It's like a potluck back at the Hodge. Only it's more of a traditional feast—hunters always share their catch with the whole community. Gifts are exchanged, too, especially at Christmas. We do potlatches for all special occasions, not just holidays. The elders are honored guests, and there's dancing. You'll love it." He smiled, eager to be off to the tribal house.

By evening, Lila was too stuffed from the feast to move. When Paul convinced her to try dried fish called *akutaq*, the salty taste surprised her with its pleasant tang. When she asked for another piece, Paul beamed. She became too full of stories and music to do more than languish at Paul's side on one of the

214

wide, fur-cushioned benches stationed along the perimeter of the big room. Huge fireplaces at each end of the room crackled, adding to the light from the bare bulbs suspended every few feet on electrical wire across the center of the ceiling. At her question about what appeared to be a long, pointed spearhead displayed along one wall, Paul explained that it was a *nunarpaq*, an ancient hunting tool still used by hunters today.

Relaxed and lazy after the afternoon's ride in the fresh air and the big meal, she declined the frequent invitations to join the shuffling dancers who moved across the smooth wooden floor in big circles, stomping rhythmically to the beat of drums. Two fiddlers tried to outdo each other, their bows dancing across the strings of the gleaming instruments tucked beneath their chins. The dangling feathers on the dancers' clothing and boots and the chanting of the singers nearly hypnotized her.

When the music stopped, a stooped old man wearing a wide-brimmed, woven fiber hat with a square top shaped like a chimney, stood. All hushed. He walked the perimeter of the room, handing out small white carvings to all adults. He placed one in Lila's hand, too, to her surprise. She dipped her head to him with a smile of thanks, then looked to Paul for an explanation.

"It's a tradition for an elder to hand out gifts. This is scrimshaw, walrus ivory" Paul said. "John's a master at scrimshaw. Some of his carvings are even on display at the museum in Anchorage. These are treasures. He gave you one, too—that's a sign of acceptance." He beamed approval at Lila. "Mine's a seal. What's yours?"

Lila examined the piece in her hand. "It's a polar bear. Wow! Look at the detail. All those little marks for the fur. This is beautiful!"

Paul took the piece from her hand. "Yup. A polar bear. This is one of his specialties! You've been accepted. You got your first piece of scrimshaw." Paul beamed and gave her a hug.

Just then, a pounding at the door announced Santa. The children squealed and made a mad dash for him. Paul and Lila watched with the other adults while the little ones unwrapped gifts and tore into their plastic-coated red and green bags of peanuts and hard candy.

Paul turned to Lila, his eyes soft with tenderness. "Next Christmas, we'll have one."

"I love you, Paul," she responded, her eyes shining. How lucky she was that he wanted the baby.

He put a protective and possessive arm around her shoulders. Lila cuddled into him, feeling a pang of homesickness that brought a vision of home and her mother. It also brought a familiar stab of fear. Where was Lou tonight? Was he still in Minnesota? Or was he already trying to come back to Alaska? She couldn't squelch biting anxiety, even though the colorful, chanting dancers seemed to be performing just for her and there was no way Lou could get to her here in Alukiak.

Lila burrowed deeper into the shelter of Paul's arm around her shoulder. Her sleep was fitful that night, as if Lou had cast a shadow over this new life in Alaska she was beginning to love.

Chapter 27

LILA WOKE ALONE the next morning and dressed to the murmur of voices and the aroma of coffee. Paul and his mother stopped talking when she pushed aside the blanket door and entered the kitchen.

Paul turned to her. "Good morning, Lila. We were talking about Tatiana. Mom says Tat's been acting funny ever since she heard we were coming for Christmas. She's stayed over at an aunt and uncle's house the last few nights and not come home at all. She even skipped the potlatch last night. We decided I should go see what's up with her."

"*Cha Ma*, Lila" Georgia added with a smile. "Sleep okay? Want some coffee? There's oatmeal, too."

It was a long hour until Paul returned. Lila helped in the kitchen as best she could, then settled into Sergei's empty rocking chair and watched the village come to life. Sluggish gray daylight struggled to overcome the lingering darkness. An occasional pedestrian passed by the window, bundled like a mummy, bent against the wind and a light snow that filtered from the invisible foggy sky.

Paul arrived with a blast of frigid air, stomped snow off his boots and called to his mother. "Hey, Mom, I found out what's bothering Tat."

"Well, son?"

"I talked to Uncle. He said Tatiana told Aunt that she's afraid Lila will take me away from all of you. She thinks we might move to the Lower Forty Eight after the baby comes. That we'll go back to Lila's people and she'll never see me."

Georgia made a disgusted sound. "Oh. That's it. Well, I'll talk to Aunt and have her—"

"Wait," Lila interrupted, rising from her chair. "I'd like to talk to Tatiana. We need to get to know each other. I know we should communicate with her through Aunt, but I really want to spend some time with her and just talk. Would that be all right?"

Georgia and Paul looked at each other. Lila held her breath. Had she made a mistake suggesting a break in traditional ways of communicating by wanting to go directly to Tatiana?

Georgia finally shrugged. "Well, maybe. Paul?"

Paul looked hard at Lila and thought for a long moment. "Let's go together. We can talk to her ourselves." He glanced at his mother for her reaction, but when she lowered her eyes without comment, he went on. "I guess I didn't think about her missing me. Tatiana and I did everything together when we were growing up, Lila. And she and Hilli were friends, so she lost Hilli, too. So much happened in these last few years, I guess I've kinda pulled away from her, and I didn't even realize it. Now she's afraid I'll leave for good. I never thought about that."

Paula and Lila were soon walking the narrow, weathered boardwalk through the village. They walked, without knocking, into a house very similar to Paul's and when Paul called out, "Auntie Ruby? You here?" Lila felt awkward about not knocking first. But Paul seemed not to notice.

A short, husky woman appeared from the kitchen, clapping flour from her hands. A huge smile split her round face. "Paul!"

After greeting each other and introducing Lila, Paul spoke. "We're here to see Tatiana. Is she here?"

"Yes. What can I tell her for you?" Aunt asked, still beaming at Paul. "She's still sleeping, I think."

"We want to talk to her ourselves," Paul answered.

Aunt's eyes widened, then squinted in puzzlement. She cocked her head, then slid her eyes to Lila, and her eyes narrowed as if suddenly understanding. A hint of disapproval flashed across her face. It was apparent that Aunt considered this request offensive and blamed Lila for not honoring traditional ways of communicating. She remained silent, staring at the floor.

But Paul stood firm. "Please go wake her up, Auntie. Tell her I'm here and I want to talk to her. Will you?"

Aunt shrugged and turned away to shuffle toward a blue and white striped blanket draping a doorway adjacent to the kitchen. Paul reached for Lila's hand. Neither spoke while they waited.

"She's coming," Aunt announced when she came back into the room, finally meeting their eyes. "Would you like coffee? Sweetbread?" Her voice was cooler than it had been when they arrived, but her manners obviously prevailed over her disapproval

Paul gave a small shake of his head and Aunt turned away, burying her hands in the mound of dough on the counter.

Ten long minutes later, Tatiana pushed aside the blanket and stood staring at them.

"Hey, Tat. Haven't seen much of you since we got here, so we came over. Want to come home and see us for a while?"

With a pouty expression, Tatiana shook her head and dropped her eyes. Paul's grip tightened on Lila's hand and she felt him tense.

"Get your coat. Mom says you're supposed to come home. We came to get you. Besides, I missed you. And Lila wants to get to know you. So come on, let's go."

Tatiana walked past them and yanked a red parka from a wooden hook in the entry, her eyes downcast. She shoved her arms into the sleeves and stomped out the door ahead of them.

"Hey, wait up," Paul called, running after her. He pulled at her arm. "Come on. What's wrong? What's the matter?"

"Didn't Auntie tell Mother?" Tatiana asked in a tight voice. She glared past Paul at Lila.

"Yeah," Paul answered. They faced off. "C'mon, Tat," he ordered. "Jump off. We're going for a walk. Here, Lila, I'll help you down." He reached for Lila and helped her step off the boardwalk.

Tatiana began walking away, kicking at clumps of snow, head down, every move announcing her displeasure. Paul and Lila hurried to walk beside her onto the rippling, snow-swept tundra stretching to the horizons in every direction.

Paul tugged at his sister's sleeve after a few minutes. "Hey, Tat, stop. We need to talk."

"Nothing to talk about," she answered, voice petulant, expression sullen. She continued to look at the ground.

It wasn't fair to make Paul try to fix this by himself. After all, Lila was the reason Tatiana was sulking and fearful of losing her brother. "I'm so glad to be here, Tatiana," Lila began. "And to meet all of you. Paul has a wonderful family."

Tatiana stole a sidelong look at Lila.

Lila smiled at her and went on, "Do you think you might want to come and stay with us for a week or so after the baby comes? I know I'll need all the help I can get. And it might be fun for you to see what Whittier's like, too. Right, Paul?"

Paul looked at Lila, eyebrows lifted in surprise, then quickly answered, "Yup. It's about time you finally came to see me. And we need to come to Alukiak a lot more, too. I've missed the place."

Now Tatiana was studying her brother. Her face held a vulnerability that hadn't been there before.

"Come to Whittier?" she asked in a small voice. "Me?"

"Yes," Lila answered. "We'll be getting married as soon as we can, and you'll be family. You'll be an aunt and the baby will need to get to know you."

"Will you bring him here?" Tatiana asked.

"Sure. We'll bring him to see you all lots," Paul responded, his eyes shining. "And all of you should come to Whittier, too."

"So you're not leaving? Not going away?" Tatiana asked. Her eyebrows lifted with hope.

"No promises," Paul replied. "I can't predict what'll happen in the coming years, but, no, we're not planning on going anywhere."

When Tatiana looked to Lila for confirmation Lila smiled and added. "I like it here."

Tatiana's brilliant smile flashed for the first time. Her teeth gleamed white and her face lit with happiness. She rushed for Paul and they met in a tight hug. Soon, that hug included Lila and before long, the three of them were hustling back to have breakfast at Georgia's.

IT SEEMED THE whole village gathered to see Paul and Lila off when they prepared to leave Alukiak two days later.

And as they were about to leave the house, Georgia handed a folded piece of fabric to Lila. Her eyes shone. "I made this for you. It's a *kuspuk.*"

Lila unfolded a knee length dress in the same loose style as the ones Grandma and Georgia and the other village women wore. The multi-colored, flowered garment was trimmed in brilliant yellow, red and blue rickrack. It was just Lila's size.

"Oh, thank you, Georgia. I'll always treasure this. I can't wait to wear it. It's beautiful," Lila managed through the tears that sprang to her eyes. "I can even wear it now. With the way I look…" her voice trailed off.

"Yes," Georgia agreed. "It will be useful until the last month or so."

Lila called her thanks to the tiny woman by the stove who answered with a big smile.

The warmest goodbye hug of all came from Tatiana, whose eyes shone with the promise of being an aunt.

Even Sergei gave Lila a brief hug, murmuring, "You have brought the sparkle back to my son's eyes. He is happy again. Thank you. You are good for him, and good for our family. Welcome."

Lila's heart sang to the hum of the plane all the way back to Anchorage. Lou never entered her mind

until a dark shadow passed between her and the sun.
At that, a fleeting worry captured her attention.

Where is he?

Chapter 28

THAT SHADOW CAST by the thought of Lou at Christmas lingered, fitting in well with the monotonous gray winter days of January and February. Eagles circled over Whittier's shoreline and crying gulls soared through the frigid skies, providing a constant, raucous chorus. Activity in the harbor died to almost nothing. Most of the boats were dry docked on wooden pallets in the parking lots or had been covered tightly with tarps and secured to the docks with heavy ropes for the season. The bay turned deeper blue as the weeks passed, and was often ruffled with white-capped waves. The color of the sea matched the slate blue of the sky.

Lila still pondered notifying the Minnesota authorities about what she'd witnessed, but couldn't get past the fear that it would likely require her to travel back to Minnesota. It would be best to wait until after the baby came like she and Paul had decided. Maybe they'd even have caught Lou by then. Paul and Nan didn't mention what she'd told them about the murder, as if they understood that bringing it up worried her. So Lila pushed it from her mind as best she could, always hoping that the next Sunday call to Mom and Judy would be the one that told her Lou had been captured and this ordeal was over. The fascination of life in Whittier helped distract her, too.

Lila learned that the Hodge's eight children didn't need coats to go to school—they simply walked out their apartment doors and rode the elevator down to the basement. From there, they scampered through an underground tunnel and popped up inside the entry of the nearby school house.

Nights were so quiet that the slamming of a door in the Hodge could be heard from one end of a corridor to the other. Dogs and cats, let out of the apartment building to do their business, scooted outside, crouched in the frosty air, then dashed back inside. A tale was often retold about the sixty-five pound dog that had been caught by the wind a few years back and blown like a bowling ball down the ice-covered road all the way to the mouth of the tunnel.

Skis and skates lay propped against the walls of the lobby just inside the Hodge's entry doors, and everyone knew whose were whose. The musty smell of wet wool permeated the lobby. Snowshoes and sleds lay tossed willy-nilly in snow banks along the front of the building. Forsaken cars, buried in snow, dotted the parking lot. It snowed and blew almost every day, sometimes only a scattering of flakes, sometimes in great, howling blizzards that went on for days at a time.

Lila loved it when Paul burst through the store's door in the darkness of late afternoon calling, "Northern lights! Come and see!" She'd grab her parka, rush out and stand beside him, awestruck. The front steps of the Hodge would become crowded as the sky flooded with shivering, twisting beams of green, red and gold lighting up the horizon and sky above the mountain tops. Curtains of undulating light tumbled and whirled, illuminating the northern half of the sky. Everyone watched the monstrous spears of glowing emerald and crimson that shimmered and danced, arching across the black canopy above them. Brilliant dancing lights flitted, whirling, glowing white before transforming into zinging rays of red. Lila never tired of watching this amazing display of nature.

During the second week of February, the *Ed Sullivan Show* introduced the *Beatles*. Everyone chattered about it during the days preceding the broadcast, and a party atmosphere prevailed in the lobby the night of the show. Excited residents milled around the room until the long-haired group took the stage. *"I Wanna Hold Your Hand"* held the crowd mesmerized and they clapped spontaneously when it finished. Paul took her hand during the song and she gripped his in return, content.

Lila had settled into the routine of winter life in Whittier by this time, and her apartment became cozier after every trip into Anchorage. She acquired brightly-colored throw rugs, a shower curtain covered in daisies, a red-checked tablecloth just like her mother's, and frilly white lace curtains to replace the ones she'd salvaged during her first days in the Hodge.

She grew familiar with the department stores and grocery stores in Anchorage, and stopped into a beauty shop to have twelve inches cut off her hair. The new pageboy style suited her well and was much easier to care for, especially now that being so pregnant made every movement harder than it used to be. Lila was thrilled with the new style and gloated with satisfaction at defying Lou's insistence that she never get her hair cut.

Nan had insisted that Lila get established with a doctor in Anchorage and have regular checkups when the baby was due in only a few months. She accompanied Lila to the appointments at the new stucco clinic adjoining the hospital in the heart of the city. Lila had confidence that she was receiving the best care Alaska could provide since its furnishings and equipment were less than a year old.

Doc Simpson, a soft-spoken, elderly doctor with neatly trimmed white hair and beard, told the women that everything looked normal with the pregnancy. He estimated the due date would be around the first of April, and cautioned Lila to make arrangements to

229

stay in Anchorage after the third week of March to be near medical care, advising her not to risk being trapped in Whittier in case the baby came early.

Nan always treated them to ice cream cones from her favorite shop on Fifth Avenue and the women did their shopping before heading back to Whittier after the appointments. Nan was a good companion, but often, when discussing the baby, Lila noticed a flicker of what seemed to be anguish or sorrow flash across her face. Although Nan remained evasive if questioned about it, Lila grew ever more certain there was something in Nan's past to cause this elusive emotion.

Judy and Margaret were nearly beside themselves with worry and excitement, and had been trying to figure out a way they could afford to come and see Lila soon after the baby was born. Jerry volunteered to work extra, a night shift janitor job at the elementary school, in order to save enough for plane tickets for them. He enjoyed being spoiled by their grateful attention. Lila's Sunday night phone calls to them were full of girl talk, chattering, and plans, and all three women looked forward to seeing each other in the spring. Eventually, nobody brought Lou up in the phone conversations, and that was fine. But Lila still worried. Lou wouldn't give up. He was just biding his time. The thread of anxiety about him never left her mind. She still jerked awake, struggling for breath, soaked with sweat, dreaming about what she witnessed that night and how his hands had closed so tightly around her throat. Paul's warmth next to her in bed comforted her and she tried not to wake him. If only they'd catch Lou, she could stop worrying and get on with her life.

Chapter 29

THE OTHER RESIDENTS of the Hodge slowly warmed to Lila while winter passed. Now there were murmurs of greeting in the elevator, smiles of acknowledgement when they passed in the corridors, and most people became less reserved than they had been at first.

A young woman introduced herself to Lila in the lobby one morning. "Hi. I'm Colleen. Me an' my husband, Bob, we live two floors up on the back side of the building—cheaper that side, you know. We look out on the waterfall..." she paused.

Hopeful, friendly brown eyes matched the tumble of dark curls held back from her face by a worn black velvet headband studded with rhinestones. She looked at Lila, waiting for a reply.

"Would you like to have coffee or something?" Lila asked, pleased at this overture of friendship.

Colleen nodded and two young girls stepped out from behind her, peeking shyly at Lila. One looked remarkably like Colleen, the other was sandy-haired with bright blue eyes. Both wore thick braids tied with red rubber bands, faded plaid blouses, and jeans patched at the knees and just a bit too short. On their feet, they wore identical scuffed red canvas tennis shoes.

"These here are Patti and Sally," Colleen explained. "Me and Bob have the two girls. We got two dogs, too, black Labs. Duke and Daisy. Bob already had 'em when we got married, so I kind of inherited 'em. Two dogs and two kids keep me hoppin'!"

"Hi," Lila greeted the girls. The girls ducked back behind their mother.

Colleen and the girls followed Lila to her apartment. "Oh, you get good light here!" Colleen exclaimed when they entered. "It's darker on our side. We can hear the waterfall day and night, but the mountain's so close, it kind of shadows things. The sound's nice to go to sleep to, though. You should come up sometime."

"Sure, I will," Lila responded. "Do you want coffee or Kool-Aid?"

"Kool-Aid!" Colleen's eyes lit up. The girls' faces brightened. Soon, all four were sitting at Lila's kitchen table, sipping the cherry drink.

"Well, I really said 'hi' to you 'cuz I noticed you're expecting," Colleen began. At Lila's acknowledgement, she continued, "I have a bunch of baby clothes and stuff left from the girls. We're not gonna have any more. Bob says these two are all we can afford. So, well, if you'd be interested, you can have the baby stuff. Unless you'll be buying new," she added with a hint of hesitation in her voice.

Lila was touched. It was obvious this young family didn't have much. And, yet, Colleen was offering to share with her. What a kind person. She seemed so young to have two children already.

"Sure, I'd love to look at what you have. Thanks."

"Well, how 'bout right now?" Colleen asked, eyes lit with eagerness. "I just cleaned the apartment this morning, so you can come on up."

Before long, Lila found herself in one of the Hodge's back apartments. The windows on this side of the building looked out on a high, narrow and powerful waterfall that rushed down the side of a close mountain to splash onto jumbled rocks at the bottom. The sides of the falls sprayed, feather-like, along the rocky gorge down the mountainside. The rushing sound, even dimmed by distance and window glass, filled Lila's senses. It was the most beautiful waterfall Lila had ever seen, far surpassing Minnesota's Minnehaha Falls.

"Wow!" she exclaimed to Colleen. "How beautiful! I have to show Paul. Oh, I'm sure he's already seen it. Things are so different on this side of the building. The waterfall is just beautiful—it's so tall!" Lila turned to Colleen, awed.

Colleen grinned back, "Pretty nice, huh? Well, the baby stuff's in the bedroom. I'll get it,"

The girls scampered after her, leaving Lila alone. She looked around at the cheap plastic end tables and the worn tweed sofa that had seen better days. A leg of the scarred wooden kitchen table bent outward, looking ready to give way. Colleen and the girls returned before Lila could see more, this time followed by two silky black Labs who scurried directly to Lila.

"These here are Daisy and Duke," Colleen said.

The dogs nudged and bumped against Lila's legs, then sniffed her thoroughly before deciding she was acceptable.

Lila returned to her apartment a half hour later, arms filled with used but clean and fresh baby clothing and blankets. She felt warmed by the young wife's friendliness, and decided to pick up something for her as a thank you on the next shopping trip. Maybe an assortment of envelopes of Kool Aid or the makings for Rice Krispy bars.

ON SUNDAY, A few days later, after finding himself in the elevator with Paul and Lila, old Tom invited them to "stop down" to his apartment for a minute. He opened his apartment door, reached inside, and handed out a hand-carved, satiny cradle of dark wood.

"Been wantin' to give this to you two youngsters," he explained with a grin. "Been in the family fer ages. But I ain't got nobody to pass it on to. I'm the last a' the line. Ain't a soul I care enough about Outside to give a dang thing to. Figgered you young folks could use it, bein' as yer jest getting' started out an' all." His wrinkled face beamed as he spoke.

At Lila's profuse thanks, Tom stepped back into his apartment and motioned them into the entry. Both stopped in their tracks, speechless, watching Tom work his way toward the kitchen. He shuffled through what was only a skinny path between six-foot high stacks of newspapers, magazines, boxes, and indescribable junk lining every wall. A strong, musty smell assaulted them as if the windows hadn't been opened in years. A large, ornery-looking, striped orange cat wound its way from behind a stack of old books. It glared at them and hissed, tail arched high above its back.

When Tom realized they weren't following him, he turned around. "Well, I know it's a mess. Hard for me to let go of stuff, ya know. Might need it someday."

Paul and Lila stepped further in along the hall, too amazed to reply. The floor beneath the living room window was covered with clumps of clothing, piles of flattened cardboard boxes, and brown paper grocery bags overflowing with empty glass bottles. A torn yellow curtain with raggedy ruffles hung precariously over the top half of the dust-covered window. On the coffee table, a dingy ball of string the size of a basketball balanced next to an overflowing ashtray. The only place anyone could sit down was the lone, faded gold fabric armchair in front of the TV. A stack of newspapers lay squished at its feet.

The kitchen counters were piled with crusted, food-stained dishes, silverware, and unwashed cooking pots. All other counter space overflowed with cans, boxes, bags, mail and paperwork in haphazard piles, a collection of empty coffee cans, and wadded-up towels. The sour, stale smell in the apartment was overpowering, and Lila had to fight the heaving of her stomach.

"Got every issue a' the *Anchorage Times* since it started up," Tom reported, his voice filled with pride, unaware of their reaction. "Ya ever want to look something up, come on down and just ask me. I got 'em all.

Paul and Lila thanked Tom again and Paul, still clutching the tiny cradle in both arms, began backing out with Lila close behind him. Both of them, trying not to breathe too deeply.

"Thanks again for the cradle," Lila managed, as they squeezed themselves out the door. "The baby will be able to use it right away. It's just the right size for a newborn. Are you sure you don't want it back?"

"Naw. Keep it. Maybe you'll need it agin, too," Tom called out from the kitchen. "Come back anytime, ya hear?"

Paul and Lila hurried to the elevator, at a loss for words. They entered the elevator car, looked at each other in amazement, and burst out laughing.

"Wow! Ever seen anything like that?" Paul asked.

Lila shook her head. "Nope! Whew! The smell!"

When they stopped at Nan's to show her the cradle, Nan was amazed to hear that they had actually been invited into Old Tom's apartment. "He must like you pretty well, to invite you in. Nobody's even been inside there for maybe ten years, best I know.

She glanced at Lila with wide eyes. "He's got a reputation as a hoarder—guess I believe it now. It was quite a mess, huh? I'd sure like to see it for myself."

"Yeah. I guess so," Lila answered. "He's been good to me. It seems like he likes me. And he said he'll let me have as much time off as I need after the baby comes. But seeing his place was really something!"

Paul and Lila returned to Lila's apartment a half hour later, still stunned at the condition of old Tom's place. They began straightening up the living room as soon as they walked in the door, looked at each other after the first few minutes of silent and frenzied activity, and burst out laughing.

"Well, that was something we'll never forget," Paul said.

"I know," Lila giggled. "I've never seen anything like it. His apartment was unbelievable!" After a moment, she teased, "So you better stop trying to save stuff."

"You, too!" Paul exclaimed. "Except you. I'm going to save you and keep you forever."

Chapter 30

PAUL BURST INTO the store one afternoon a few days later. "I just talked to my mother on short wave. They're coming to Anchorage for the games in three weeks. I asked 'em if they wanted to come to Whittier, too, and Mom said they did. So, they're coming to see us!" Paul's flashing eyes told Lila how much this meant to him.

"The games?" Lila asked.

At her questioning look, Paul went on, "The Governor helped get the Eskimo Games started a couple of years ago. They've been held in Fairbanks before, but this year they'll be in Anchorage, same time as the Fur Rendezvous. The games are kinda our Olympics," Paul explained, his face bright with enthusiasm. "They let other people learn about us. And it gives give us a way to celebrate our culture There's the blanket toss and a stick pull and the one-foot high kick. And music and dancing and storytelling. Our early people needed special skills for hunting and finding food and shelter in this harsh climate, so these contests have been part of our history and celebrations for a long time."

"Fur Rendezvous?" Lila repeated.

"Oh, yeah. In the old days, the trappers brought their furs into Anchorage every February to trade. It always turned into a big bash. Now, it's a state celebration still called the Fur Rendezvous. There are dog sled races, dances under the stars, drinking, parties, fireworks, and food booths, all downtown. It's a big deal. I was planning to take you. Now, with the games here, too, we have to go."

Paul grabbed Lila to him in an excited hug and went on. "Mom said Tatiana is Alukiak's candidate for Eskimo queen. She was a princess last year, so Grandma's been beading and embroidering and working on her costume all year. Guess Tat will do the traditional hunters' feather dance. She's pretty good at it. I can't wait for you to see her. And our neighbor kid, Johnny Igniknak, will be representing Alukiak in the blanket toss. Mom said he's been practicing at the meeting house every day and can bounce really high. There'll be traditional foods, lots of crafts for sale, and everyone will be in their best clothing. You can have caribou jerky again, and *akutaq*. You won't believe the fur coats and the beadwork!"

Lila's mind raced. "Your folks are coming to visit us? We'll have to have Nan help us figure where they can stay. Maybe Tatiana can sleep on my couch.

Maybe you can give your bedroom to your parents since you have a double bed. Nan'll help with everything, I'm sure. And I bet she'll love your Mom."

Paul beamed. "Let's go tell Nan!"

Nan leaped into the planning as expected. She and Lila cleaned a recently abandoned apartment that still had furniture, supplied bedding and towels, and stocked the kitchen with coffee and other essentials. Lila and Paul grew ever more excited as the day for his family to arrive at Merrill Field approached.

Paul's hand covered Lila's all the way through the tunnel in what had become a tradition between them now. They parked along the edge of the runway at Merrill Field and had to wait only a few minutes until a tiny speck in the distance took on the shape of a small plane. Soon Paul's family poured out of the aircraft, and the hugs were enthusiastic. Even Sergei reached for Lila and pulled her to him without shyness. Tatiana glowed, dancing with excitement, twirling in her fur parka until the hood fanned straight out from her shoulders. Georgia's face shone with delight as she hustled about, gathering their bags.

They loaded the luggage in the truck bed, and put Georgia in the middle of the front seat between Sergei and Paul. Tatiana and Lila squeezed themselves in on laps and into empty spaces as best they could amid giggling and grunts. Everyone finally settled into the packed cab, and spirits were high despite the

241

crowded conditions. The drive through the city streets of Anchorage and south to Whittier went quickly while Paul explained Potters' Marsh and the waters of the Turnagain Arm, as they passed by. Despite his explanation about what to expect from the tunnel, there were gasps from Tatiana, Sergei and Georgia when they first entered the dimness.

Everyone gathered in Paul's apartment to talk and watch TV that night after a supper of dilled halibut and frozen French fries at Nan's. It was midnight before anyone headed for bed.

PAUL'S FAMILY GOT their first look at Whittier the next morning, guided by Paul and Lila. They explored the Hodge, strolled through the underground tunnel to the school building, toured the vast emptiness of the Buckner Building, walked the entire length of the wharf, and marveled at the gigantic, snow-covered mountains ringing the bay. Sergei, with a faraway look, told them the sound of the gulls brought back memories of the sea. Georgia marveled at how people could live so close together, all in the same building. Tatiana, who had never been farther from home than Anchorage, took it all in with wide eyes.

Tatiana demonstrated her feather dance that night, in Paul's living room. Her graceful bends, sidesteps and supple arm movements to music from Paul's stereo, all the while waving a feather-filled fan, mesmerized them all. They went to bed late again, anxious not to waste a moment together.

Lila and Paul had to go back to work on Monday, so Nan took charge of the guests. Her supper of halibut and potato salad was followed by a spirited game of rummy and lots of laughter at Lila's inexperience with the game.

Sergei, Georgia, and Tatiana rode out through the tunnel Tuesday with Paul's coworker, Jeff, who had to make a trip into Anchorage and was willing to drop them off at Georgia's brother's house. The rest of the week dragged for Lila and Paul until the weekend allowed them to head into Anchorage for the games and Fur Rendezvous.

Lila had never seen such crowds in the city streets. Rowdy men, huge furry hats stuffed on their heads, stumbled between the bars. Women in ankle-length fur coats traversed between J.C. Penney and small specialty shops, their arms laden with packages. Steaming street corner carts proclaimed the virtues of smoked reindeer sausage and clam chowder. The vendors sold aromatic bags of hot popcorn, and people lined up for snow cones in flavors of cherry, root beer and blue raspberry. Cotton candy-makers and beer vendors added to the carnival atmosphere.

Several blocks of Fourth Avenue had been cordoned off for the upcoming dog sled race. Dogs twirled on chains in their straw beds along the route, yipping with excitement. A dozen, remarkably calm reindeer, tethered with red leather harnesses,

243

watched the goings on from their temporary corral in a nearby park. Children in bright knit scarves and hats dashed everywhere, calling to one another.

By late afternoon, Tatiana had to report to the auditorium where the coronation would be held. She'd remained calm and intense all afternoon, and displayed no nervousness. When everyone wished her good luck at the door to the auditorium, Tatiana's eyes blazed. "I'll do my best," she vowed. "Just watch me. I can do that dance with my eyes closed. And Grandma's costume's incredible. She worked on it so hard—I have to win for her. I'm sure my costume will give me added points. I'm gonna show up all the other girls!" She gave a confident smile and disappeared through the door.

The family was glad for the distraction of the rest of the events while they waited for the evening coronation. Lila listened while Paul and Sergei and Georgia explained each event.

They laughed along with the crowd while two contestants grunted through the stick pull. The men sat facing each other, feet together and knees bent, trying to pull a stick out of the other's hands. Lila couldn't believe how high the winner kicked his foot in the one-foot-high event where men demonstrated their agility by kicking a suspended object with one foot and landing on the floor with the same foot. Sergei explained that the event was based on the custom of a messenger from a hunting group coming within visual distance of a village, and giving a high kick to signal that caribou were running near. Lila covered her eyes at the ear pull in an effort to drown out Paul's explanation about pain and endurance. She grew fascinated at the traditional displays of endurance, strength, and agility.

The Alukiak boy placed second in the blanket toss, reaching twenty-four feet as he was tossed high on an eight foot-round sealskin blanket. Georgia told Lila that this was how her people used to spot game over the horizon.

All contestants performed with enthusiasm, and Lila couldn't help being caught up in the excitement of the crowd.

Tatiana's performance captivated the audience that night. From the moment the willowy young woman entered the stage, she held the audience mesmerized. Tatiana blazed onto the stage in a striking, white caribou-skin dress her grandmother had soaked and scraped to clinging softness. The dress sparkled with reflective red and gold beading. Long white fringes covering her wrists and knees trembled in time to her every movement. When her traditional hunting dance gestures mimicked the crack of rifle shots, everyone watching gasped at her skill. Not a single person remained in their seat when she finished. Tatiana tossed back her shining mantle of dark hair at the ovation, grinned widely, and gave a final swing of her hips followed by another rifle crack gesture. The crowd roared. Everyone was certain they'd just witnessed the performance of the night. And they were right. The white ermine crown matched Tatiana's dress as if it had been planned that way. Georgia and Sergei basked in the congratulations surrounding them as they left the building.

Tatiana's picture appeared on the front page of the *Anchorage Times* the next day. The most important thing to her, though, was Paul's assurance that she could return to Whittier as soon as the baby was born. She couldn't wait to start being an aunt.

Chapter 31

THE NIGHT AFTER Paul's family left for home, Paul and Lila lingered over grilled cheese sandwiches and dunked Nan's chocolate chip cookies in milk.

Hey," Paul said. "You know, you never finished telling me about getting here. Remember, you got too tired to talk anymore that night you first told me about what happened?"

"Oh yeah," Lila replied. "The trip. And how could I forget the day I met you? You were the cutest guy I'd ever seen. Well, the most handsome," she added in a playful tone, noticing Paul grimace at the word "cute."

"I remember seeing you for the first time, too," Paul answered. "Your hair caught my eye first. So shiny and thick and exactly the color of the fireweed honey my mother makes. I'd never seen hair that color before. I loved the way it waved down your back, too, just like a movie star. Then I saw your face.

And your blue eyes. I was lost from that minute on. I could hardly talk when you first looked at me."

Lila laughed. "Well, I was exhausted and scared. But I did notice you, too."

"So tell me about the drive from Minnesota. I still can't believe you did it all alone," Paul urged.

"Well, the days just fell into a pattern after I crossed the border into Canada," Lila explained. "I just drove hard following the Alcan Highway signs, filled the car with gas, and ate only when I was hungry. Found a pullout when I was too tired to drive anymore, spread the sleeping bag across the seat, locked the doors, and snuggled in."

She told how other travelers spent their nights the same way. Gravel turnout areas held parked eighteen-wheelers, as well as various other vehicles that pulled in and parked for the night. Lila told Paul her fear of being alone in unknown country was lessened by the presence of these other travelers and by the comforting lack of darkness. She'd been awakened on the first night by a noisy semi that pulled into the turnout at midnight, and was surprised to see that it wasn't dark outside, but more like dusk. And no matter how early she awoke in the mornings, it was always light.

"The first stop for gas was my chance to use the station's restroom to brush my teeth and wash my face and comb my hair," she told him. "It felt funny to sleep in my clothes, but the old sweatshirt I'd left home in was comfortable and warm. I just wrestled clean underwear and socks from my suitcase every morning and changed into them in the restrooms. It was pretty easy to take care of myself. I was so upset and scared that I never got really hungry, so meals weren't a problem."

Lila explained that after two days of steady driving through Edmonton and Grande Prairie in Alberta, she was just reaching Fort Nelson in British Columbia when the sun began to fade below the horizon of distant mountains and the dashboard clock read ten o'clock. Since she'd been too long without a bed and shower, a motel was needed for the night.

Fort Nelson was a small and dusty town with most of its clapboard buildings in need of repair and painting. The single story, eight-unit Yukon Motel, its walls hungry for white paint, was set back from the highway behind a grove of trees and flashed a sign for rooms at only nine dollars ninety-five a night. Perfect.

"I'd never stayed in a motel before," she said. "I checked in, paid with cash, and signed the register as 'MaryAnn Wilson' so I couldn't be traced. And I wrote one digit of the car's license number wrong on the registration card, too."

At the lift of Paul's eyebrows, she shrugged. "Well, I was afraid Lou was after me and might be able to trace the license plate. Or have the police do it. I was way out in the wilderness by then, but I was still afraid."

"Go on," Paul said.

"Well, that motel hadn't been remodeled, or cleaned much, since it was built. Every step I took, dust flew up from the wood floor. There was a musty double bed sitting in the middle of the room with a deep sag in the middle. The straggly curtains couldn't hide the dirt on the window, so it was pretty dim in there."

Lila told Paul what a gas station attendant had told her the day before while he washed her windows—how the Alcan Highway had been built by the military just before World War II. He said most of the establishments along the road had been built to serve support groups for the road project.

"I think that motel was one of those," Lila said.

She told how she awoke early the next morning, discomforted by the stuffy closeness of the room and the vague odor of other people. "The shower had felt great that night, and it was quiet there, but I couldn't get out of that room fast enough in the morning."

While the towns of Watson Lake and Whitehorse in the Yukon Territories fell behind her during the long day of driving, her thoughts had turned home. "I knew my mother would be very worried about me by then. But there weren't any pay phones out there in northwest Canada."

Since it hadn't been possible to get anything other than static on the car radio on the isolated Canadian roads and she hadn't seen a TV or newspaper since she left Minnesota, she began to worry about a missing persons report. Had Lou put out an alarm? Or had Mom or Judy? Was her name or face on the news? She had no way of knowing.

"That was all I could do," Lila said. "I knew if Lou even had a clue about where I was headed, he was just mad enough to come barreling after me."

Lila explained that the tiny, scattered communities on Alaska Highway were so far apart she learned to study the atlas in order to gauge the next gas stop. Lou's money was holding out and she had well over three-fourths of it left even though gas here in the wilderness cost twice as much as back home. Lou had always grumbled about paying thirty-five cents a gallon for gas in St. Paul. What would he say if he knew she was paying almost twice that much now?

Lila had concentrated on the road ahead, trying to push thoughts of Lou away. The dry, sunny days made driving easy, even though the gravel roads were rough and dusty. Waning sunlight lingered so long she often found herself driving late into the night without even realizing it.

Paul gave a tight smile when Lila explained how two semis had adopted her on the day she crossed the highest peaks of the Canadian Rockies in western British Columbia.

"One was parked at the same turnout I was the night before, and he left the same time I did in the morning, He stayed ahead of my car and then another eighteen wheeler joined us and drove behind me. Then those two stayed with me all the way through the mountain summits that whole day. The roads were slippery then because it rained off and on and even sleeted when we got up high, and the curves were steep and icy. They stayed right with me, one in front of me, and the other one in back. We never even talked or anything. It was kind of like they thought I needed protection or something. Maybe they talked to each other by CB, do you think?" Lila gave a small smile at the memory.

Her heart had hammered the following afternoon when a road sign alerted drivers to prepare to stop at U.S. customs a mile ahead. What would she do if they wouldn't let her through into Alaska? There was no record of her entry into Canada. Were they able to track such things?

"I'd never even been out of Minnesota, so I was pretty nervous. I'm kind of shaky a little right now, just remembering how worried I was."

Paul moved over, and put an arm around her shoulders. "And then what? How did it go getting into Canada?"

Lila told Paul how, when she reached the border a few minutes later, she saw the driver of the lone car ahead of her hand some papers to the uniformed man in the glass-walled booth. She'd watched with growing anxiety and tried to figure out what they were saying as the driver responded to questions from the customs agent. All too soon, it was her turn.

The agent, in an official dark green uniform with gold shoulder badges, leaned his head slightly out the window when she approached, and waved her forward. Lila's heart began pounding while she came to a stop and rolled down her window with a trembling hand.

"Good afternoon, Miss. Your identification, please," the agent had ordered in a firm voice.

"I kinda fumbled through my purse," Lila said. "My hands were shaking so bad. Finally, I found my driver's license and handed it to him. He asked me where I was headed. I just said, 'Whittier, Alaska.'"

"By yourself?" the agent had asked, his eyes widening. "You're the only occupant of the vehicle?"

"I was afraid my voice would show him how nervous I was, so I just nodded. He studied my face for a long time, and I almost died, I was so scared. Then he asked in a real formal tone where I had crossed the U. S. border, and how many days did I spend in Canada."

"I know I kind of stuttered and stammered, but I managed to get something out about northern Montana. I told him I couldn't remember the name of the town but I thought it was near Wolf Point or something like that…"

Lila hesitated until Paul leaned his cheek in next to hers. "Go on. What next?"

"The agent just kept waiting for me to say more. So I told him it took me four days to drive from Montana. By then, I had wild butterflies in my stomach. I had no proof of crossing into Canada. I didn't know what I'd do if he asked for it. He seemed to think for a while and then asked if I had any firearms, alcohol, or tobacco in my vehicle."

"When I shook my head no, he just gave a shrug and handed my license back. While I was putting it in my purse, he leaned further out and asked if I had any questions about how to get from there to my destination. I hesitated, so he told me to just stay on that same Highway 1, the Alcan, all the way right into Anchorage and then on down to Whittier. He explained that the road would split off in a few hundred miles and to be sure not to take the turnoff north to Fairbanks."

"After I thanked him, he said I should be able to make it to Tok that night if I drove steadily. He said there was a good, clean restaurant there and a safe motel. He asked if I understood I was heading onto treacherous mountain roads that were isolated and dangerous this time of the year. He seemed kind of worried about me."

The agent, before waving her on, had added, "Be careful, Miss. Do not pick up any hitchhikers. Not under any circumstances. And be sure to stay on this main road where there are other travelers. Try to make it to Tok tonight, for sure. Always keep your gas tank at least a quarter full, too. The gas stations are few and far between." With a final, concerned look, he'd waved her past his booth.

"I'd made it to Alaska. I was really here."

Chapter 32

LILA SIPPED HER water, then went on telling how she'd pulled away from the customs station onto the gravel highway stretching far ahead into the mountains of Alaska. Sobered by the custom agent's warnings, she became anxious to reach civilization. When her worries were interrupted by a rock that smacked against the windshield with a loud crack, she'd ducked instinctively while a web of tiny cracks quickly circled the point of impact. Then, stunned and awed by the splendor of the Alaskan wilderness, she became distracted from what she'd left behind. As the road fell away down a steep curve ahead, the beauty of this Alaskan portion of the trip surpassed even the scenery of the Canadian Rockies.

"For a city girl who'd never been farther from St. Paul than a northern Minnesota lake, it was a whole other world," she exclaimed to Paul.

White-capped mountain ranges rose majestically in every direction as far as she could see, their slopes multi-colored green, gold and orange in the brilliant September sunlight. Valleys far below held twisting, silver ribbons of water, and miniature evergreen forests crowded the shores of pristine lakes dotted with forested islands and peninsulas. Monstrous cliffs on the other side of the road thrust upward in reddish-tinted splendor. The gleaming yellow and gold leaves of birch trees on mountain slopes could have been made of sunlight. Occasional flashes of fear brought by thoughts of Lou were quickly overcome by the vast, grand, amazing scenery.

Plump black bears with shiny coats looked up with curiosity while she passed their meadows, then calmly settled back to munching the vegetation. Moose wandered nearby, even right up onto the highway. A huge dark cow on spindly legs strutted across the lanes before her, twin calves trailing in single file behind. A solitary bull moose looked up from a marshy area bordering the road, shaking droplets of water from the long, shaggy beard dangling from his chin. One misty morning, a wolf materialized in the ditch and ran alongside the car, its stare fixed with hers.

There were no guard rails along the narrow gravel highways, no billboards, no signs, and hardly any traffic. The car became covered with dust so thick she could hardly see out the windows. It didn't take long to realize it was best not to fight the bumpiness of the gravel road, but simply allow it to jiggle her comfortably along. The mesmerizing noise of the tires crunching on the gravel let her mind wander into a nearly hypnotic state where the cares and concerns of the life she'd left behind almost floated away.

Paul's eyes widened when she told how, on a straight stretch of highway later in the day, she had to stop right in the middle of the road for a herd of reindeer that filed two and three abreast in a steady stream across in front of her. The beautiful animals all looked straight ahead, seemingly unaware of her vehicle, focused completely on getting where they were going.

"They all looked exactly the same, with brown bodies, white shoulder capes, and fluffy, white, furry socks on their ankles," she said. "Their long, branching antlers had dark velvety covering and all the antlers were tipped forward at the very same angle when they passed in front of the car. When I rolled down the window, I could hear the clickety-clackety of their hooves on the road. It was incredible! Was that one of those reindeer migrations?"

"Yeah, those were caribou," he explained.

She'd watched for an hour until the herd of thousands finished passing before her. Several cars ended up backed in a line behind her and the occupants appeared as fascinated by the migration as she was.

As she drove on again, gravel and rocks spun out from the car's wheels, and dust billowed in a thick tail behind her. Once more, a flying rock smacked the windshield, leaving another crackled spot just to the right of her vision. She kept going, thoughts of Lou distant for now. Despite the relentless, slanting, late afternoon sun in her eyes, she pulled down the visor and just drove on, desperate to get to Tok.

"The car was like a warm cocoon. All I could think about was to keep driving hard, every hour was further toward Whittier. It was a long afternoon and early night of driving, and the gas gauge got close to empty, but I finally made it to Tok."

Lila sighed. "I got gas right before the only station closed for the night. Tok sure isn't much of a town. I got a room at the Musher Motel like the custom agent told me to. And I was really hungry so I spent some of Lou's money on a steak dinner, which was just what I needed. It was wonderful to take a shower that night. I let the hot water pound my shoulders and back for about fifteen minutes. Then I sat on the bed and watched Walter Cronkite talk about the war getting worse in Vietnam. I was afraid there'd be a news item about a missing Minnesota woman, but there wasn't. Did you know there's a standard twelve-hour news delay—it takes that long to get newsreels to remote locations like Tok?" she asked Paul.

He smiled. "Sure."

Lila went on to describe the long morning of driving steadily after leaving Tok. The gas gauge had dropped dangerously close to empty again before Lila spotted the Long Gun Café and Fuel and pulled in for a fill.

"The grilled cheese sandwich I ordered in the café was the best I've ever tasted—there were thin slices of dill pickle in the hot cheese. I was surprised at such an unusual taste. And I was hungry again, so I finished with a huge piece of warm blueberry pie with a scoop of ice cream melting on top."

Paul nodded encouragement. "What else?"

"The view from the huge picture window along the dining room's back wall looked like a picture postcard!" she said. "An icy-blue glacier was kind of nestled between two mountains. The peaks soared up under the brightest blue sky I've ever seen. Inside, the dining room was full of old, dusty mounted animals—a huge brown bear rearing on hind legs, a moose head with massive, spreading horns, a wolf crouching on all fours, a mink, and two caribou heads with tall, complex sets of antlers. The walls were crowded with fish and birds of all kinds mounted on plaques and branches, and grainy black and white pictures of old Alaska. It was a neat place!"

"Yeah, I've heard of it," Paul responded.

Lila went on to tell how the wiry, gray-haired man in a stained apron who waited on her also cooked her order, and then took her payment While making change, this jack-of-all trades proprietor assured her she could make it to the small town of Palmer, located about thirty miles from Anchorage, by ten or eleven that night if she drove steadily. He cautioned her about the steep, sharp, winding mountain curves ahead and warned her of falling rock that might not be cleared off the highway yet, since rock slides happened almost every day and highway crews couldn't keep up with them all this far out.

Worried a bit by what lay ahead, her confidence wavered. The spark of uncertainty triggered memories of what she'd left behind, and Lou's face flashed before her again. A biting pang of anxiety swept through her, but she determinedly shook it off and headed out the carved wooden café door. Lou was far away. She had to concentrate on the road ahead.

Chapter 33

LILA DROVE THROUGH the early evening, gaping at glaciers, forested mountain slopes, and plunging canyons. Square-faced, white mountain goats cavorted on steep crags high above the road, and an occasional eagle swept majestically through the pink-streaked golden horizon ahead. Minnesota felt far behind and this was all surreal, like being in another world. And for the first time, as darkness began to fall, Lila felt lonely, and wished for someone to share this splendor.

Despite having to navigate hair-raising curves bordering deep canyons and having to be on the alert to make last-minute swerves to avoid frequent rocks in her lane, Lila drove on. She fought off doubts about being alone on the unfamiliar and dangerous roads, and was glad for the company of other vehicles that infrequently passed her, even though they left her in a choking cloud of dust. Immersed in the splendor of her surroundings, determined to make it to Whittier, more sure than ever that she could do it, Lila drove steadily on.

Before she knew it, a small wooden road sign announced that Anchorage was only a hundred and eighty miles ahead.

Several hours later, Lila rolled into the tiny town of Palmer that lay nestled in a scenic bowl of mountains. A strip of reddish dusk lingered along the shadowy mountaintops. She felt nearly drunk on the beauty of her surroundings. And Anchorage was just ahead. Only forty more miles.

"I stopped at a Shell station and used the hose along the building that offered free water for car washing. The dirt and dust just rolled off my car until it was white again and the windows finally got clean. I'd hardly been able to see out of them anymore. I couldn't resist turning into an A & W next to the station for a root beer float and my favorite Teen Burger and fries. It was so good to get a taste of home."

She smiled at the memory. "A few minutes later, when the waitress trotted out and clipped the food tray to my window, it felt like I'd made it back to civilization. I gobbled the fries and hamburger, and the float tasted exactly like the ones in Minnesota. But I couldn't stop worrying about finding my way to Whittier. During those long, lonely days on the road, I finally had time to really think through what had happened and what lay ahead. I wondered what Lou was doing after all this time with no word about me.

It was possible he'd already traced me and was on the way. But nobody at all knew where I'd gone. Well, except Chuck and Dee in Montana and the border agent. So chances of him being already on my trail were slim, I hoped. I still felt kind of out of it, like I was watching someone in a movie or something. Like it wasn't really me doing it all. Weird, huh?" She spread her hands.

Paul grinned. "Yeah."

"It was getting late by then, so I stopped at a little motel that night. I didn't want to get into Anchorage at midnight and have to try to find a place to stay. The next morning, just out of Palmer, the gravel highway became hard-packed and the white metal road signs said it was the Glenn Highway to Anchorage, so I knew I was close. That Matanuska River with its wide, flat muddy banks sure was different from Minnesota rivers. Then I drove through a place called Chugiak, but it didn't look at like a real town, just some scattered houses. I twisted around a few small lakes, and drove past a place called Moose Horn Lodge and the Golden Grizzly Auto Shop. Log cabins and wood shacks along the road got closer and closer together. I wondered about all the miniature log buildings standing on stilts in almost every yard. Caches, is that what you said they were?"

"Yup, that's right," Paul replied.

"Well, Packs of dogs that looked like wolves swirled around their chains in lots of yards, so that must have been sled dogs, right?"

Paul dipped his head. "Yes."

"A half hour south of Palmer, I saw the city skyline. It looked so small compared to the Cities. I couldn't believe that right on the edge of town there were dozens of small planes parked in a field along the highway. They were all colors, clustered around metal buildings under a huge sign that said Merrill Field."

"Those were hangers. Hangers for the planes. Alaska has more private planes and pilots than any other state." Paul interrupted.

"Oh. Well, I was surprised to see an airport so close to the city border. In Minnesota, the airport's huge and it's way out south of Minneapolis. Anyway, when I got closer to Anchorage the traffic got heavier every minute, and the highway merged into what looked like the city's main street. Fifth Avenue, right?"

Paul nodded.

Lila told Paul how surprised she'd been to find that Anchorage looked nothing like Minneapolis/ St. Paul. There were no tall buildings, no stoplights, no freeways, very little traffic, none of the hustle and bustle she expected to find. The rough, blacktopped city streets were full of deep potholes with jagged edges. Wide cracks crisscrossed the pavement, and odd grooves were worn right down the middle of the traffic lanes. Instead of the skyscrapers she was used to, most of the downtown buildings were plain, with painted wood siding. The two or three-story wood-frame buildings with small windows were crammed close together beneath a maze of neon signs. Some of them sported huge, colorfully painted murals of the ocean or Eskimo life on the flat side walls facing the street. A familiar J.C. Penney sign in the window of one store had brought a smile of recognition to Lila's face.

The streets weren't at all crowded like they were in St. Paul and the few small parking lots were nearly empty. A corner sidewalk café with red and white striped umbrellas over the tables advertised fresh crab legs, but was nearly deserted. Gift shops advertised Eskimo parkas, antler carvings, native art, scrimshaw, furs and gold nuggets.

"I didn't know what scrimshaw was. The fur coats in the store windows amazed me." Lila recalled. "Anchorage was so small and different from St. Paul."

Lila told him how surprised she'd been when Fifth Avenue curved southward into L Street after only twenty downtown blocks, the buildings dwindled, and another larger, commercial airport came into sight. Its narrow two-story terminal and spindly air traffic control tower looked insignificant compared to the airport back in Minnesota.

"I noticed the red logo for Pacific Northern Airlines on one of the parked planes. Pacific Northern flies into the airport in Minneapolis, too, so I was glad to see it," she informed Paul. "I knew I better fill up with gas and get directions to Whittier then. It was exciting to be so close. I pulled into the first gas station I saw."

The attendant, a talkative old guy in oil-stained blue coveralls, pumped her gas and pushed a dirty rag around the windshield. In response to Lila's question about how to get to Whittier, he looked at her with curiosity in his eyes and asked where she was from.

He'd pushed back his dirty cap at her brief answer, and replied, "Well, don't that beat all! A young gal like you making it all the way from Minnesota by yourself! Never heard of such a thing. Pretty little thing, ya are, too. Bluest eyes I ever saw. Musta had a good reason…" his voice trailed off.

He'd waited for an answer, an explanation, but Lila had remained silent.

Finally, he'd shrugged and continued, "Yup. Whittier. 'Bout a good hour south. You gotta go back east over to the Seward Highway and then just keep on it south all the way to the train depot for Whittier. So, jus' go left at the next corner, hang a right when the street sign says Seward Highway, and you'll be on yer way. Ya gotta go a ways past the Girdwood cutoff, maybe fifteen minutes more. After that, stop at the Portage depot where they load the train. It'll take ya a good hour or so from the city limits. There's them big blue and gold signs that say Alaska Railroad at Portage. Ya can't miss it."

"Hey," he'd added. "Do ya need an oil change? Did ya get one along the way? Ya put a lotta miles on this Galaxie, young lady."

Lila had started.

Oh, cars need to have oil changes.

She remembered something about drivers having to watch the oil, but, since she'd never had a car of her own, it hadn't occurred to her.

"Yeah, good idea. I'm sure it's due. Can you do it now? Can you check the tires, too?"

"Yup. You can wait in the station. There's a couple a chairs and some magazines, mostly about cars, though. Should take only about twenty minutes. We're not that busy right now. Go on in now. I'll call ya when it's done."

When he called Lila back to the car, he continued talking as if he'd never stopped. "Oil's changed. Tires look fine and dandy. It's easy to work on a new car like that. Air filter was pretty dusty so I put a new one in."

He looked at Lila for a reaction. When she thanked him, he handed her the keys. "Trains only go through the tunnel to Whittier twice a week, ya know, so ya gotta be there for the ten-thirty train tomorrow morning or you'll end up waitin' 'til Saturday. Ya know ya gotta drive your car right up on the flatcars of the train, right? It's the only way to git through the tunnel."

Lila had indicated she understood and felt lucky she didn't have to wait in Anchorage until the weekend. Another good sign. How much would the train trip cost and how it would work to get her car actually loaded onto the train? It would be best to find the Seward Highway, get a cheap room, and then head south early in the morning and do whatever it took to get through the tunnel.

But the flash of terror she'd felt back in Palmer reignited, and her stomach had tightened with tension by the time she checked into the Black Bear Motel along the Seward Highway. The room had no shower, so after a quick bath in the rust-pocked tub, she walked to the café next door for a bowl of soup and then settled in for the rest of the day. She slept fitfully that night, afraid of not waking up in time to get down to the train station, and rose at the first sounds of traffic outside her window. Getting to the train consumed her thoughts.

"That early morning drive south out of Anchorage on the Seward Highway nearly took my breath away!" Lila explained, her tone high with wonder.

Paul grinned in agreement, "I know."

She slid into memories of how the two-lane gravel highway hugged vertical mountain cliffs on the left. The cliffs, scarred by huge slashes where the rock had been blasted away to make the road, rose reddish and steep. Brisk waterfalls poured from them, nearly splashing onto the highway. Within ten feet of the right shoulder of the road, a long body of water lapped against the rocky shore. Icy glaciers of shimmering blue snaked between snowy peaks across the water. Lila remembered having to squint against the brightness, not wanting to miss anything.

"That fresh clean smell through the open window was different from Minnesota's air. I wondered if I was smelling the ocean. I'd never imagined such a pure and glorious place. It was so vast, so grand. I'd never seen anything like it. I hoped Whittier would be half as beautiful."

"Before I knew it, I was passing the sign for the turn to Girdwood, like the gas station man told me. I knew I was almost to the train then. I was just amazed by everything that morning. Some traffic whizzed by me in places the highway straightened enough to let 'em by. It was like they were so used to the scenery, it meant nothing to them. But I thought it was gorgeous! Pretty soon, I saw the signs for the railroad. And then, there you were!"

"And, well…you know the rest," Lila mumbled, overcome by a sudden weariness and a dry and scratchy throat. She couldn't keep her eyes open and her shoulders ached with fatigue. The clock said one-thirty. She never stayed up this late.

Paul rose and pulled her to her feet. "You're worn out. I'm tired, too. Let's go to bed." He steered her toward the bedroom.

Chapter 34

THE NEXT DAY while Lila waited on a customer, the man suddenly stumbled, then grabbed onto the counter, his eyes flaring. Canned goods tumbled off their shelves and rolled in all directions across the floor. Loaves of bread fell from the rack, glass jars tinkled against one another, and Lila's head bobbed uncontrollably until the shaking subsided a full minute later. She looked, wild-eyed, at the man across the counter.

He shook himself. "Whew! That was a four, I bet! Maybe a five! Haven't had one like that for quite a while." He straightened his cap and took a swig of the beer bottle he'd clutched when the shaking began.

"What..." Lila managed to croak. "What was that? What happened?"

"Ain't you never felt an earthquake before?" he asked. "Hell, we have tremors like that here all the time. Been kind of quiet this winter, though, now that I think about it. Most of 'em ain't as strong as this one. This was a good one, all right. They'll report it on KFQD tonight, I bet. We gotta listen an' see how bad it was in the rest of the state."

With that, he took his change and banged out the door, leaving Lila still breathing hard. An earthquake! What would Mom and Judy think about that?

Just then, a cramp in her stomach bent her double. She pushed her hands hard against it until it subsided a moment later, then straightened up. Shaken and unnerved by the painful twinge, she took several deep breaths before beginning to pick up the groceries from the floor. She had to stand and rub her aching stomach every few minutes until the faint, recurrent pain finally went away. She finished putting the items back on the shelves, then rested on the stool behind the counter until she felt back to normal.

The rest of the afternoon dragged. No customers came in. She counted the morning's receipts and jotted them down in the ledger, polished the cooler fronts and swept. But, unsettled by the earthquake and the unusual cramp-like pain she'd experienced, Lila found it difficult to stay busy while she waited for closing time.

Paul arrived just as Lila was shutting the cash register drawer for the night. His face was filled with concern as he hustled through the door. "The earthquake?" he began. "Were you standing next to something to steady yourself? Did it hit here very

271

hard? I wanted to come right away, but we had a train due in, and we had to take measurements of the tracks to make sure there was no damage."

He strode to Lila and took her in his arms. "Are you okay? I was worried about you."

Lila cuddled against him. "Yeah, I'm fine now. But that was a first for me. It was scary! I was at the counter with a customer so we both grabbed on. It was really something. I still feel shaken up."

"But are you fine?" Paul asked, pushing her back from him to look into her face.

"Yeah. I really am. I had a little cramp in my stomach right after the earthquake, but it's gone now. Will there be another earthquake?"

"You had a cramp!" Paul's eyes widened.

"Yeah, but it was just a little one and I'm fine now. I almost forgot about it," Lila replied, and then hesitated, remembering.

That's right, Paul's wife had lost a baby. And now I've worried him. I shouldn't have mentioned the cramp.

Lila put a smile on her face and reached out to hug Paul. "I'm fine. Fine. It was nothing. All this is new to me, you know. Come on, let's go. I'm hungry and I left chili in the crockpot. Sound good?"

Paul seemed to relax a bit. "Well, if you're sure. Yeah, chili sounds real good. Come on then. Here, I'll help you with the parka."

They climbed into Paul's warm pickup and when they parked, Lila smiled at the hump that was her car on the far edge of the lot. The Galaxie was completely buried in snow since she hadn't driven it at all during the winter.

I sure haven't put many miles on it. Hope it starts in the spring. Oh, well, Paul will help me if it doesn't.

The walk to work every noon did her good, but by now, the parka wouldn't zip over her big belly, so she first wrapped herself in one of Nan's old stretched-out sweaters. The leather mittens lined with rabbit fur that Paul had given her for Christmas kept her fingers toasty, even on the most bitter of days. Since there were now only weeks to go before the baby was due, Lila felt sure she'd make it through the Whittier winter just fine.

The winter had been just like everyone described. Snow drifts covered the main floor windows of the Hodge so the office, lobby, post office, and other rooms on the first floor had to keep lights burning all day or they would have been in complete darkness. The train brought very few vehicles when it did make it through from Anchorage, and she and Paul had been prevented from driving into town three times by blowing snow, icy roads, avalanches, and blizzards.

Their long, snug evenings in Lila's apartment became the place for Lila and Paul to plan for the future and look forward to a life together. When Paul expressed concern about the prejudice Lila would face as his partner, she always answered the same. "It doesn't matter to me. We'll deal with it. Those people are the ones with the problem. I've started staring them down until they look away. They know they should be ashamed of themselves."

"But—"Paul would begin.

"Don't worry about it," Lila always answered. "I love you. Let's not let those jerks get to us."

SOMEONE ELSE WAS making plans, too. A bitter Lou, still in hiding in Artie's basement apartment in Minneapolis, had by now convinced himself that the blame for his situation lay entirely on Lila. After all, she was the only one besides Artie who knew what had happened. The only one who could screw up his life. And Artie would never dare tell. So things would be fine if Lila was taken care of. Lou brooded constantly, convinced that Lila would eventually report witnessing the murder in the parking lot. Since she was the only witness other than Artie, Lou became more obsessed every day with getting back to Alaska, finding Lila, and taking care of her before she talked.

When he heard through the grapevine that Twin City police were still searching for him for the attack on Margaret, he remained in hiding, becoming more bitter about his situation every day. He plotted his revenge during the long Minnesota winter, shaved his head, and grew long sideburns and a goatee. He obsessed over plans to drive as far as North Dakota in the used car Artie would buy him, dump it, slip across the border, and hitchhike through Canada as soon as weather would allow. He was certain he'd be able to get through the tunnel to Whittier this time after so long, and with such a changed appearance. He would finally get that thieving little bitch.

Chapter 35

ALMOST EVERYONE IN the Hodge gathered in the lobby on St. Patrick's Day weekend for a potluck dinner—a storm had raged for four days and cabin fever had set in hard. It was the first time a neighborly event like this had occurred since Kennedy's assassination, and that one had been a somber affair.

The residents gathered to share whatever they'd been able to rustle up from their kitchen cupboards. The great variety of gelatin salads—cherry with sliced bananas, lime with crushed pineapple and miniature marshmallows, plain orange, raspberry topped by whipped cream, amused Lila and Paul. There were two kinds of homemade moose sausage, six cakes, smoked salmon, and a loaf of crusty banana bread that didn't last long. Nan contributed a crockpot filled with meatballs in barbeque sauce, and Paul helped Lila put together a roaster full of moose burger and baked beans. Colleen and Bob and the girls brought a cake pan piled high with peanut butter cookies that the little ones had helped bake. Duke and Daisy were there, too, green bows tied snugly around their necks, cruising the edges of the crowd, tails whipping the air. The dogs sniffed everyone and everything industriously and generally made nuisances of themselves by begging for food, which they wolfed down as if another scrap of food would never come their way. Nobody seemed to mind.

Frail old Agnes, in a prim black dress, pearls at her neck and ears, surprised everyone with an enormous box of specialty chocolates that she passed around, beaming at the expressions of appreciation for such a treat. This lobby was Agnes' territory. She didn't speak or greet people from her chair in the corner every morning, just appeared to enjoy watching what was going on.

"She's kinda nosy, if ya ask me," Nan had remarked wryly a few weeks ago, her comment eased by a smile. "But we're sorta her family, and I guess she likes to keep track of us."

Everyone lingered after eating, reluctant to retreat to the apartments that had held them captive for the previous four days. The main topic of conversation was of how the *Beatles* now had the country under their spell.

"What kind of name is that? The *Beatles*!" old Tom asked scornfully of anyone who would listen.

People shook their heads in pretended agreement. But the room was abuzz with talk of the group's long hairstyles and how often their unique songs played on the radio. A few people argued that the *Beach Boys* had a better sound, but discussion about the *Beatles* monopolized most of the conversations. Some Hodge residents dawdled along the edges of the gathering, not really participating in conversation, but seeming to need the brief, mild, social interaction that being in the company of others provided.

Lila ate way too much, and that night had trouble getting comfortable next to Paul on the couch as they cuddled side by side watching Ed Sullivan. For the first time since Paul began sleeping in her bed, it felt crowded. It was impossible to sleep on her back or front and there didn't seem to be enough room for her to stretch out on her side without rolling against him.

At her last appointment, the doctor had assured Lila that the pregnancy was progressing normally. He reminded her to be sure to find accommodations in town by mid-month, although it now looked as though the baby wouldn't come until after the first week in April. Paul's aunt and uncle in Anchorage graciously offered Lila their spare bedroom, and she'd already dropped off a nightgown, a few other pieces of clothing, and a blanket and terry-cloth sleeper for the baby.

She'd registered at the hospital and was relieved to learn that a normal delivery would cost about six hundred dollars. She had more than enough money.

Paul spent three nights sanding and staining a wooden crib with twirled spindles that had been abandoned in a storage room at the Hodge - a beautiful and unique piece of furniture that would be all ready to go when the baby outgrew Tom's little cradle. Colleen's husband, Bob, who worked at the railroad office with Paul, helped carry it to Lila's apartment. When it was finished, its presence in the corner of her bedroom made the upcoming birth become more real. Paul insisted on paying when she picked out three receiving blankets, two boxes of thick white diapers, a six pack of rubber pants, diaper pins, and a set of crib sheets on the next trip to Anchorage, and she loved him for it. The corner of her bedroom was soon filled with terry cloth sleepers, rattles, a wide-eyed teddy bear, and piles of tiny clothes.

Nan began showing up at Lila's door almost every morning, hovering, bubbling with advice. "You'll have to get bottles and nipples and a bottle sterilizer. A dozen bottles and nipples, at least. And plastic pants—lots of them. And what about formula and baby food? Do you have bibs? Babies spit up a lot. You should have a warmer blanket, too. Wait, I have one that'll work. I'll wash it tomorrow and bring it down. We'll need a stroller as soon as the weather gets nicer, too, you know."

Her advice and expertise surprised Lila, but Nan ignored any comments Lila made about it. Once, when Lila asked how Nan knew so much about sterilizing formula, Nan's pinched face betrayed pain she couldn't hide. She made an abrupt turn out of the room, leaving a thin trail of smoke behind, and avoided Lila for a few days after that. Lila decided to stop asking, fearful of losing Nan's support or bringing up what was obviously a troubling subject.

A yearning to be with Mama intensified as the reality of the upcoming birth hit. All of Nan's chatter eased it somewhat, but Lila longed to have her mother by her side as this unknown experience loomed. She was grateful for Nan's involvement, and felt very sure the baby would be in good hands when she returned to work at the store, but she couldn't help wishing her mother were here.

She and Paul discussed names. He wanted Natasha after his Russian grandmother, or Ann, which was Lila's middle name. Lila, almost positive it would be a boy, suggested Matthew, simply because she liked the name. The intimate task of naming "their" baby drew them closer than ever.

Paul suggested giving up both of their apartments, and moving together into a corner two-bedroom unit on the top floor of the Hodge. But Lila wanted to wait with any kind of move until after the baby came, much too uncomfortable to even consider packing and moving. There was also the nagging, growing reluctance to move in with Paul, since she knew that her mother, and society, would disapprove. Her mother would surely love Paul, but Lila couldn't shake the feeling that living with another man while she was still married to Lou was wrong. Her conscience was finally kicking in, but the upcoming birth had priority in her thoughts. After the baby came, then she'd call the detective and do what was necessary to get her life back on the right track.

That brought to mind the looming problem of how to get a divorce without having direct contact with Lou. A divorce would surely be easier if he was in custody. It was all too much right now and Lila chose to put off any further action until after the baby came. She'd have to get divorced somehow, so she and Paul could get married and live together properly. It would be so nice to live in a bigger apartment up on the top floor and really be a family.

Lila was also nervous about leaving the security of Whittier and moving into Anchorage to await the birth as the due date drew nearer. There would be no easy way Lou could find out she was staying with Paul's relatives, but Lila grew anxious for the whole thing to be over. It was unlikely that Lou could get back into Alaska so soon after being kicked out of the state, but it was only a matter of time before he tried again. She couldn't wait to bring her baby back through the tunnel, and tuck him safely into the crib in her bedroom.

As soon as the delivery was over and she was settled back in Whittier, it would be time to call the police in St. Paul and tell them about witnessing the murder. She could face the risk of becoming a known witness to murder with Paul by her side for support. They discussed how her details of the murder might spur the police to look even harder for Lou. The additional danger it would bring for Lila when Lou found out she'd talked went unsaid.

LILA WASN'T AWARE Paul had recently bought a small, semi-automatic pistol he wore holstered just above his ankle. She never saw him unstrap it and conceal it in his folded pants leg when he undressed each night. She didn't know how much he worried about Lou, and how sure he was that knowledge of the gun would greatly increase her anxiety.

Chapter 36

MARCH TWENTY-SEVENTH, Good Friday, was a busy day for Lila. She felt unusually weary by the end of her workday and decided to leave the store a little early. She'd spent the entire week stocking shelves, ordering inventory, cleaning and polishing, and taking care of details for Tom in preparation for her absence. The six o'clock train through the tunnel that night would deliver Lila to Paul's aunt and uncle's home.

Paul let himself in Lila's apartment door about a half hour after she arrived home. "Store was closed when I stopped. Took off early, huh?" Without waiting for an answer, he continued, "Almost ready to go? Anything I can do?" he asked, tossing his jacket on a chair.

"I think I'm ready," Lila answered, rushing to him for a brief, excited hug. She pulled back at once and continued chattering. "I almost don't want to go. Leaving this place feels funny. I've felt so safe here. I know I don't need to worry, but I still do. And, I'm a little scared about having the baby, if you want the truth. I'm afraid of the pain, and I don't know what to expect—"

Paul interrupted her. "Hey—settle down. You'll do fine! Women do it all the time. The doctor says everything's normal. You're healthy, and you're getting the best care in the state. By this time next week, we'll be back here with her, safe and sound." His eyes twinkled. "I can't wait to see her."

Lila replied, "He's going to love it here, don't you think? Matthew—what a perfect name."

Paul laughed and reached to pull her back into his arms. "Very funny. Now remember—I'll take care of everything here, water the plant, and call you every day. And before you know it, we'll be back. Everything's gonna be fine. Aunt Zona and Uncle Dale are waiting for you and, knowing them, they'll spoil you." He looked around. "Hey, let's eat. We're having the leftovers, right?"

Lila turned to put the leftover spaghetti in a small pan on the stove and began to unwrap the garlic toast from the previous night's supper. She glanced out the living room window at snow beginning to fall beneath a low, gray cloud cover while the food warmed.

"Is the snow going to be a problem getting to Anchorage?" she asked.

"Nope," Paul replied. "Look how smooth the bay is and there's no wind at all. The weather report said heavy snowfall is expected to begin during the night, but we'll already be in Anchorage by then. I'll stay there with you 'til Sunday morning. Maybe we can go to a movie tomorrow night. The theater on Fireweed has that *Blue Hawaii* movie with Elvis showing, I think. You'd like that, wouldn't you?"

Lila brightened. "Yeah, that would be fun."

As she spoke, the pan on the stove rattled beneath its cover and her feet registered a slight tremble in the floor. She turned. "What was that...what?"

Before she could finish, the floor rolled. She swayed with it and grabbed the edge of the counter.

"Earthquake!" Paul hollered. "Here! Lila!"

Lila turned toward him, reaching out in desperation while the world began to churn around her. The pan slid off the stovetop and crashed onto the floor, spraying tomato sauce everywhere. Lila fell hard onto her knees. The television cabinet in the living room teetered on its legs, toppled with a crash, and the TV set skidded across the room, just missing her. Books tumbled from shelves. Everything on the kitchen counters slid back and forth before crashing to the floor into the mess of tomato sauce.

Paul stumbled toward Lila, fell to his knees, and began to crawl toward her with outstretched arms. He scrambled and lurched, finally reaching her, and they clung together while the world rocked around them. Neither could even manage to stay on their hands and knees. They rolled with the tumult as everything crashed around them. It was all they

285

could do to cling to each other while the floor rolled beneath them and tossed them from side to side.

From outside the apartment, loud bangs clanged over the screech of crumpling metal. The rolling and crashing seemed endless. Paul's jacket suddenly flew past Lila's face, just before the chair it had been on collided with her side. A searing pain followed, and Lila doubled over as her abdomen contracted.

"Oh, no! The baby!" Lila gasped.

She grabbed Paul's arm with such a powerful grip that he winced in surprise. Another tremor rolled them both toward the window wall before she could say anything else. Paul cushioned Lila with his body as the heavy coffee table slid toward them and crashed against his back.

Lila screamed when a sharp pang shot through her middle. Panicked, she felt sweat pop out on her forehead and clutched at Paul. Pain now came in unrelenting waves. She was tossed to and fro and finally torn out of Paul's grasp to land hard again against the wall beneath the window. At last, the frenzied shaking slowed, and Paul again began crawling toward her.

"Lila! Lila! Are you okay?" he wheezed, his face a white mask of concern.

Lila rolled onto her side on the hard floor. Before she could catch enough breath to answer him, a piercing pain, stronger than the others, shot through her back. She couldn't stop the wail that escaped her lips. Paul's eyes grew wide with terror, and he crawled toward her, his face frantic.

"Lila! You're hurt! Oh, God! You're hurt! The baby! Is it the baby?"

Lila managed to nod, before her body was racked by another wave of pain. She rolled onto her back on the hard floor and curled her knees toward her chest to try to stop it. Tears poured from her eyes.

Paul's face went red. "Is it the baby?" he yelled. He knelt beside Lila just as a mild tremor shook them again. When the shaking slowed and stopped, he lifted Lila's head, supporting her cheeks between his strong hands.

"Look at me. Look in my eyes. Answer me, Lila! Is it the baby?" he demanded. "You have to answer me! Lila! Answer me!"

The sharp tone brought Lila's attention to his face. "I think so," she whispered. "It hurts so bad.... I can't....Oh, Paul... What happened?"

"An earthquake. A big one. But you...you're hurt!"

Before Lila could respond, she was overcome by a pain so great she couldn't breathe. Droplets of sweat trailed over her face as she tried to writhe away from it. Her stomach became hard and she screamed again at the agony overwhelming her body.

"Paul...oh, Paul," she moaned.

She didn't notice the change that came over Paul at that moment. He regained his feet and stumbled toward the bathroom, returning in a few seconds with an armful of towels. He knelt beside Lila, his voice gentle but firm. "Lila, I think the baby's coming. Here put a towel under your head. Better? I'll help you…" He paused while another spasm wracked Lila's body.

Before he could continue, the floor trembled beneath them, mildly this time. He spoke in a reassuring tone and swept Lila's sweat-soaked hair away from her face with careful fingers. "You're doing fine. The earthquake's over. These are just aftershocks now. The baby's coming and we're gonna have to do this ourselves. I'll be here every second. We have to get our baby born now," he explained.

Lila locked her attention onto his strong and reassuring voice.

With great care, he eased Lila's pants and socks from her legs, then her underwear. "We can do this. Right?"

Lila murmured. "Just don't leave me, Paul. Please don't leave me. Will the baby be…" She couldn't finish the sentence, as another wave of pain washed over her.

Paul leaned over her and massaged her abdomen, trying to ease the pain. "Don't fight it," he instructed. "We can do this."

Lila was in no condition to notice the shakiness in his voice or the whiteness of his face.

A sudden noise at the door drew their attention. Nan came stumbling through, stepping over broken pieces of wood, her face ashen. A trickle of blood ran from her forehead down her cheek.

"Lila!" she hollered. She stopped short at the sight of the two on the floor. "What the hell?" She rushed forward.

"Is she hurt?" she cried to Paul. "Is she hurt? Is it the baby?"

She fell to her knees beside them. Lila reached for Nan's hand and clutched it.

"The baby's coming," Paul said. "Am I glad to see you!" He moved a bit aside to let Nan squeeze in beside him. Just then, Lila was stricken with another wave of pain. She cried out and squeezed Nan's hand tighter, her face clenched in agony. Paul and Nan's eyes locked over Lila's head.

"Do you know what to do?" Paul asked. "What about the earthquake? This was the big one, wasn't it?"

Nan agreed. "Yeah, it's bad out there, I'm afraid. But we have to help Lila. Go see if you can find any blankets. We have to keep her warm. And put some under her. The floor's hard. God almighty! What a mess here!"

Paul scrambled to his feet and returned in a minute with several bunched-up blankets. They made Lila as comfortable as best they could while wave after wave of pain washed through her. Their murmured words of reassurance barely registered.

Before long, the pains began to come regularly, sharp, deep, and relentless. Every time they subsided,

Lila regained her breath while Paul wiped the sweat from her face. The floor trembled again beneath them occasionally and Lila feared another quake was coming.

"Just aftershocks," Paul reassured her.

"You're doin' good, Dearie" Nan added. "You're doin' just great. We'll help."

Paul remained crouched next to her, gathering her to him whenever possible and murmuring words of encouragement.

After another hour of agony, with Paul and Nan crouched beside her, Lila felt the need to push harder, and a whoosh of warm water swished out along her legs, soaking the blankets beneath her.

Nan murmured, pulled away slightly and massaged her back. She moved up onto her haunches, "Dearie. This is good. Your water broke. Push if you can. Push as hard as you can. Can you do it?"

Lila, barely able to respond, concentrated on pushing. The pain was different now—not so sharp, not as searing. But it was unrelenting. The minutes dragged until a massive fatigue overcame her.

"Push, Lila. Push, Dearie. You have to keep pushing," Nan said.

"I can't. It hurts too much. And I'm too tired," Lila responded. "I can't. I just can't."

"Lila. Do it. You have to keep pushing." Paul spoke this time.

290

A bigger pain swept through her, like it was something she could overcome if she could only push hard enough. She grunted. A second later, searing pain like she had never known overcame her. Lights danced beneath her eyelids. She planted her heels on the floor and screamed. "Get it out!" Waves of pain washed over her and she shrieked, "Get it out! Please! Get it out!"

Nan moved to kneel between her feet. "Push it out. Push your feet down against the floor as hard as you can," she ordered. "Keep it up. It's coming. You're doing it!" Her voice took on a pitch of excitement. "It's coming! I can see the head!"

At her words, Lila took a deep breath, gave a mighty push through the biting pain, and collapsed. She lay exhausted on the hard floor, panting and trembling, unable to move.

Paul yelled, "It's a boy! You got your Matthew!" A tiny squeak confirmed his words. "Listen! He cried!"

Lila swam in and out of consciousness for a moment. She didn't notice when Paul pulled out his pocketknife and cut the umbilical cord. When she felt him place the warm, squirming, wet baby on her front and looked down for her first glimpse of her son, the tears came.

Paul settled on the floor beside her, tucking the blankets around her and the baby. "Look at him! Wow! A fine, big boy. You did great, Lila," he murmured.

291

His eyes, as well as Nan's, were tear-filled. He settled himself down beside Lila, his cheek next to hers, and snuggled close, placing a tender, protective hand on the baby's back. They lay like that, resting together, now oblivious to the mild aftershocks rippling through the apartment every few minutes.

Nan struggled to her feet, and stood, breathing hard, gazing in amazement at the three on the floor.

Lila stirred, the hard floor beneath her now uncomfortable. "I have to get up. I have to get cleaned up. We have to take care of him." She struggled to get up and support herself on her elbows.

"Here, I'll take him," Paul replied.

He laid two towels on the floor, and transferred Matthew onto them with gentle hands. Lila rolled to watch, fascinated, drinking in the sight of her son, transfixed by Paul's tender hands cradling the baby's head when he lifted him. As Paul wrapped the towels snugly around the infant, Matthew began to squeak. Within seconds, his cry became a strong, angry-sounding wail.

Lila and Paul looked at each other in delight, then up at a grinning Nan.

"Listen to that!" Paul exclaimed. "He's mad! He didn't like being taken away from you. I bet he's hungry. Just listen to him."

Lila's face lit up—she couldn't look away from her baby. He was perfect. Dark hair matted a perfectly-formed little head. He waved clenched fists and gave vigorous kicks against the nest of towels. His face grew scrunched and reddish under tiny, definite black eyebrows, and his wail grew louder.

"We need to clean him up. And feed him," Lila began.

She struggled to her knees, halted, and looked around in amazement. For the first time, she realized the extent of the earthquake's damage to her home. Everything she owned was strewn about, tossed into heaps, broken, and smashed. She gasped in shock.

Paul reached for her. "Don't worry. We'll get it cleaned up."

Nan took charge. "Right now we need to find the bottles and nipples and diapers somehow in this mess. Look, there's a can of formula over by the door. Paul, check the bathroom and see if the shower still works so Lila can clean up. Just stay where you are for a minute, Dearie."

Paul rose and stumbled toward the bathroom door through the debris covering the floor. Lila heard the squeak of the bathroom faucet, followed by a mumbled word she couldn't make out. Paul appeared in the bathroom doorway, and tried to yank the door upright where it hung at an angle on its single bent hinge.

"No water. Pipes must be broken somewhere. At least we don't have water spurting all over in here. No lights either, electricity must be off."

Nan looked down at Lila. "We have to clean you two up somehow. And keep him warm. And find some water to mix with the formula. It has to be sterile. We'll need to get you and the little one to the doctor as soon as we can to make sure everything's okay." She looked at Paul. "Maybe somebody has water. Go find out."

Paul's face betrayed his concern. "Yup," he answered, turning toward the door.

Lila sank back onto the floor. Matthew had quieted and was resting in his nest of towels, his little face calm now.

"Hurry back, please, Paul." She looked around in dismay. "This was the big one they talk about, wasn't it?"

Paul looked back from the doorway. "Yes. I've never seen anything like it, ever, or even heard about one this bad." He drew a deep breath. "I'll be right back, as soon as I can. Just stay there. Don't try to get up. There could be more tremors. Nan'll stay with you and the baby. I'll get some help, and be right back." His voice cracked slightly and his gaze lingered on Lila before he stepped toward the broken door frame.

Lila settled back down beside Matthew and watched Paul throw his shoulder hard against the apartment door to get it to screech open far enough for him to squeeze out. He looked back at Lila. "I'll leave it open enough so if you have to get out, you can. It's stuck." His voice shook. "I'll be right back." With a final long look of concern, he disappeared into the hallway.

When his footsteps had died away, Lila gave a deep sigh and murmured, "I can't believe it. I have a baby. I have a son." At that, familiar fear replaced her excitement.

Lou has a son. What will he think about that? What will he do?

Chapter 37

LILA'S HEART SKIPPED a beat. Lou's son had been born, and he didn't even know she'd been pregnant. What would he do when he found out? A vision of his angry face overtook her, and she gave an involuntary tremble. Maybe he'd never have to know. Maybe she could figure out a way. And she'd just been through an earthquake. She couldn't quite believe it. Mama and Judy would be beside themselves when they heard about it this on the news. She'd have to call them as soon as possible. With these thoughts, Lila felt her strength returning.

"I have to get up and get dressed and take care of things," she said to Nan, surprised at the weakness of her voice.

"No, Paul said to stay where you are. Just rest. The baby looks fine. I think he's sleeping now. Lay back. I'll see what I can find around here," Nan ordered.

Lila shifted onto her side, laid a sheltering hand over Matthew, and drifted into light, exhausted slumber.

It seemed only seconds had passed before she was awakened by Paul and Nan's voices.

"Oh, Dearie. Oh, Lila! What a day you picked to have a baby!" Nan knelt beside Lila, her voice warm with reassurance. "Here. Paul found that the faucet works in the laundry room, and he brought a jug of water. I'll help you get cleaned up. He's gonna try to put your bed back together, and we'll get you into it soon as we can find some clean clothes. Here, hold my arm. I'll help you up. Think you can stand?"

"But, Matthew..." Lila protested.

"I'll get him," Paul answered, and knelt to gather the towel-wrapped bundle up off the floor and into his arms. He stood, mesmerized, gazing at the miniature face, while Nan helped Lila to her feet.

"Bring him into the bathroom," Nan ordered. "Bring all the towels, too. Wrap him in them and tuck him in the sink for now. Keep him snug and covered and warm. We'll use the tub to get Lila cleaned up, and you can get to work on setting up the bed."

With an obedient and relieved sigh, Paul did as he was told. While Nan helped Lila, they could hear Paul dragging the bed frame, box spring and mattress back into place in the bedroom.

"Here, I found this," he called, handing Lila's nightgown through the bathroom door. Moments later, Lila found herself being tucked into her bed with Matthew snugged in beside her. She closed her eyes in relief.

"Now," Nan continued, "You need something to eat and drink. I'll scrounge around and get somethin' together. Are you hurting?"

Lila shook her head. "Yeah, and I'm thirsty."

"I'll find something for you to drink," Nan replied. "Paul, get downstairs and go outside the building. This sure as hell is a major disaster, and I have no idea how things are out there. We need to find out. We gotta try an' sterilize a bottle and boil water for the baby's formula soon. We better get him into a diaper and warm clothes, too. So first, look around out in the living room and bring me whatever baby stuff you can find. Then go outside, and get back up here with a report."

Paul's distress had eased now that Nan was in charge. He returned in a few minutes with both packages of diapers, still in their unopened plastic wrappers, and an armful of baby clothes. He moved with care, holding two glass baby bottles and a torn cardboard package of nipples tucked beneath his chin.

"Here's all I can find right now," he said after setting them down on Lila's bed. He turned to Nan and his eyes grew wide. "Nan! You've been hurt! There's blood on your face!"

"What? I don't feel nothin'." Nan turned to look in the mirror over the dresser, but found only shattered shards of glass clinging to the mirror frame.

"Oh, what a mess! Look at this place!" she cried. "What does my face look like? It doesn't hurt at all." She put her hand to her right cheek. "Oh, here. Now I can feel it. Is it deep?"

She turned to Paul. "No, it looks more like a scratch," he said. "There's a bump on your forehead, too. What happened?"

Nan shrugged. "Don't know. I don't remember bein' hit or gettin' hurt. But then, I was gettin' tossed around like a goddamn rag doll."

She paused for a moment and shook her head. "Lordy! It was something! Never in my wildest dreams did I think we'd have somethin' like this happen here in Whittier! I wonder how the rest of the state is? And Paul, ask everybody you see what they know. We have to find out when we can get through the tunnel to get Lila and the baby to the hospital. I wonder if cars and trucks...and the train...if anything's working?"

At that, she and Paul hurried toward the window. Lila heard their simultaneous gasps.

"What?" she called out from the bed.

Paul spoke first, without turning from the window. "The cars in the parking lot! They're tossed all over the place! Most are on their sides, and some of them are even upside down! The windows are broken out of every single one of them! The snowplow's twisted right in half! And the docks! The docks are gone! Some pilings are all the way up on land, and they're smashed into the sides of the oil

299

tanks. There's oil in the water, and it's burning! So much black smoke! And the boats! The boats are all over the place up on shore, and the ones still in the water are half sunk! The wharf's gone! It's disappeared! God, I hope nobody was out there!"

Paul turned to Lila, his face ashen. "Whittier's destroyed! Telephone poles are broken in half, just laying in the dirt! Electrical wires are on the ground all over the place! And the store—it's half collapsed, and all the windows are broken out! God! My God!"

Nan turned from the window to look at Lila, her face ravaged. "This is bad. Real bad. We won't be able to get out to the doctor in Anchorage anytime soon, that's for sure. We gotta figure out how to handle things here 'til help gets through. If we can find a working phone, we need to call Doc Simpson and ask him what to do."

Her voice faltered, and she put her hands to her face. "Lordy, Lordy. We are in a pickle, that's for sure."

Then, as if realizing her words would be upsetting to Lila, she squared her shoulders. "But we'll figure it out. You and the little one are healthy and strong. Where are those diapers? Get goin', Paul. Get down there. See what you can find out, 'specially if there's a phone that works."

Paul, his face contorted with shock, hustled out the door without a word. Lila lay back, trying to absorb what she'd just heard. She watched Nan diaper Matthew with expert moves and tug a yellow terry sleeper over his tiny head. Nan tied it beneath his feet and handily wrapped him back up in one of the blankets Paul had brought in. Matthew stirred, but didn't waken when Nan tucked him back in beside Lila.

"Here he is, warm and dry. Not cleaned up the best, but fine for now. Next we better get a bottle ready. When he wakes up, he'll be hungry."

She headed out the bedroom door and returned a minute later, shaking her head. "Not a chance. The stove's tipped over an' the plug's snapped right off at the wall. Even if we had electricity, we couldn't boil water, or even heat anything." She looked speculatively at Lila. "So, how do you feel about breast feeding?"

"What?" Lila asked. "Breast feeding. But, how…"

"You're gonna learn," Nan replied. "Just do what comes natural."

When Matthew awoke, he had needed only a few seconds to find what he was after, and his first feeding began. Nan rummaged through the rest of the bedroom, setting whatever she could to rights, folding, straightening, sweeping, and keeping a watchful eye on the new mother as she experienced the first feeding of her newborn.

That was how Paul found them twenty minutes later. He halted in the doorway, and his eyes softened with tenderness. But a few seconds later, that look vanished.

"It's bad," he reported with a grimace. "Really bad. They say the waves were unbelievable. They think a dozen people mighta been swept out to sea. Nobody knows for sure, but they can't find one family. The Carlsons were having a bonfire and picnic by the shore—nobody's seen 'em since. There's not a single car or truck running. The tracks are bent and twisted, too, so the train is worthless."

He stopped to take a deep, shuddering breath, "There's no phones. Quite a few people are hurt. Tom's one—broke his hip, they think. The power plant's damaged. All radio contact's out. Everybody's wondering about the rest of the state and Anchorage. It's a disaster, for sure!"

Chapter 38

THE NATIONAL NEWS burst with reports of the devastation in Alaska following the strongest quake ever registered in North America. Landslides and tidal waves had taken the lives of more than a hundred people in the state. The city of Anchorage lay in ruins; its streets buckled, many buildings collapsed. An entire neighborhood on a bluff was lost in a landslide. Nationwide, the story dominated the news.

Whittier was in chaos. The town had sustained five million dollars in damage and thirteen lives had been lost during the violent four-minute quake. Metal plates in the joints between the Hodge building's sections had worked as planned, but the metal had bent and curled under the tremendous force of the twisting earth. The banging together of the building's sections had cracked some interior walls, but the earthquake-proof design had saved it, as well as the lives of its occupants. By the time a reconnaissance plane established contact with Whittier the third morning, everyone knew their community would never be the same. During the middle of the third night, as residents hunkered down in the dark, cold building, the electricity flickered back on.

Massive, violent waves had wreaked havoc, leaving the shore in total disarray. Both of the huge docks and the wharf had vanished, swept out to sea. Buildings along the shoreline had caught fire and burned to rubble. Wisps of black smoke lingered from oil that continued to burn over the surface of the harbor. Caring for the injured and attending to the still smoldering fires claimed everyone's attention.

Radio contact had been established, power restored, and the injured flown to Anchorage by helicopter by the end of the fourth day. It took four more days to remove fallen rock from the tunnel, replace and realign the damaged train tracks, and repair the bridge on the other side. A light snow fell intermittently during the days following the earthquake, giving the entire scene an eerie, ghostly dusting of white.

State work crews, first dropped by helicopter and then brought in on the train, scampered like ants over the scene, clearing debris, fighting still smoldering fires, and beginning the repair and restoration of Whittier. Maintaining the security of the tunnel was impossible as work crews poured in and out.

A SCRUFFY STRANGER pulled into Anchorage five days after the quake. The car he drove was mud-covered, its radiator hissing, when he parked it outside the Alaska Railroad's main office in downtown Anchorage. The brick building, one of the few structures that had escaped major damage, buzzed with activity. The stranger melted into a line of job seekers, requested assignment to Whittier, and exited with a job.

LILA WAS BUSY that day, too. She had seen Paul for only a few precious moments since the disaster. All able-bodied men were spending every waking minute working to restore order to Whittier, and Paul was on the front lines. He stopped in a few times each day, though, to check on her and Matthew, his face blackened with soot, eyes red-rimmed with fatigue. Lila would assure him that she and the baby were doing fine, push sandwiches and cookies into his jacket pockets, and tell him not to worry.

Paul let Lila know it looked like the train would be able to take vehicles out through the tunnel in a few more days, and assured Lila that she and Nan and the baby would have a place on the first train out so they could get into Anchorage to the doctor. Paul's truck was one of the few that had sustained minimal damage and was still in working order, so he said it would be available to use for the trip. Under the circumstances, it didn't occur to either one of them to worry about Lou.

Lila continued with the cleanup of her apartment, and reveled in her new role as a mother. Matthew was an easy baby, according to Nan. Lila wasn't so sure, when she was awakened every few hours during the night by his hungry wails, but Nan told her not to worry, that the interval between feedings would get longer and longer with each passing week. Lila learned to handle diapers and tuck her baby snugly into his receiving blankets. She settled into nursing Matthew with little problem.

"How do you know so much about babies?" Lila asked Nan one morning.

When Nan's usual chatter didn't follow, Lila looked over to see Nan's face contorted, her lips pursed into a hard line. Something was very wrong. This was the look Lila had noticed so many times before. What was wrong?

"Nan? What is it? Tell me—I know something's bothering you."

"I had babies," Nan choked out, her voice breaking. "Two babies. They were only fifteen months apart. TB got 'em both within a month of each other. Back in Seattle. My old man split on me then. Couldn't take it, I guess. Never even said goodbye. Was just gone, even before I buried my little girls…" She tried to stifle a sob.

Lila rushed to Nan and enveloped her in a hug. The woman sobbed against Lila's shoulder for long moments, then pulled away. "It was a long time ago. I'm over it," she said unconvincingly, and turned back to the dishes in the sink.

Lila walked into the bedroom, picked up a sleeping Matthew, returned to the kitchen and placed him in Nan's arms. "Here, Grandma Nan."

Nan's eyes filled with tears as she hugged Matthew to her breast and buried her face in his blankets. Her shoulders shook. Finally, she lifted her face, a big smile shining through the tears streaking her cheeks.

Lila felt a desperate need to talk to her mother and Judy after Nan left. She couldn't wait to tell them about Matthew's birth and to assure them she and little Matthew were fine, but the phones were still out of order.

Mom has a grandson and she doesn't even know it yet. I wish she was here. I miss her so much right now.

Lonesome and homesick for the first time in many months, Lila puttered around the apartment while darkness claimed the world outside her windows. Snow swirled beyond the windows, but it was cozy inside the apartment since the windows had remained intact and the heat was back on. Matthew slept in a corner of the living room, tucked into the tiny cradle old Tom had provided, content and warm beneath a soft, crocheted blanket Nan had contributed.

A short time later, with Matthew snuggled in her arms during a feeding, Lila contemplated her life. She had it pretty good, despite the quake and the unfinished business with Lou. Tom, nursing a badly bruised hip from the quake, said the store would reopen as soon as they finished putting glass back in the windows and fixing the roof. Maybe in a couple more weeks or so. And he'd need her as much as she could possibly work until he was up and around again.

This was the perfect time for her to just rest, and Lila was surprised how good she felt already. The water was turned back on, as were the heat and electricity. The apartment was pretty much back in shape and workers had already fixed the stove plug for her. Everyone else seemed to be settling back into their routines, too. Even Nan had her place put back together. Lila liked it that Nan had to come and watch TV with her every night since hers got smashed. She felt lucky to have Nan in her life. Now that Lila knew why Nan had always looked so sad before when they talked about the baby, Matthew had become Nan's adored, honorary grandson. And Lila had Paul, too. He'd helped deliver the baby. He'd been there for her, just like he promised. How she loved him. And she had no doubt he loved her just as much.

Lila hummed while she washed the dishes. At Nan's familiar knock, she called out, "Come on in, Nan," and reached for the popcorn popper.

They settled on the couch with a big bowl of popcorn between them. Nan laughed with Lila at *The*

Jetsons, and admired Little Joe, their favorite, during *Bonanza* while the evening hours passed. Nan did her nightly check of the earthquake's bruises on Lila's back and side, pronouncing them "ugly as sin, kind of greenish now, but healing." Nan rocked Matthew until he fell asleep, and even then was reluctant to put him back into to his crib.

Nan left for her own apartment after the ten o'clock news, and Lila slipped into bed and immediate sleep, not even waking when Paul nudged in beside her at midnight. She handled Matthew's three a.m. feeding with drowsy contentment, and tucked him back into his crib in the semi-darkness, barely wakening.

Neither she nor Matthew woke when Paul got up and slipped out the door in the morning.

THEY WERE STILL asleep when the crew of blue-clad workers from Anchorage hustled onto the train at the Portage Station for the ride through the tunnel to Whittier. Nobody looked twice at the man with the baseball cap pulled low over his eyes. Nobody noticed the fierce gleam in his eye or the hunting knife in the black leather case that hung from his belt loop. The worker kept to himself the first day, molding himself into the crew unobtrusively. He couldn't believe his good fortune when he overheard a coworker explaining that everyone in Whittier lived in that one big apartment building over there.

Chapter 39

LILA AND PAUL had their first supper and evening together in almost a week that night. Paul had been to his own apartment after work to shower and put on clean clothes, and now sat at Lila's kitchen table, shoulders drooping with weariness He wore a loose-fitting, faded, red cotton pullover with tiny geometric designs that Lila had never seen before and she recognized his need for the comfort of what were obviously old, familiar clothes. Most likely, Georgia, or maybe Paul's grandmother, had made that shirt for him.

"I'm as hungry as a grizzly," he smiled. "What do we have?"

"Not much," Lila answered. "When Nan and I go to Anchorage tomorrow we both need to stock up. We plan to pick up groceries after the doctor appointment. I can warm you up some beef stew from a can and make toast now. Does that sound good?"

"For a start," Paul laughed. "I'm so hungry I feel like I could eat anything that isn't moving right now." He gave a weary sigh and laid his head on his arms on the table top. "Anything—I'll have anything you can put on the table. I'm so glad we're back to a normal work schedule."

After a moment, he raised his head. "Matthew? How's he doing? I've hardly seen him. Is he in his cradle?" He rose, face lighting with eagerness and anticipation. Lila pushed the toaster lever down and followed him. They walked together to the cradle in the corner of the living room. Matthew lay wide awake and unblinking, staring up at them. Lila bent to pick him up, but Paul touched her arm.

"Let me," he murmured. "Look at the little guy. He was awake and just laying here, quiet. Look at all that hair—we'll need to start combing it pretty soon."

He leaned over and lifted the baby from the cradle and into the crook of his arm. The two stared at each other for long silent moments. Then Matthew gave an abrupt thrust of his tiny fist and whacked Paul in the cheek. Lila and Paul burst out laughing.

"Well! Guess he'll be able to take care of himself," Paul chuckled.

Lila's heart overflowed with love by the time she tucked Paul and Matthew into bed an hour later. It felt so good to have a normal supper with Paul. And how good he was with Matthew.

She couldn't wait to tell her mother and Judy how fantastic Paul was. She smiled, remembering how tired he'd been after supper, and how he fell asleep almost before his head hit the pillow. And Matthew loved all the attention, she could tell. It was like they were a real family. She drifted toward sleep with thoughts of how happy she'd be when Mom and Judy come to visit and could finally meet Matthew and Paul. Life would be just about perfect then.

At the idea of just about perfect, Lila remembered Lou. A shudder overcame her as she realized she needed to call the police in St. Paul now and tell them about witnessing the murder. She'd been so afraid for so long that making contact might end up giving Lou a clue about where she was, but it was time to do the right thing. Maybe Lou had moved far away by now. Her mother and Judy never mentioned him anymore. But Lila didn't dare hope he was gone out of her life for good. She knew better. And she had to figure out a way to get a divorce.

Chapter 40

A CHILL APRIL wind blowing frozen raindrops sideways greeted the railroad work crew when they stepped off the train in Whittier the next morning. Most of them had known enough to listen to the weather forecast and were bundled in heavy jackets, warm hats and thick work gloves. But one of them shivered in the damp air and shoved his bare hands deep into his pockets, cussing this God-forsaken place under his breath. He sauntered away from his fellow workers who were crowded around a rusty barrel during the ten o'clock coffee break, their hands held to the warmth of the brisk fire.

Nobody noticed the shadowy figure who crouched down and ran hard, focused on the tall apartment building fifty yards away. Nobody was on the Hodge's entry steps when he slipped through the front door.

Once inside, he paused to get his breath. He didn't notice the withered old woman until she asked in a high, whispery voice "Looking for someone?"

He started, and turned toward the voice from the bench in the corner. "Yeah," he replied, trying to hide his irritation. "I'm thinking of living here. Where's the office?"

With a sniff, the old woman asked, "Considering living here, huh?"

"Office?" he repeated, his voice brusque and dismissive.

The old woman looked at him with a shrewdness he found disconcerting. Finally, she shrugged, and pointed a crooked finger down the hall. Just as he reached an elevator alcove, the doors pinged open and two boys ran out, headed toward the lobby.

"Hey, guys!" Lou called out. "I'm trying to get to Lila's apartment and I forgot the number. Know her?"

"Yup," one boy answered. "Lila's on eight. But I don't know the number. Take a left off the elevator and then go down the hall. Almost all the way. She's got a picture of flowers on her door. You know the number, Jimmy?"

"Nope," the other boy answered. "Hurry up! They're going to try to roll the big boat back into the water and I wanna watch!"

The boys took off running, and within seconds, Lou was in the elevator, heading upward.

LILA CUDDLED MATTHEW to her breast, studying him as he ate.

His eyes look so wise. He looks at me like he knows I'm his mother. He stares at me like he's memorizing my face. He's so handsome. So cute. What a perfect baby. He's sweating because he's working so hard to eat.

With a contented smile, she settled deeper into the cushioned rocker Paul had surprised her with. From its place by the picture window, she could watch what was happening below, even though today's sleet dimmed the scene. The water in the harbor roiled gray and agitated, and frenzied scraps of clouds whipped back and forth across the rapidly darkening sky. Even the gulls had settled elsewhere rather than fight the winds this morning. The windows rattled continuously. It was be a good day to be snug at home, especially since Paul would be back in a few hours. She planned an easy supper of macaroni and the reindeer sausage from Paul's freezer, and she would make toast with the homemade bread Nan had brought up this morning. That would have to do until she could get to Anchorage tomorrow and do the grocery shopping. She sighed with pleasure and turned to her baby.

Because of the sleet and wind at the windows, Lila didn't hear the scrabbling noise at her door. But she did hear the knob turn and felt the change in the air of the apartment as the door was opened. Paul was home early. Good. She hugged Matthew to her, turned toward the door, and started to rise from the chair.

Lila froze at the sight of the man who stepped inside. He kicked the door shut behind him. She gasped as terror, then shock, washed over her. She took an involuntary step backward, clutching Matthew to her chest.

Lou stared. "Hello, my little darlin," he snarled. "Surprised to see me? Hey, what ya got there? A baby? What the hell?" His face contorted in puzzlement. His scowl grew and he stood stock still as he absorbed what he was seeing. His face turned crimson. "That has to be my kid! You bitch! You went and got pregnant. How dare you…" His eyes burned with fury. He reached to his belt and unsheathed a wide, gleaming hunting knife.

Lila's heart began thundering at his movement and the glint of the knife blade. Her mind reeled.

Oh my God! He has a knife! A big one! He found me! Oh my God! Matthew!

She looked around, frantic. But there was nowhere to run. She was trapped in the apartment. There was no other door. She pressed Matthew to her chest so hard that he began to whimper.

"Get out of here," Lila screamed. "Get out! Right now!"

Lou grinned and took a step forward, his gaze locked with hers. "Not before I finish what I came for, you little bitch!" he sneered. "You shouldn't of done what you did, my little darlin'. You made a big

316

mistake when you left me. Stole my car and my money. You know you gotta pay for what you saw and did. And now you went and had a kid. Kept it from me, too. Don't tell me to get out! Don't tell *me* what to do, you little bitch!"

He advanced into the living room. Lila stepped backward, then with a quick turn crouched and slid Matthew, blanket and all, beneath the end table, pushing him back under it as far as she could. She leaped up, overcome by sudden and surprising defiance. She grabbed the newspaper from the end table, and rolled it into a tight rod with quick, decisive movements.

Lou snorted. "Hah! Little darlin'—gonna fight, huh? If that's the way ya want it, All righty then, have it your way. I like it when they fight, makes it more fun for me."

He began to stomp across the room toward her. Lila reached down and grabbed the heavy coffee table, sending books and magazines crashing to the floor. Matthew began to wail at the noise. She hurled the table at Lou with every bit of her strength. He halted in surprise when the table grazed his shins. His face turned purple with rage.

"Ow! Sonofabitch!"

Lila darted toward the kitchen, wheezing. If only she could get to the knife drawer. If only she could get a knife! She had to fight back! Her heart pounded as she scuttled along the wall.

Lou turned and rushed toward her, knife raised. When Lila spun on her heel and dashed back toward the big window in the living room, Lou bellowed like a mad bull and lunged for her. But as he began to take his first step, his legs suddenly caved out from under him and he slammed face-first onto the carpet. His outstretched fist gripped the knife even as he tried to break his fall.

Lila couldn't believe her eyes. There behind Lou stood frail old Agnes, a heavy cast-iron frying pan clutched in her hands. The old woman panted from the effort and struggled to hold the pan upright. A long white tendril of loose hair trailed over her shoulder and one long black stocking puddled at her ankle. She looked at Lila in triumph, grasping the frying pan with both hands.

Too astounded to react at first, Lila gasped. Agnes! Agnes had whacked Lou's knees from behind and knocked him down! How did Agnes know Lou was here? And there was Nan behind her, too. Before Lila could take it all in, there was a scuffling at the open apartment door. Colleen and her two black Labs blasted into the room behind Nan.

"Stay! Stay!" Colleen shouted at her dogs, but both charged at Lou, who was scrambling to his feet. The dogs surrounded him, snarling. Lou sank back to the floor, cringing. The dogs moved over him, growling deep in their throats, teeth exposed by curling lips, the hair on the back of their neck and shoulders standing tall and thick.

"Stay. Hold!" Colleen ordered from the doorway. The dogs obeyed, their attention never wavering from the man on the floor.

Nan reacted first, hustled over and reached under the end table to slide out a now wailing Matthew. She cuddled him to her and soothed him. Lila took in the scene, shocked at the events of the past few minutes. She looked at Agnes and Nan and Colleen and the dogs in wonder.

"How…How did you…" she began.

"Agnes noticed him…" Nan began to explain.

"I saw this man come into the building a while ago…" Agnes interrupted, her voice surprisingly strong. She lowered the heavy frying pan to the floor, straightened up, and continued, "I sensed something amiss when he walked through the lobby. I had a very uneasy feeling about him and then I remembered your story, Lila dear. So I went to Nan's and told her about him. We hurried down to the office and made a call to the railroad office to get the men over here, but nobody answered."

Nan took over. "We knew we better check on you, and we thought about Colleen's dogs. So I went and got her and, here we are."

Suddenly, the dog closest to Lou gave a high-pitched squeal and lurched back from the man on the floor. A stream of blood spurted from its neck and the animal pitched sideways, struggling to stay upright. Lou sprang to his feet and viciously kicked the other dog while stabbing at its shoulders and side. The dog stumbled into a small puddle of blood beside the other dog, and sank to the floor.

Colleen screamed, "Duke! Daisy! My God! He stabbed my dogs!"

She fled out the apartment door, screaming. "Bobby! Bobby! Come help! The dogs! The dogs!"

Nan, still clutching Matthew, darted into the bedroom and slammed the door. Through her terror, Lila heard the faint click of the doorknob's lock.

Lou was on his feet now, brandishing his knife. His eyes burned wild, his face grew contorted. He snarled, "Gotcha now, little darlin'. It's just you and me an' the old hag. You don't have a chance."

He took a step toward Agnes and bellowed, "Get out of here, you old piece of shit! Get out while you can."

He took another step toward her, reached out and shoved her hard toward the door. Agnes stumbled through it and Lou flung the door shut with a bang, flipping the lock. Cocky now, confident, reveling in Lila's fear, he took a step toward her, waving the bloody knife back and forth, an evil grin on his face.

Lila had never known such terror. She stood rooted in place, frozen, trying to breathe, but her breath wouldn't come. Her heart hammered. She felt light-headed. All she could think of was Matthew.

Matthew...Paul...Mom. I have to live for them! I can't let this happen!

She looked around in panic. The only thing she could think to do was scoot behind the sofa, so she dropped to her knees and scrambled behind it.

Lou laughed, his tone wicked and menacing. "Trying to hide, huh? Won't do you no good!"

He grabbed the sofa and slammed it back against the wall, crushing her. Lila gasped at the impact, but an unexpected anger overtook her. She scooted her back against the wall, drew her legs against her chest, and kicked against the sofa with all her strength. It hit Lou hard in the legs and he staggered backward trying to keep his balance. A look of astonishment filled his face.

All at once, there was a loud crash at the door and Paul charged in, his face crazed with fury and terror.

"Lila! Lila! Where are you? Paul shouted, his eyes seeking hers.

Lila screamed, "He has a knife! A big one! Watch out!"

Lou whirled and bounded toward Paul, knife outstretched, slashing the air. Paul stooped, jerked up his pant leg, and whipped out his gun. The sight of the gun halted Lou in his tracks.

"Back off! Right now! Drop the knife! Back off or I'll shoot!" Paul roared in a voice Lila had never heard before.

"Who the hell are you?" Lou bellowed. He took a threatening step toward Paul.

"Down! Down on the floor! Drop the knife and hit the floor! Right now! One more step and I shoot!" Paul commanded, his voice now deadly calm.

As Lou stood undecidedly, there was a commotion at the door. Colleen's husband, Bobby, kicked the broken door aside. He was followed closely by two more men from the railroad office. They took in the scene, then hustled over to stand beside Paul.

"Drop it. You're outnumbered," one of them ordered. "Drop the knife and get on your face on the floor. You have three seconds before we take you down. Do it!"

Lou hesitated only a second before dropping to his knees and letting the knife fall at his side. Paul rushed forward and kicked the knife against the far wall. "Down! All the way! On the floor! Now!" he hollered.

With obvious reluctance, Lou lay down, turning a furious, purple face to Lila. One of the railroad men jumped on Lou's legs, whipped the belt off his own waist, and began tying Lou's ankles. The other man knelt across Lou's shoulders and tied his hands together with a dishtowel he'd grabbed off the kitchen counter, giving a rough final twist to the knot.

Paul rushed to Lila where she crouched on the floor and pulled her to him. "Are you okay?" His voice was frantic. When she didn't answer, he pushed her from him and inspected her. "Matthew?" he exclaimed, his eyes filling with fear.

Before Lila could answer through her too-dry throat, Bobby's cries filled the room. "Duke! Daisy!

Oh, God! He stabbed them!" Tears poured down Bobby's cheeks as he knelt and gathered the animals to him, murmuring words of comfort in an agonized voice. "Duke, my puppy! Good dog! Daisy, Daisy, good girl."

He whipped off his shirt and wadded it against Duke's neck to stop the bleeding. Daisy nuzzled her way under his arm, still whimpering, and he tucked her close against his side.

Paul pulled Lila to him and sheltered her from the scene on the floor. "Matthew?" he asked again.

"Nan. Nan has him. In the bedroom," Lila replied woodenly. The room had become too bright. Black spots swirled before her eyes. She tried to get up but her knees buckled. She collapsed against Paul.

WHEN SHE AWOKE, she was in her bed, with Paul lying beside her, holding her tightly. She snuggled into his warmth, then bolted upright as the memories rushed in.

"Matthew? Matthew!"

"He's fine. Taking a good nap. Nan fed him. She gave him a bottle and he took it right away." Paul pointed to the corner of the room. Lila's racing heart calmed at the sight of the little bump beneath the blanket in the crib.

"How… How did you know Lou was here? Where is he? Where's Lou?!" Lila's voice rose in panic and she struggled to get up. Paul pushed her back down with a firm touch.

"Lou's taken care of. You won't have to worry about him anymore. Troopers are on the way. There are enough witnesses to put him away for a long time. Bobby and the other men trussed him up pretty good. They're practically sitting on him over in the office 'til the law gets here."

"But...you... How did..." Lila stuttered.

Paul explained how he and his coworkers had their heads bent over the train schedule earlier that morning when the train hooted its arrival out of the tunnel with the day crew. He had glanced up to see how many arriving workers could be sent over to help move boxcars.

"One of 'em caught my eye," he explained. "There was something about the way he moved and looked around. Kind of shifty, or something. My skin got all prickly when he walked by the office door. Something seemed familiar about that face. It was something about his eyes."

He patted Lila's back and went on. "I let it go while we worked out the schedule, but it nagged at me. I couldn't get him out of my mind—had a bad feeling since I first noticed him. Then, all of a sudden it hit me. I knew the guy had to be Lou! I yelled to the guys to follow me. God!"

He pulled Lila up tight against him. "You were a tiger! You sure were fighting!" He looked at Lila in awe.

324

"I had to. For Matthew. For us," Lila answered, and melted into the arms of the one she loved. She'd found her Alaskan refuge.

Epilogue

TWO WEEKS LATER, Lila handed Matthew to Paul and tore to the terminal door to be enveloped in the arms of her best friend and mother as they hurried in from the windy tarmac. Although Judy and Mom had been on the plane for over seven hours, excitement overcame any weariness and the three women danced and squealed through a long group hug. Minutes later, Paul had been introduced and Matthew was cradled in his grandmother's arms for the first time. Judy's eyebrows shot up in a sign of silent approval to Lila the instant Paul grinned a hello at her.

During the next week, Lila and Paul showed Mama and Judy life in Whittier. Nan and Margaret discovered much in common, not the least of which was the baby they both loved, and Margaret ended up choosing to stay in Nan's extra bedroom. Judy slept on Lila's couch, but the two young women talked nonstop, giggled, told secrets, and hardly slept at all. Matthew basked in the attention, and so did Paul.

Already, a formal legal notice from an Anchorage attorney had been filed with the court system in Minnesota. The divorce would happen within months.

A letter with a Montana postmark arrived while Margaret and Judy were in Whittier. Even though Dee and Chuck's written words assured Lila that everything was fine with them, all agreed that a call to them was in order. When Paul got through and handed the receiver to Lila, Chuck's surprised voice told her how the rebuilding of their house had gone well and was covered by insurance. Lila was comforted to learn his burns from the house fire were more minor than first thought and he'd been able to be back in the café cooking within two weeks. He said Dee was fine, but out of town this week helping care for a newborn grandson in Helena. He said she enjoyed having a nice new house that was much easier to clean and take care of than the old one had been. Margaret got on the phone to Chuck, too, and thanked him profusely for helping her daughter. The call ended with everyone promising to stay in touch.

Nan's Sunday potluck in the lobby gave Judy and Margaret a chance to meet Colleen and her family, Tom, Agnes, and the many other residents who were curious about these visitors. Judy at first turned up her nose at caribou and moose, but soon relented and helped herself to a bit of everything. Duke and Daisy, red bandanas wrapped around the bandages still on their throats, roamed the gathering and didn't lack for attention or treats. A surprise tribute was arranged for Agnes, who beamed while everyone took turns praising her spunk and courage. When she unwrapped the shiny, silver frying pan from Paul and Lila, she laughed out loud for the first time in everyone's memory.

CPSIA information can be obtained
at www.ICGtesting.com
Printed in the USA
FFOW03n1509081217
43946607-43035FF